CW01655943

Death By Jogging

ALSO BY P.F. FORD

SLATER AND NORMAN MYSTERIES

Book 1: Death By Carpet
Book 2: Death By Plane
Book 3: Death By Night
Book 4: Death By Kitchen Sink
Book 5: Death By Telephone Box
Book 6: Death In Wild Boar Woods
Book 7: Death In The River
Book 8: Death In A Skip
Book 9: Death Of A Pensioner
Book 10: Death Of A Long-Lost Son
Book 11: Death By Takeaway
Book 12: Death By Caravan
Book 13: Death by Jogging

THE WEST WALES MURDER MYSTERIES

Prequel: A Date With Death
Book 1: A Body On The Beach
Book 2: A Body Out At Sea
Book 3: A Body Down The Lane
Book 4: A Body At The Farmhouse
Book 5: A Body In The Cottage
Book 6: A Body Under The Bridge

DEATH BY JOGGING

P.F. FORD

A Slater & Norman Mystery Book 13

JOFFE BOOKS

Revised edition 2024
Joffe Books, London
www.joffebooks.com

First published as *Deceptive Appearances*
in Great Britain in 2018

This paperback edition was first published
in Great Britain in 2024

Cover art by Dee Dee Book Covers

ISBN: 978-1-83526-777-6

To my amazing wife, Mary — sometimes we need someone else to believe in us before we really believe in ourselves. None of this would have happened without her unfailing belief and support.

PROLOGUE

The young woman was in her late twenties. An attractive girl, she had one of those faces that broke into a smile at the slightest excuse, only now her face was twisted with fear as she ran for her life, her long blonde hair flying out behind her. The usually gleaming-white trainers she was so proud of were now thick with black mud, which was splashed up the legs of her red tracksuit bottoms. Her red T-shirt was torn in several places where she had rushed headlong through the undergrowth in panic.

Now she broke cover in the darkness and found herself on what she thought was a road but was in fact just a lay-by only used by the occasional trucker looking for a quiet stop. She could see a large truck over to her right. Its red tail lights glowed in the dark, and the engine seemed to be running. She reasoned there must be a driver inside, and if she could only attract his attention maybe he could save her.

Convinced she was doing the right thing, she changed direction and headed towards the truck. Not far to go now and she would be safe. Despite the confusion brought on by her panic, she noticed the truck seemed to be getting nearer much too quickly, but it was only in the final second or two she realised why.

But by then it was too late. The truck was reversing so quickly she had no chance . . .

CHAPTER ONE

'So I just need double top for the game, right?' asked Slater.

'Only because you cheated,' protested Norman.

'How could I have cheated? It's just simple subtraction.' Slater pointed to the blackboard they had nailed to the wall next to their dartboard. 'You can see for yourself.'

Now Norman pointed to the suspiciously smudged numbers chalked on the board. 'Anyone can see you changed those figures when I was in the loo.'

'I don't need to cheat to beat you at darts, Norm. You're rubbish, and you know you are!'

'I'll have you know I used to play for my station when I was in the Met.'

'And how many games did you win?'

'I dunno, I didn't keep count. Anyhow, it's not all about winning, it's the taking part.'

'That's just as well,' muttered Slater.

'I heard that! What are you suggesting?'

'Let's be honest, Norm. If we enter a contest as a doubles team, we aren't even going to get through the first round — unless we're up against a short-sighted pair and we steal their glasses.'

'You really think so? Only you're pretty good. I was sort of hoping you could make up for me being not so good.'

'I don't want to put you down, Norm, but even a "not so good player" ought to be able to hit the board with every dart. You waste at least one dart every throw. You need to accept it's just not your thing. That's how it is sometimes.'

Norman heaved a sigh. 'I suppose you have a point. Okay, I admit I'm crap at darts, so how about we make this last game more interesting?'

'More interesting?'

'We know you're going to win, right?'

'Right, so?'

Norman produced a ten-pound note from his pocket and held it up for Slater to see. 'Ten quid says you can't get that double top with your first dart.'

'Really?' said Slater. 'You know I never miss those.' He held his hand out. 'You might as well give me the money now.'

'Arrogance,' said Norman, placing his money on the table. 'I like that. You do know it's a weakness, don't you?'

'There's a whole world of difference between arrogance and confidence,' said Slater. 'I'm confident we both know I'm going to win this bet and collect the cash, but just to make you happy, I'll match your ten.'

He took his wallet from his back pocket and removed a ten-pound note, which he slapped down on the table alongside Norman's. 'There you go.'

Slater watched as Norman adjusted the notes so Slater's was on top of his own.

'It'll make it easier for me to collect,' Norman explained.

Slater laughed. 'Yeah, right,' he said as he took careful aim at the board. Slowly, he pulled his arm back, ready to throw. 'The only way you're going to win this is if you cheat.'

'Yo!' called a voice from the next room. 'Anyone home?'

The timing of the shout couldn't have been better and was just enough to take Slater's eye away from the prize as he threw the dart. There was a familiar "thwock" as the dart plunged into the board.

'I'll be there in just a second,' called Norman. He stepped forward to look at the dartboard, his face breaking into a broad grin. 'Oh dear, what a shame. I think you'll find that's a treble, not a double. That means I win the bet.'

'I was distracted,' said Slater. 'You've got to let me have another go.'

'Why would I do that?'

'That voice. It put me off.'

'Yeah, it's a shame about that,' agreed Norman, 'but, as you told me not two minutes ago, that's how it is sometimes. So, you lose, and I collect the cash.'

'Wait a minute,' protested Slater. 'You can't do that.'

'Sure, I can,' said Norman, stuffing the two ten-pound notes into his pocket. 'See? It was easy.'

'Yeah, but—'

Norman grinned at him. 'I told you arrogance was a weakness. Anyhow, I don't have time to argue — we may have a new client out there in reception, and it would be rude to ignore them. Are you coming?'

Slater snorted in good-humoured disgust and then followed Norman from the room. That was one up to Norm, but it wasn't even lunchtime yet. There was plenty of time to get even.

CHAPTER TWO

'Good morning,' Norman was saying as Slater entered the room. 'My name's Norman Norman, and this is my colleague, Dave Slater.'

Norman was addressing a man wearing jeans, a white T-shirt and a black bomber jacket. Slater was surprised to find his immediate impression was that this guy could get away with a lot. Apart from being shifty-looking, he seemed to have no distinguishing features, and because of that, most people would probably have difficulty describing him — or even remembering him.

As the man introduced himself and they shook hands, Slater wondered why he had viewed the newcomer in this way. Was it gut instinct or was he simply smarting over the loss of a tenner and knew this man was responsible?

Norman led them over to their informal seating area, and they sat down. 'Now, Mr Davies, or can I call you Adrian? How can we help you?'

'Everyone calls me Adie,' he said. 'I need some help finding someone. Can you do that sort of thing?'

'We are detectives. Finding people is one of the things we do.'

'Who do you want us to find?' asked Slater.

Davies fished a photograph from his pocket and passed it across to Norman. 'Her name is Martha Dennis. She's my sister.'

Norman studied the photo, then passed it to Slater.

'She looks a bit young to be your sister,' said Slater.

'I'm afraid it's an old photo, but it's all I have.'

'How long has she been missing?' asked Norman.

'A year to the day,' said Davies.

'Where did she go missing? Was it somewhere local? Only I can't recall anything like that from a year ago.'

'The last time anyone saw her she was getting on a train in Portsmouth, heading for London.'

'Portsmouth?' said Norman. 'Was she living there?'

'Not exactly.'

Slater had been gazing silently at the photograph, but now he spoke. 'What does that mean?' he asked, looking up at Davies.

'She was a bit of a nomad, you know, liked to move around a lot. At the time she disappeared she was living somewhere around here.'

'You're her brother, but you don't know where she was living?'

'I know the area, but not the exact address.'

'And what was the area?'

'The postal town was Tinton.'

'That's a bit vague,' said Slater. 'It's a small town, but as a postal district it covers quite a large area and includes at least a dozen villages. Are you sure you don't know her address? Where did you send birthday cards and things?'

'We weren't that close,' said Davies. 'We didn't do birthdays. It's just that she's the only family I've got.'

'What about her husband?'

Davies looked confused. 'Husband?'

'Your name is Davies, and you said her name was Dennis. I'm assuming that means she was married.' Slater got the feeling he had inadvertently thrown Davies a lifeline.

'Oh, that. Yeah, she was married, but it didn't last five minutes.'

'So she's divorced?'

'I don't think she ever got around to that. I believe she left him but didn't bother with a divorce — that's the sort of thing she would do.'

There was an awkward silence before Norman spoke again. 'Did you report her missing to the police?'

'Oh, yeah, I told the police, but they're no help. The Portsmouth lot seemed to think that as she didn't live in Portsmouth, and she was seen getting on the train, it wasn't their problem, and the local lot weren't much better. They say as she's an adult, there's no sign of any foul play, and she moved around a lot anyway, she probably just fancied a change.'

'And what do you think?' asked Slater.

'Even though we weren't close, she always used to tell me when she was moving. She must have moved twenty times or more, but she always told me.'

'What I meant was, what do you think happened to her?'

For the first time, Davies looked him in the eye. 'I have no idea, but the fact she didn't tell me she was moving worries me.'

'It can't have worried you that much if you've waited a year before you tried to find her?'

'It's not like that. I've been looking everywhere, and I thought the police would be a lot more help than they have been.'

'So, now you've come to us,' said Norman.

'Will you help me?'

Norman looked at Slater. 'What d'you think, Dave? Can we help Mr Davies?'

Slater studied Davies for a moment. 'I think I might be a bit more inclined to say yes if Mr Davies were to tell us what he's holding back.'

Davies swallowed hard and his tongue darted out from between his lips. His eyes flicked between the two detectives, but all he got in return was a cold stare from Slater and a half-hearted smile from Norman.

'We'd be pleased to help you, Mr Davies,' said Norman, 'but as my colleague says, I'm sure you can appreciate we need to know all the facts before we make such a decision.'

Davies licked his lips again. 'The last time I spoke to my sister, she told me about a new friend she was hanging out with.'

'Does this friend have a name?' asked Slater.

'Alex.'

'Alex what?'

'I have no idea. All she said was the name Alex.'

'Is Alex male or female?'

'I'm pretty sure he was a he.'

'Do you know what this Alex looks like?'

'No. I'm sorry, I have no idea.'

'That's not exactly going to help us much,' observed Slater.

'That's why I didn't mention it before.'

'Can you think of anything your sister said about Alex that might help us?' asked Norman.

'Are you even sure they were friends?' Slater added.

'They were definitely friends,' insisted Davies. 'Apparently Alex liked to go jogging every morning, and Martha had taken to going along too. According to her, they even had matching red outfits.'

'Maybe Alex was a fitness coach,' suggested Norman.

Davies smiled. 'My sister never, ever worried about keeping fit. She used to smoke, live on fast food, and drink like a fish. She was even known to snort coke from time to time.'

'But you just told us she was going jogging every morning. Maybe she turned over a new leaf,' said Slater.

'Or maybe they were a bit more than friends,' said Norman.

Davies considered the idea for a few seconds. 'That's always a possibility, I suppose, but I've never heard her mention a boyfriend before.'

There was an awkward silence as they all considered the situation.

'You're sure you've told us everything now?' asked Slater suspiciously.

Davies held his hands up. 'That's everything, trust me. As I said, the only reason I didn't mention Alex before was because it's just a name.' He looked pleadingly at Norman. 'Will you help me find my sister?'

Norman looked at Slater, who gave an almost imperceptible nod.

'Okay, Mr Davies, we'll try to find your sister, but first you'll need to agree to our terms and give us some more details.'

For the first time since he had entered the room, Davies looked relaxed. 'Of course. Fire away. Anything I can do to help.'

CHAPTER THREE

Slater watched through the window as Adrian Davies walked across the car park, climbed into his car, and drove away.

'What did you make of him?' he asked, turning to Norman.

'How d'you mean?'

'Maybe it's just me, but I thought he was feeding us a lot of bullshit.'

'He was pretty vague at times,' agreed Norman. 'And he didn't want to make eye contact, did he?'

'I couldn't see any resemblance between him and his sister.'

'That's hardly conclusive proof of anything. This is going to sound weird, but he didn't seem to resemble anyone, did he?'

'You noticed that too? He'd be hard to describe, right?'

'No distinguishing features, that's for sure.'

'And he was insistent we shouldn't waste our time with the police,' said Slater.

'Yeah, that made me suspicious,' agreed Norman. 'That's why I fed him the line about the police being a waste of space and how we wouldn't go near them with a bargepole.'

'I have to admit, that was a cute move on your part,' Slater said. 'I'm not sure I would have thought of that.'

Norman acknowledged the compliment with a slight nod. 'I guessed it was what he wanted to hear.'

Slater reached into his pocket and found a pound coin. He flicked it into the air. 'Call it, Norm,' he said, catching it on the back of his right hand and covering it with the left.

'Is it my turn again?'

'You know the rules: whoever wins the toss gets the casting vote.'

'Heads,' called Norman.

Slater uncovered the coin. 'It must be your lucky day. That's twice now.'

'We don't have to take the job if you don't want to.'

'I didn't say I didn't want to take it. Anyway, we just took a deposit.'

'Yeah, but with all these doubts, why would you want it? I can see you don't like the guy. We can still change our minds and turn it down.'

'I don't have to like him,' said Slater. 'Anyway, we can't really turn it down, can we? I know we've both got other income, but this place will become a money drain if we're not careful.'

'It's not that bad, is it?'

'We're not going to go under any time soon, but we can't keep working for nothing. We seem to be pouring money in without getting anything back. We need to start making some money. And besides, aren't you just a little curious to know what this is really all about?'

'You smelled it too, right?' asked Norman.

'Definitely enough bullshit to make me want to find out what's really going on. Either he's up to something, or he knows exactly how to reel us in.'

'It's intriguing though, right? And as the guy's just paid a big lump up front, I think we're more or less obliged, don't you?'

'You're right,' agreed Slater. 'I think there may be more to this than first meets the eye, but let's take it and see where it goes.'

'As long as he's paying, I don't think it matters where it goes,' said Norman. 'It might even make it more interesting.'

* * *

'Okay, let's have look at what we've got so far,' said Slater.

'It's not much,' said Norman. 'We have a photograph that must have been taken at least ten years ago. We know she lived somewhere in the Tinton area. We know it's possible she kept herself fit by jogging and that she used to wear red running gear.'

Slater sighed. 'That photograph is as good as useless. She's ten years older now. She might have changed her hair colour and who knows what else might be different. Hell, she could have a shaved head, be wearing glasses . . .'

'Don't forget the mystery jogging partner called Alex.'

'Oh, well, that narrows it down, then,' said Slater. 'We're looking for someone called Martha, but we have no idea what she looks like. She might go jogging, and perhaps wears red when she does. And she could be with a friend called Alex, whose appearance is even more of a mystery than Martha's.'

'I admit it's pretty vague,' said Norman.

'Vague? That's an understatement.'

'You forgot something else.'

'I did? Go on, then.'

'She has a year's head start.'

'Oh, yeah, I forgot about that.' Slater heaved a big sigh and slumped back in his chair. 'Let's be honest, Norm, she could be anywhere on the bloody planet by now!'

Norman grinned. 'Is that it, now? Have you finished whingeing?'

Slater looked across at Norman, and his face broke into a smile. 'Yep,' he said. 'That's all the negatives we're up against. Now, where shall we start?'

'Seeing as our man was so insistent we shouldn't go to the police, how about you get in touch with that nice DI from Winchester?'

Slater laughed. 'I take it you're referring to Stella Robbins, whom I haven't spoken to since the day we walked her mother's dog in Wild Boar Woods.'

'That's her,' said Norman. 'Maybe she can find out if Martha Dennis was ever officially reported missing.'

'But I hardly know her! Besides, she's at Winchester, not Portsmouth.'

'Yes, and Tinton CID is now based at Winchester, isn't it?' said Norman. 'Besides, she's the only contact we have who might be able to find anything out for us.'

Slater pulled a face.

'There's no harm in asking, now is there?'

'No, I suppose not,' said Slater reluctantly.

'While you're doing that, I'm going to place an ad in the local newspaper. Maybe someone will recall seeing a woman looking like Martha with a man called Alex.'

CHAPTER FOUR

'DI Robbins.'

'Oh, hi. This is Dave Slater. Remember me?'

'Of course I remember you,' she said, with a smile in her voice. 'I was hoping you might call.'

'You were?'

'Shirley misses you.'

'Shirley?'

'My mum's dog. We walked her together, remember?'

'Ah. Right, yes, the walk.'

There was a brief, awkward silence before she spoke again, her tone now quite different. 'That's not why you're calling, is it?'

'Well, not exactly. I was wondering if you might be able to help us out?'

'Help you out with what?'

'We have a missing person to find, and we're not convinced she was reported missing to the police.'

'Why do you think that?'

'Just a hunch.'

'Why should I waste my time on your hunches?'

Slater thought she was being rather belligerent about what he thought was a simple enough request. 'I thought as we're friends you might be willing.'

'I still haven't got over what happened the last time I went near one of your cases.'

'I'm not with you.'

'When the shit hit the fan, and I got the blame.'

'I thought that would have been sorted out by now. You said it would be a case of a slapped wrist.'

'Well, it isn't. I'm still stuck behind a damned desk while they make their minds up what to do with me.'

'That's not good. I'm sorry,' said Slater. 'I had no idea.'

'Yes, well, I thought you might have called to find out, *as we're friends*.' The last three words were delivered with heavy sarcasm.

Slater was squirming with embarrassment. 'Fair enough. I'm sorry. I should have called.'

'I thought maybe Shirley had pissed you off or something. I mean, she was pretty wet, and when she shook herself all over you, there was mud everywhere.'

Slater smiled at the memory. 'That wasn't a big deal. It washed off easily enough.'

'Perhaps it was me, then? Was it something I said? Or maybe it was something I didn't do.'

'Stella, can you stop this? I mean it — Shirley didn't annoy me, and you didn't say anything wrong.'

'So it *was* what I *didn't* do. Well, I'm sorry, but I'm not like that. I need to get to know someone before I'm prepared to—'

'Stella! You didn't do anything wrong. I enjoyed the afternoon with you, and I'd like to do it again.'

'You would? So you didn't mind that I didn't want to come back and—'

'I actually respect the fact that you didn't. That's not the problem at all. It's just that I've been a bit busy, and well, it's a bit complicated.'

'A bit complicated? You told me you were single.'

'I *am* single.'

'So why is it complicated?'

'Because I like you, and I know how it will end up.'

'That's not a very good explanation. You'll have to do better than that.'

'I'm not sure I can, and I certainly can't do it now, over the phone.'

She thought for a moment. 'How about we make a deal, then? I'll look into your missing person report and, in return, you buy me dinner tonight and explain why it's complicated.'

Slater felt trapped. 'Yeah, but—'

'Take it or leave it. It's the only way I'm going to do you a favour.'

'I don't seem to have much choice.'

'Correction,' she said. 'You don't have *any* choice.'

'D'you bully all the men you come across?'

'It's not bullying, it's negotiating. It just so happens my negotiating skills are much better than yours.'

'Hmmm,' was all Slater could say to that.

'Now, does your missing person have a name?'

CHAPTER FIVE

It was 8 p.m. Slater had already been waiting nervously for fifteen minutes, and now Stella Robbins was officially late. A waiter shuffled up to him at the bar, carrying two menus.

'Your table is ready, sir.'

Slater looked past the waiter towards the entrance, but to no avail. 'I'm afraid my partner isn't here yet. Would it be okay to order another drink and wait here for a few more minutes?'

'But of course, sir. I'll bring your drink over in a moment.' With a little bow, the waiter backed away.

Slater sighed and wondered why he felt so nervous. It was just a date with a woman, for goodness sake. He had been on hundreds of dates before, so what was it about this one that made him so nervous?

A tinkling bell announced the arrival of another customer, and as he looked across the room, their eyes met, and hers crinkled at the corners as she smiled. Slater had seen Stella Robbins in her work suit and dressed for warmth in her dog-walking gear, but now she looked quite different as she walked across the room to join him. It took him a few seconds to realise it wasn't just the way she was dressed, but as he stood to greet her, he understood: she'd had her hair cut short.

'I thought I'd be fashionably late and keep you waiting,' she said.

'I suppose that's no more than I deserve,' he conceded. 'I nearly didn't recognise you with the new hairstyle.'

'Do you like it?'

'Yes, I do. It suits you.'

'I thought I'd do something girly to cheer myself up.'

* * *

Once settled at their table, it wasn't until they had ordered their food that Robbins mentioned the deal.

'I'll tell you what I managed to find out about your runaway,' she said, 'and then you can tell me about your problem.'

Slater had been hoping the second part of this arrangement could have been avoided, but it was obvious he had no chance. 'Okay. If you insist.'

She flashed him an impish smile. 'Oh, I do, believe me.'

She produced a sheet of paper from her handbag and unfolded it on the table before her. 'Right then. I dug out the report that was filed for Martha Dennis. She was reported missing on 12 March 2018.'

'That's not a year ago,' said Slater.

'I'm sorry?'

'Are you sure that's right? We were told she had been missing a year to the day.'

She pulled a face. 'I can only go by the date on the report, but if anyone's lying, my money would be on your guy.'

'I had a feeling he was feeding us a load of crap,' muttered Slater.

'What's that?'

'I'm sure you're right. We think our guy is up to something — we just don't have any idea what it is. Go on, please.'

'Well, don't get too excited,' she said. 'There isn't a great deal to tell. It turns out Martha spent most of her teenage years running away from home—'

'So, with resources being what they are, she wasn't exactly a high priority,' finished Slater.

'Not only that,' said Robbins, 'she also happens to be twenty-eight years old, and as an adult, she can come and go whenever she pleases.'

'What about the friend, Alex? Did they find him?'

'There's no mention of an Alex in this report.'

Slater's mouth dropped open. 'That's weird. Her brother said she had talked about this guy Alex. It seems he was her only friend.'

'Not according to the file.'

'Are you sure?' he asked.

'Has anyone ever told you how annoying that is?' she asked sharply.

'How annoying what is?'

'Asking me if I'm sure every time I tell you something. I can promise you I double-checked everything, especially the stuff that didn't agree with what you told me.'

Slater felt his face turn red. 'Actually, yes, it has been mentioned once or twice before.'

'Oh, so it's a habit, is it?'

'Apparently, yes. I'm sorry.'

'You will be if you keep on doing it,' she teased.

'Okay,' he said, sheepishly. 'Point taken. I apologise again. It's just that I didn't expect quite so many discrepancies between what we were told and the official version.'

She smiled at how easy it had been to wind him up. 'Apology accepted. So, what's going on?'

'As I said, we knew the guy wasn't exactly being straight with us.'

'Why do you think he came to you?'

'My guess? He thinks we're two country bumpkins who don't know their arses from their elbows.'

'Are you going to keep working for him?'

'I'm not sure. The thing is, he's already paid us a pretty big wedge as a retainer.'

She looked amused. 'I didn't have you down as a money-grabber.'

Now it was Slater's turn to be amused. 'It's not about money-grabbing. We're not like you lot, paid for by the public. We're a business.'

She nodded. 'Good point. I hadn't thought of it like that.'

'The thing is, my bullshit radar was twitching when we spoke to the guy this morning. Now it's well and truly engaged,' he said. 'And we're not exactly overwhelmed with clients who would be pushed to the back of the queue.'

'If you don't mind me asking, how long is the queue?'

'This guy is it.'

'I see. I didn't realise you were so . . .'

'Close to the breadline?' finished Slater. 'Actually, it's not that bad. Norm has his pension, and I was left a bit of money. But, even so, we're not a charity. We can't pay the bills with fresh air.'

There was a brief silence as Robbins let this sink in. 'Did this Adrian Davies tell you anything that was actually true?'

Slater smiled ruefully. 'Ha! You have to wonder, don't you? At least we know there were a couple of partial truths. He got Martha's name right, and he did report her missing, even if he got the date wrong.'

'Are you going to confront him?'

'I'll have to speak with Norm first, see what he thinks.'

'But he's obviously up to something.'

'Of course, he is,' agreed Slater, 'and the first question is, why is he looking for her?'

'Jilted lover?'

Slater tilted his head. 'My gut tells me it's not that. I think there's only one way we're going to find out, and I suspect Norm will feel much the same as me.'

'What does that mean?'

'It means the only way we'll find out what he's up to is if we carry on as if we're the two know-nothing idiots he thinks we are and see what we can dig up.'

'I can check him out if you like?'

Slater held up a hand. 'I can't ask that.'

'You didn't ask. I offered.'

He shook his head. 'When we spoke earlier, you told me you were still flying a desk after last time. What would happen if someone found out you were doing extracurricular stuff for me and Norm again? That wouldn't help your case, would it?'

She pouted thoughtfully. 'I'd be careful.'

'Yeah, and you could still get found out. I don't want that to happen, no matter how small the risk.'

'Well, if you change your mind.'

Slater smiled and returned her gaze. 'I won't.'

* * *

Slater watched as Stella sipped at her glass of wine. He really fancied a pint but had stuck to mineral water all evening as he was driving. They had passed the time over dinner with idle chitchat, and he found her very good company. He felt totally relaxed and was beginning to think maybe he was going to be spared from having to explain himself. Then coffee arrived, and instead of drinking, she placed her elbows on the table and studied his face.

'What?' he asked.

'You told me you were going to explain something to me,' she reminded him.

'Did I? What was that?'

She gave him a look that told him she knew that he knew very well what she meant. 'You were going to explain why this is complicated.'

'Oh, that.'

'Yes, *that*.'

'It's pretty boring.'

'I don't care how boring it is. A deal's a deal. I did my bit, now it's your turn.'

'It's not—'

She held a hand up. 'Stop making excuses. You told me you knew how this would end. I think, having said that, you owe me an explanation, don't you?'

'I don't know where to start.'

'How about you start by telling me what "this" is?'

'Us?' he said. 'You and me?'

To his horror, her face seemed to be telling him he may be jumping to conclusions, but then she looked down at her coffee.

'If we were to start dating, I mean,' he added hurriedly.

She appeared to be studying her coffee, but he could see the corners of her mouth lifting.

'I think you know exactly what I mean,' he said.

Now she looked up at him, her smile infectious, her eyes sparkling. She placed her elbows on the table again, put her hands together, and rested her chin on them, still studying his face. 'Is that what we're doing now? Dating?'

It was quite clear she was teasing him, but two could play at that game.

'I thought this was just a deal,' he said. 'An information trade.'

She pouted again. 'I thought that was just an excuse to take me out to dinner.'

'Dinner was your idea,' he reminded her.

'Was it? Oh, yes, that's right, it was. But you are enjoying my company, aren't you?'

'I am,' he admitted. 'Very much.'

'Does that mean you would like to ask me for a date?'

'It wouldn't end well, Stella.'

She looked at him enquiringly. 'How can you possibly know that?'

'Because it always ends that way.'

'But why?'

'I seem to have a problem making long-term commitments with women.'

'Whoa,' she said. 'Hang on a minute. Who said anything about long-term commitments? I'm talking about going on a date, not getting married.'

Slater felt his face redden again. 'I know that. The thing is, if we started going out, and it got serious, there would come a point where I would end it rather than see it through.'

She looked vaguely offended and considered his words for a moment before she spoke. 'Why do men always assume they are the ones who would get to make that decision? It's very arrogant to assume women are simpering idiots who don't have any say in what happens.'

Slater hadn't assumed any such thing and certainly hadn't intended to offend her. But he was rather thrown by the unexpected question, and before he could think of an answer, she was off again.

'What makes you so sure I'd stick around? How do you know I wouldn't dump you first?'

'I didn't mean it like that,' he said. 'I started with "if". I wasn't assuming anything. And don't worry, I'm well aware women can make those decisions.'

She was trying to look serious, but there was no hiding the smile that threatened to engulf her face.

'And of course you could very easily decide to dump me first, but why are you talking about that when we haven't even started dating yet?'

She gave him a condescending smile. 'Actually, I think you'll find *you* raised the subject first. I was just making sure you understand there is an opposing point of view.'

Slater nodded his acceptance of her right to have an opinion. 'Okay,' he said, grinning. 'That's fair enough. You might dump me, but why on earth would you want to?'

'Ha!' She rolled her eyes and laughed. 'You mean your arrogance wouldn't be enough? Okay, let me see. We've only been here for a couple of hours and I've already identified one annoying habit. There could be loads more for me to find.'

'Yeah,' he said sadly, his mood suddenly darker, 'you're probably right about that. It comes from spending years on my own.'

'Are you telling me you don't go out with women?'

'I'm here, aren't I? Of course I go out with women, but the thing is, I like you, and I wouldn't want to hurt you.'

'And there's a reason that always happens, is there?' she asked.

'I don't know what it is. It just happens every time.'

'Trust me, I'm quite a tough old bird. If you ended up dumping me, I'm sure I'd cope.'

'Maybe it's me. Perhaps I'm just a complete arse and I don't see it.'

She snorted. 'I don't believe that for one minute,' she said. 'Besides, you couldn't possibly be as bad as my ex-husband was.'

He looked at her enquiringly.

'Oh, don't worry, he's long gone from my life,' she said. 'He was the man who put the arse into arsehole. You couldn't possibly match him.'

'I'm not sure if that was a compliment or not,' he said.

'It's definitely a compliment,' she said. She looked at her watch. 'I don't want to be a killjoy, but I've got an early start in the morning. You know what it's like.'

'Yes, of course,' he said. 'Have you got far to go?'

'Well . . . it's just that—'

'I'm offering you a lift, Stella, that's all. I'm not expecting anything else.'

She looked doubtful, and Slater wondered what was bothering her.

'I promise you I'm not assuming anything,' he assured her. 'I'm not that kind of man.'

* * *

The atmosphere in the car on the ride to her house could best be described as tense. The easy atmosphere between them in the restaurant had been replaced by a nervous silence. Slater wondered what her problem was and spent the journey wracking his brain trying to understand what he'd done wrong. The only thing he could think was that she thought he was going to try something on. He decided that if she had doubts about whether she could trust him, he intended to make sure he didn't give her reason to feel they were justified.

It was barely ten minutes before they were outside her house. He made sure his movements were slow and deliberate as he stopped the car and put the handbrake on. Then he placed his hands on the steering wheel and they sat in the darkness, both staring ahead.

'Thank you,' she said. 'It's very kind of you to go out of your way.'

'Nonsense. It's no trouble. I couldn't leave you to make your own way home. I know it sounds old-fashioned in these days of independent women, but it wouldn't feel right.'

'I've really enjoyed this evening. It's been fun,' she said.

'Would you like to do it again?' The words were out of his mouth before he had even realised what he was saying.

In the darkness he couldn't see her reaction, but he was sure she had frozen, just for a second or two before she spoke. 'It's been a long time since—'

She stopped abruptly in mid-sentence, and he wondered what she hadn't said, but a little voice in his head told him to mind his own business.

'Maybe you'd like some time to think about it,' he said gently. 'I mean, there's no rush, is there? If you decide you'd like to, you know how to get hold of me.'

She had the car door open now. 'Yes, thank you, I think that's a good idea,' she said as she slipped from her seat. 'I'll call you.' And then she was out of the car and walking away.

He watched as she walked across the pavement and through a small gate. He realised he had been holding his breath, and now he let it out in one long, slow whoosh, then he let the handbrake off, put the car into gear, and pulled away. As he headed for home, he wondered what that was all about. What had happened to the cool confident DI he had got to know? She had been fine when they had walked her mother's dog. She was all warmth and fun in the restaurant, and then what?

She said it had been a long time since . . . Obviously, something had happened to her somewhere along the line, and whatever it was had made her very wary. He had a nasty feeling he could guess what it might have been. If he was right, she probably had a right to be wary of any man.

CHAPTER SIX

When Slater arrived for work next morning, he was carrying a large bag stuffed with clothes.

'Having a clear-out, huh?' asked Norman, nodding at the bag. 'I'm sure the charity shop will appreciate the donation.'

'It's not a donation,' said Slater indignantly. 'My washing machine's broken down. This is my washing.'

'Oh, right. I'm sorry.'

'I'm going to whizz down to the laundrette once I've had a cup of tea, if that's okay?'

'I'm sure we can spare you for a while,' said Norman. 'So how was the hot date?'

'It wasn't a date, as you well know,' said Slater. 'DI Robbins did us a favour, and I bought her dinner in return.'

Normally he might consider sharing his thoughts about Robbins' behaviour with Norman, but he felt he owed it to her to keep quiet on this occasion. Whatever her problem was, he didn't feel it was his place to share it. Not even with Norm.

'But you wanted an excuse to take her out, right?' Norman persisted.

'Dinner was *her* idea.'

'But you didn't say no, did you?'

'It was just part of the deal. That's all there was to it, alright?'

Norman wasn't convinced, but recognised Slater was like a bear with a sore head this morning and backed off. 'So what did we learn from this deal?'

'We had our suspicions about Davies confirmed.'

'In what way?'

'He did report Martha missing, but in March, not a year ago.'

'D'you think she went missing in March, or did he just wait until March to make the report?'

'That's exactly what I thought, but hang on a minute, because it gets worse. There was no mention of anyone called Alex in the police report.'

'So, the police would have been looking for a woman on her own when she might have been with a guy,' said Norman. 'No wonder they didn't find her.'

'They didn't find her because they didn't really try to. Davies told them she had a record of going missing ever since she was a kid. Besides, she's twenty-eight years old, and there was no sign of foul play.'

'So, because she was an adult, they told him she's free to disappear any time she feels like it,' finished Norman.

'Exactly,' said Slater.

'Did Davies actually tell us *anything* that was true?'

'Well, he got Martha's name right, and he did report her missing, but that's about it.'

'What's he up to?' asked Norman thoughtfully. 'This is sounding more like a wild goose chase every time you open your mouth. Are we wasting our time here?'

Slater smiled. 'It looks as if that's a possibility, but don't forget, if we are wasting our time, we're at least being paid for it.'

'You think we should carry on?'

'Aren't you intrigued?'

'Well, yeah, of course I am,' said Norman, 'but if Davies is just going to feed us more crap . . .' He took in Slater's face. 'Did we actually learn something useful?'

'Robbins gave me an address.'

'Is it far?'

'I'm not certain, but I think it's not far from the laundrette.'

'What? Here in Tinton?'

Slater nodded. 'That's what she said. I thought I'd check it out when I go down there later. It's somewhere to start.'

'What about Davies?'

'I suggest we let him carry on thinking we're too stupid and greedy to work any of this out. And, as you said, he'll probably just feed us more bullshit.'

'But what if he was lying when he said he didn't know where she was living? I mean, he's lied about almost everything else. He could have been there and cleaned the place out.'

Slater nodded again. 'That's a possibility, but the chances are the place has been cleaned out anyway, as she's already been gone for six months.'

Norman was reading Slater's mind. 'But you think there might be a landlord or neighbour who could tell us about Martha, right?'

Slater smiled. 'So you're on board with this?'

'Hell, yeah! I'll come with you. I wanna know what this guy's up to, same as you do.'

'Okay, drink your tea, and then let's go see if we can find us a landlord — or a helpful neighbour.'

'Give me ten minutes,' said Norman. 'I have something I set up last night I have to check.'

* * *

'Holy crap!' muttered Norman a few minutes later.

'What's up?' asked Slater.

'You'd better come and have a look at this.'

Slater strolled across the room and peered over Norman's shoulder. 'What am I looking at?'

'This email from Vinnie.'

Vinnie was Norman's friendly computer wizard. Slater knew Vinnie was something of a genius but considered him to be a hacker and was always wary of using his help. 'Vinnie? Are you serious? You've brought *Vinnie* into this?'

'We've been through this before,' said Norman irritably. 'You know we don't have the resources we had in the police, and you know Vinnie can save us a lot of time. Isn't that why we approached Robbins?'

'That's not the same.'

'It saved us time, didn't it?'

'Well, yeah, I suppose so,' admitted Slater. 'But Vinnie cuts too many corners!'

'Look,' said Norman patiently, 'I get that you find Vinnie arrogant and cocky and that you don't like him, but just try to forget that for a minute. The thing you need to focus on is not his personality, but the fact he saves us shedloads of time whenever I ask him for help. And, just to prove my point, he's done it again. We're not going to argue about this, just read the damned email.'

Tutting loudly, Slater read the message. Norman had asked Vinnie to check out Davies. The result wasn't good news.

'Shit!' said Slater. 'A false address and phone number. That explains why he paid us in cash.'

'I bet Vinnie's going to come back to us later and tell us the guy's given us a false name as well,' said Norman. 'This stinks!'

'And then some,' agreed Slater.

'So, we have a guy with a fake address, and quite possibly a fake name, who has asked us to find a woman who might be with a friend who may, or may not, exist. The words needle and haystack came to my mind earlier, but now I'm beginning to think that would be a much easier thing to find.'

'And, just for good measure, it's quite possible we have a pile of dodgy cash in the safe,' added Slater.

'And for what?'

Slater pulled a face. 'My guess is he wants us to lead him to her. I have no idea why, but I'm sure it won't be for the good of her health. On that basis, I think we should try and find her without him finding out.'

'If she went missing to avoid him, she might be better off if we don't find her,' said Norman.

'But if he wants to find her that badly, we're probably not the only ones looking, so . . .'

Norman finished the sentence for him. 'It would be better if we found her before anyone else.'

Slater pointed a finger at Norman. 'Exactly!'

* * *

Half an hour later, they were walking up a narrow street on the outskirts of Tinton town centre. Slater stopped and looked at the house numbers.

'This *is* the right street, isn't it?' he asked.

'Yeah, this is it — Macklin Street,' Norman read from the sheet of paper he had torn from the office pad. 'We're looking for number 128.'

'Do you want to make another bet?' asked Slater.

'What about this time?'

'I bet you this address isn't right.'

Norman looked at the house numbers closest to them. 'There's 48, 50, 52.' He pointed down the street. 'We're going the right way, and we're on the right side.'

'Yeah, but already we're over halfway along. Unless someone missed out a load of house numbers up ahead, there's no way we're going to get to number 128.'

Norman looked back down the road and then up the other way. 'Crap! You're right.'

'We'd better check it now we're here,' said Slater. 'But I think we've been handed a dud.'

Five minutes later, they knew Slater had been correct. The houses ended at number 88. They had even tried number 28 without success. When another neighbour emerged from their house, they asked her if she had seen anyone matching their description, but the response only served to confirm their suspicion. They had drawn a blank.

'Bugger,' said Slater.

'I'll second that,' said Norman.

'What do we do now?'

'Well, unless you're going to take your dirty washing home with you, I suggest we may as well go back to the car, get your laundry bag, and go do your washing.'

* * *

'Okay, let's go,' said Norman, once Slater had retrieved his washing from the car. 'I can't remember the last time I went to a laundrette.'

'I'm just going to do my washing,' said Slater. 'It's not a visit to a theme park.'

'Are you kidding? This is going to be like a whole new experience for me.'

'You've lived on your own. I can't believe you've never been to a laundrette.'

'Yeah, well, maybe once or twice,' conceded Norman, 'but that was years ago. I always find them fascinating places. They're great for people-watching.'

'Well, don't get too excited. I doubt there will be many people to watch on a Tuesday morning.'

As Slater had predicted, the laundrette was deserted, and the only sign that anyone living had been anywhere near the place appeared in the form of an empty laundry basket that stood before one of the machines, which churned away noisily.

'Sorry, mate,' Slater said to Norman. 'No people to watch this morning.' He made his way across to the row of machines, chose the end one, and then put his bag down while he studied the instructions taped to the wall above the machine.

'I always wonder about people who do that,' said Norman.

Slater turned around. 'People who do what?'

Norman nodded towards the empty basket. 'Put their washing on, then walk off and leave it.'

'What's wrong with that? I used to put mine on and then go down to the supermarket and do my shopping while it washed.'

'Didn't you worry someone might steal your clothes?'

Slater looked at Norman with something approaching pity. 'You're kidding me, right?'

'What?' said Norman.

'Who steals clothes from a laundrette?'

'You never know.' Norman pointed to the machine, which was just starting a spin cycle and sounded as though it were getting ready for take-off. 'I mean, anyone could walk in here, empty that machine, and walk out again.'

Slater rolled his eyes. 'Yeah, right, except they'd have to wait for the machine to finish, and they'd be stealing a whole bunch of soggy clothes. Do you seriously think someone would steal wet clothes from a laundrette?'

'They never got the chance when I used these places,' said Norman. 'I used to sit there and watch mine to make sure.'

Slater looked Norman up and down, then grinned. 'Oh, come on, Norm. Seriously? Who would want to steal your clothes?'

'Ha! You'd be surprised.'

Slater scoffed. 'No,' he said. 'I wouldn't be surprised. I'd be astonished.'

'What does that mean?'

'How can I put this? Let's just say you're not exactly a fashion icon, are you?'

Norman looked down at his clothes. 'What's wrong with what I'm wearing?'

'Threadbare has never been in vogue to my knowledge.'

'Okay, so maybe the jacket's a bit worn,' conceded Norman. 'Anyway, I don't recall seeing your name on the latest list of well-dressed men.'

Slater smiled and winked at Norman. 'That's because they haven't seen me yet.'

'Ha! Don't kid yourself.'

Their discussion was interrupted by an exclamation from behind them.

'Well I never! David Slater. Gawd, I haven't seen you in years.'

They both spun around at the sound of the voice. A woman was standing, hands on hips, beaming at Slater. She was a little stooped, and her wrinkled face suggested she had long since waved goodbye to her sixties, and quite possibly her seventies too.

'Duchess?' he said.

'You haven't forgotten me name then,' she said.

He walked over to her and gave her a big hug, then stood back to look her up and down. 'You're looking very well, Duch.'

'You always were a flatterer,' she said. 'I look ancient, and you know it.'

'You're still looking good for your age, though, love.'

'And you're looking as handsome as ever,' she said. 'What on earth are you doing in here?'

'My washing machine's broken,' he said.

'I suppose you want me to do you a service wash, do you?'

'You don't still work here, do you? Surely you must've retired by now.'

'Officially I retired years ago,' she said. 'But I didn't know what to do with myself. Sitting around on me own's no fun. I need to be with people, so I asked if I could carry on here. Only part-time, like. They let me come and go as I please, so it's quite nice, really.'

'I suppose you've got a flock of young men relying on you to look after them?'

She blushed. 'I do a bit of washing and ironing for one or two,' she admitted. 'It earns me a little pocket money, and it keeps me out of trouble. It's so much better than being on my own.'

Norman had been loitering uncomfortably in the background, but now Duchess turned her gaze on him.

'This is my friend and business partner Norman Norman,' said Slater. 'Norm, this is the Duchess. She's an old friend of mine from way back.'

'I used to do all his washing for him, back in the day,' she said, nodding at Norman.

Norman beamed at her and stepped forward to gently shake her hand. 'He still needs someone to look after him,' he said.

'Is that your job?' she asked.

'It's not supposed to be, but someone's got to keep him clean and tidy, you know?'

She turned her attention back to Slater. 'Are you still in the police? You must be chief constable by now.'

'Ha! I think we both know there was never any chance of that happening, Duch. I got fed up with trying to work with my hands tied behind my back, so, in the end, I quit.'

'Oh dear, that's a shame. What are you doing now?'

Slater nodded at Norman. 'Norm was in the police too. Now we work together as private detectives.'

'Ooh! Like Sherlock Holmes and Doctor Watson? Which one of you is Sherlock?'

'To tell the truth, I sometimes think we're a bit more like Laurel and Hardy,' said Norman.

Duchess laughed. 'I'm sure that's not true. It must be very exciting.'

'Not very often,' said Slater with a rueful smile. 'Mostly we're just trying to find facts to make sense of things.'

'I remember when you used to come to me for stuff like that,' said Duchess wistfully.

'And very helpful you were too,' admitted Slater. 'You always knew what was going on locally.'

'I still do,' she said. 'I might not be able to get around like I used to, but there's nothing wrong with my sight or my hearing.'

'We could do with someone like you for the case we're working on now,' said Norman.

'What do you want to know?'

'We've been given an address — 128 Macklin Street.'

'That's not right,' said Duchess. 'They stop at 88.'

'Yes, we've just discovered that,' said Slater. 'Is there a 128 anywhere around here?'

She thought for a few seconds. 'No, dear. I can't think of anywhere around here that has numbers that high.'

'So that's a dead end then,' said Norman gloomily.

'Maybe I can help,' said Duchess. 'Who are you looking for?'

'A young woman called Martha Dennis, late twenties, slim, blonde hair. We've been told she was living around here up until last May.'

Duchess frowned in concentration for a few seconds. 'No, sorry, that doesn't ring any bells,' she said finally.

'She might have a boyfriend called Alex,' suggested Norman hopefully.

'I'm afraid that doesn't help,' said Duchess.

'She likes jogging,' said Slater. 'She used to jog with this guy Alex. Have you ever seen a young couple jogging around here?'

'I used to sometimes see a young woman early in the mornings, but I don't remember her having a man with her.'

'When was this?' asked Norman.

'I'm not sure. I haven't seen her recently. It was before the summer. Probably February or March.'

'Do you remember what she used to wear?' asked Slater.

'Now that I do recall, clearly. She always wore red.'

Slater and Norman exchanged a look. 'And you're sure she was never with a man?'

'I never saw her with a man, but maybe they used to meet up somewhere.'

Slater stepped forward, gently pulled Duchess towards him, and kissed her forehead.

'Duchess, you're an angel,' he said.

'Have I been helpful? Have I solved your case?'

'I don't know about solving the case,' he said, 'but so far we've had nothing to go on. At least now we know we might actually have a case to solve.'

'I'm not sure I understand.'

'It's not easy to explain,' said Norman, 'but trust me, you might just have given us somewhere to start. All we have to do now is try and work out where this woman lived.'

'I'll keep my eyes and ears open,' she said. 'If I learn anything else, I'll let you know.'

'Thanks, Duchess,' said Slater, handing her one of his cards. 'You can reach me or Norm on this number.'

She pointed to the bag of washing he had brought in with him. 'Aren't you coming back for your washing? It'll be ready this afternoon.'

'Of course. But if I can't get back—'

'If you don't get back today, I'll take it home with me. You know where I live. You can pick it up any time you're passing.'

'She's a dear old thing,' said Norman, as they walked down the street a couple of minutes later.

'Who, Duchess? Yeah, she's great. I used to see her all the time when I first moved here and was working as a PC. But then, eventually, I got my own flat with a washing machine, and I didn't need to use the laundrette any more. Seeing her now I feel guilty about it, because I should have kept in touch with her.'

'Life happens, and people drift apart,' said Norman. 'That's just how it is. She doesn't seem to hold it against you. Why is she called Duchess?'

'Her surname is Ellington. When he was alive, everyone knew her husband as "Duke", so it was only natural she would be his "Duchess".'

'Ha! I like that,' said Norman.

* * *

At six thirty that evening, Slater put his finger to the doorbell and pressed. A few seconds later, there was a sudden burst of noise from a TV as an inside door opened, and then a light was switched on.

'Who is it?' called a voice uncertainly.

'It's me, Dave Slater.'

There was a sound of locks being undone and bolts sliding across, then the door opened a crack and a beady eye peered out at him. Then the door closed again, and he heard a chain being slid back. Finally, the door swung open.

'Well, come on in,' said Duchess. 'Don't let all the warmth out.'

Slater stepped hastily through the door into a tiny hallway with three doors leading from it. Duchess swung the front door closed behind him and slid the two bolts across.

'It's a sad state of affairs, having to have all these locks, but you can't be too careful these days,' she said, as she turned to face him.

'I'm afraid you're right about that, Duchess,' he agreed.

'Mrs James, around the corner, let a man in the other week. He told her he'd come to read the electric meter. After he'd gone, she realised he'd nicked her purse. Poor thing, it was pension day, and he took the lot.'

'Did she tell the police?'

'Oh yes,' she said. 'But they as good as told her it was her own fault for letting him in. They say they'll look into it, but it won't come to anything. They always say they're going to investigate, but they never catch anyone, do they?'

Slater felt a deep-seated desire to defend the police, but he knew she was right. 'It's not that they don't care. They just don't have the numbers to investigate like they used to, so they have to prioritise.'

'That's not much help to Mrs James, is it? How's she supposed to live with no money?'

Slater had no answer for that, and he felt a stab of guilt, as if it were all his fault.

Duchess sighed. 'I'm sorry, I know it's not your fault, son. I just don't know what the world's coming to these days. Come on through.'

She led him through a door into a small, neat living room where an ancient television set filled the room with jangly sound. Slater was just thinking it was going to be impossible to hold a conversation in this din when Duchess reached for the remote control and switched the set off.

'Don't let me spoil your viewing,' he said.

She smiled a weary smile. 'Don't be silly. It's mostly repeats of repeats, so I'm only missing something I've already seen umpteen times before.' She pointed to a chair. 'It's nice to have a reason to turn the damned thing off. I don't get many visitors. Sit down a minute while I get your washing for you.'

As he settled into the chair she had indicated, still feeling responsible for the fate of Mrs James around the corner, Slater was now suffering additional guilt after hearing Duchess didn't have many visitors.

She bustled through another door into what he assumed must be her kitchen, and almost immediately she came back with his laundry.

'I've ironed it for you too,' she said, placing the bag by his chair.

'You didn't have to do that, Duchess.'

'I didn't do it because I had to — I did it because I wanted to. For old times' sake.'

Slater felt his face begin to colour and suffered yet another stab of guilt. 'Thank you, you're very kind.'

'I thought you'd left the area.'

Slater shifted uncomfortably and wondered if it was possible to feel more guilty. 'I'm sorry,' he said. 'I should have kept in touch.'

She studied his face for a moment, then smiled. 'No, dear,' she said. 'You don't need to apologise. There was no reason why you should have kept in touch. We all have friends that we drift apart from. That's just the way it is.'

Slater wasn't quite sure if she was being genuine or if this was another, much more subtle way of adding to his guilt trip, so he said nothing but decided that if she was going to continue twisting the knife, he was going to have to leave. At last, she changed the subject.

'I think I might have some information for you,' she said.

'Really?'

'I go to this afternoon club sometimes, and after you left this morning, I got to remembering someone there had mentioned having a young woman lodger. So I went there this afternoon, and I was right.'

She looked at him expectantly, her face suggesting she might just have solved his case or perhaps identified Jack the Ripper.

'Does this person have a name?' he asked.

'No, but it was definitely a young woman, and she used to go running.'

'I mean the person who had the lodger. Do they have a name?'

'Oh, yes, silly me. His name is Vernon Tisdale.'

'And where can I find this Vernon Tisdale?'

'I'll write his address down for you, if you like.'

'That would be great, Duchess, thank you.'

She went to a small bureau in a corner of the room, produced a notepad and a pen, and wrote down the address. Then she tore the sheet of paper from the pad and brought it across to Slater. He looked at the spidery writing that crawled untidily across the page.

'I suppose you'll be on your way now,' she said sadly.

'Actually, I was rather hoping you might offer me a cup of tea.'

A smile suddenly lit up her face. 'Really?'

'Why not?' he said. 'We can have a chat, catch up on old times. If that's alright with you?'

'Of course it's alright with me. I'll put the kettle on.'

CHAPTER SEVEN

'Mr Tisdale? My name is Norman Norman, and this is my partner David Slater. We're private detectives trying to find a missing person, and we think you may be able to help us. We were wondering if you wouldn't mind answering a few questions.'

The old man standing before them tilted his head to one side as if he hadn't understood. 'What questions?'

Vernon Tisdale was seventy-four years old. He was tall, white-haired, stick-thin and used a walking stick. He had an angular face, and when he smiled, Slater was reminded of a skull a pathologist had once shown him.

'We understand you used to have a lodger, a young lady.'

'There's no law against having lodgers, is there?'

'We're not the police, Mr Tisdale, and we're not here to accuse you of anything. We heard you used to have a lodger, and we believe she may be the person we're looking for. We were hoping you might be able to tell us something about her.'

'My memory's not very good, you know. I'm not sure I can help.'

'How about we ask you a few questions?' suggested Norman. 'If you can help us, that's great, and if you can't, that's okay too.'

'The questions might jog your memory,' added Slater.

'What questions?'

Norman exchanged a quick glance with Slater, who rolled his eyes.

'How about you let us come in for five minutes?' said Norman.

'How do I know who you are?'

'You've seen our cards,' said Slater, 'but if you want more proof, I can give you a phone number for a Detective Inspector Robbins at Winchester Police headquarters. She'll vouch for us.'

The old man considered for a few seconds, then stepped back. 'You'd better come inside,' he said sharply.

They followed him down a dark, dingy hallway and into a damp-smelling room on the left. He hobbled across to an armchair and sank down into it. He didn't offer them a seat, but Slater didn't mind. There was a smell in the room he didn't trust, so he preferred to stand.

'Well, get on with it,' snapped Tisdale.

From what Duchess had told Slater last night, Vernon Tisdale used to be in business and had a reputation for being a tyrant, so his impatience was no more than they had expected.

'Is it right you had a lodger?' asked Norman.

'Yes, I think that's correct.'

'You think? Don't you know?'

'I told you my memory isn't what it used to be.'

'But you had someone sharing your house?'

'She didn't share my house. She lived in the basement.'

'She?' asked Norman.

Tisdale looked puzzled. 'What?'

'You just said "she" lived in the basement.'

'Did I?'

'Yes, you did,' said Slater.

'I suppose I must have, then.'

'So you *did* have a lodger, and she was a woman,' insisted Norman patiently.

'If you say so.'

Norman sighed. 'Look, Mr Tisdale, a woman called Martha Dennis is missing, and we're trying to find her. I'm not suggesting you have anything to do with her disappearance, but if she was living here, you might be able to help us find her.'

'That name doesn't mean anything to me.'

'But you admit you had a young woman living in your basement?'

'You tricked me into saying that.'

'I don't think I did,' said Norman.

'Can we have a look in her room?' asked Slater.

'Definitely not!' snapped Tisdale. 'It's empty, all cleared out. Her stuff's all gone.'

'Where has it gone?'

'I don't know. The letting agent handled all that. He arranged for her to come and stay, and he cleared her stuff away after she left. She stopped paying the rent. I couldn't have her stuff here if she wasn't paying the rent.'

Norman produced a photograph and handed it to the old man. He stooped over the photo for a few seconds, then looked up at Slater and Norman in turn. 'Who's this?'

'Martha Dennis,' said Norman. 'Is that the woman who was living here?'

Tisdale looked down at the photograph again. 'This is a young girl, not a woman.'

'Yeah, I'm afraid it's the only photograph we have. It was taken when she was a teenager. She's coming up to thirty now,' said Norman.

Tisdale handed the photograph back. 'That's not how she looks now.'

'You mean it is Martha?'

'I didn't say that. What I mean is the woman who lived here didn't look like that.'

'Did the woman who was living here have a boyfriend?' asked Norman.

'I wouldn't allow that sort of thing here.'

'Did she ever mention a boyfriend? A guy called Alex?'

'Of course not. I never spoke to her.'

'You didn't?'

'Why would I? She lived in the basement, and I lived up here. I had no need to speak to her.'

'You say the agent handled all the details,' said Slater. 'Can you tell us this agent's name?'

'I have no idea.'

'You must have had an invoice of some sort,' said Norman. 'Letting agents don't work for nothing.'

'He took his fee from the rent.'

'Okay, so you must have had some sort of contract.'

'It was a verbal arrangement.'

'That's very convenient,' said Slater.

The old man gave him a distasteful look. 'I think you should leave now. I'm feeling very tired, and you're just confusing me with all these questions.'

Slater and Norman exchanged a look. 'Okay, Mr Tisdale. I understand,' said Norman. 'Maybe we can come back in a day or two.'

'There's not much point,' said Tisdale. 'My memory isn't suddenly going to be any better.'

'Yeah, right,' said Slater. 'Of course it's not.'

The old man gave him another disapproving look, but he didn't say a word.

* * *

'The guy's taking the piss,' said Slater as they walked away from Vernon Tisdale's house. 'I bet his mind is sharper than mine. He's hiding something.'

'Yeah, I thought so too,' said Norman. 'Let's give him a day or two to think about it and then pay him another visit.'

CHAPTER EIGHT

It was just before midday when Slater's mobile phone started ringing. As he looked at the caller ID his eyebrows raised in surprise, and he lifted the phone to his ear.

'Hi, Stella, I wasn't expecting to hear from you today.'

'I wasn't joking when I told you I had an early start yesterday. The thing is, when I got here my meeting had been cancelled but, being an afterthought at the moment, no one thought to tell me.'

'I bet that made you happy.'

'I wasn't best pleased, as you can imagine,' she said, 'but then I thought that as I was here with time to spare, I might as well do something useful, so I did a bit more digging into your case.'

'I thought we agreed you wouldn't take any risks,' said Slater.

'No, that's what *you* agreed. I didn't agree to anything of the sort,' she said firmly. 'I make my own decisions about these things.'

Slater sighed. He knew when an argument was a lost cause, and this one was exactly that. 'I assume you're calling because you have some news, then?'

'That's a very astute assumption.'

'Sharp as a knife, that's me. Come on then, what's this news? Is it good?'

'That depends what you mean by good. It's certainly interesting.'

'That sounds ominous,' said Slater. 'Go on then, let's hear it.'

'You might want to sit down.'

'I am sitting down, and I'm sure it can't be that bad.'

'I wouldn't bet on it,' she said.

'Just tell me.'

'Okay, here goes then. First of all, according to our records, Martha Dennis doesn't have a brother.'

'Well, I can't say I'm surprised to hear that.'

'Oh, really?' She sounded disappointed.

'It turns out he gave us a false address, and we're half expecting to find Adrian Davies isn't his real name, so nothing's going to surprise me about this guy.'

'How did you find out about the address?'

'We have this guy Norm knows.'

Slater stopped speaking for a moment. He wondered if it was really a good idea to tell a detective inspector he hardly knew about Vinnie. He thought perhaps discretion might be the best plan.

'He lives up in London,' he continued. 'Norm asked him to check Davies' address out. It turns out the place doesn't exist. The phone number's a dud too.'

'That rather complicates things, doesn't it?'

'Yes and no. The arrangement is for him to come to us for updates so, in theory, we don't need to know where he lives.'

'It sounds like you probably weren't supposed to find out.'

'Well, as I said before, he thinks we're two dimwits who would need a map to find our own backsides. Anyway, is that it? Did I really need to sit down for something we were more or less expecting?'

'Probably not,' she said, 'but you might want to be sitting down for the next bit of news.'

'That good, is it?'

'It surprised me.'

'Let's hear it then.'

'Okay. According to the information our mystery man submitted, Martha Dennis was twenty-eight years old and as fit as a fiddle the last time he saw her.'

'Yes, that's what he told us.'

'It's bullshit.'

'I hate to tell you, Stella, but that doesn't really surprise me either.'

'Martha Dennis had a history of running away when she was a juvenile—'

'And she was like a nomad when she became an adult,' added Slater, 'which is why your lot didn't feel the need to throw a lot of resources at it. You're not telling me anything I don't already know.'

'You won't know the next bit,' she said.

Slater yawned. He was pleased to hear her voice, and he didn't want to put her off, but if all she was going to do was tell them what they already knew . . .

'The real Martha Dennis was a teenage runaway too.'

Now she had his full attention. 'What do you mean, the "real" Martha Dennis?'

'The person you call Martha Dennis is using a fake ID. The real Martha died ten years ago.' She paused to let Slater digest this fact.

'Bloody hell,' he muttered. 'How did she die? Was it suspicious?'

'It was a road accident. No suspicious circumstances. She just happened to be in the wrong place at the wrong time.'

For once, Slater was lost for words, his mind racing with possibilities.

'I'm not sure what you two are getting into,' said Robbins, 'but I think you should be careful. When people start using fake IDs, it's unlikely to be for a good reason. Maybe you should drop this case.'

'What? Drop the case and sit twiddling our thumbs?' said Slater. 'No chance. I want to know what's going on, and I can guarantee Norm will feel the same way. I'm sure you understand that, don't you?'

* * *

Norman shook his head. He had just been listening to Slater relay his conversation with Stella Robbins.

'So, let me get this straight,' he said. 'You're saying Martha isn't Martha, and Davies isn't her brother, is that right?'

'It's not quite that simple. The real Martha didn't have a brother, but then the woman we're looking for isn't the real Martha, so Davies could still be her brother.'

'That would make her Martha Davies.'

'That's possible, but only if he's really Adrian Davies,' said Slater.

'So, she's not who he says she is, and he's not who he says he is, and he may, or may not, be her brother. Is that it?'

'That's more or less it, yes.'

'What the hell are we getting into here?'

'That's more or less what Robbins just asked me,' said Slater.

'What did you tell her?'

'I told her I'd like to find out what's going on, and I told her I was sure you would say the same thing. Am I right?'

Norman grinned. 'Are you kidding? Of course I want to know. Besides, the man paid us a deposit up front. It would be rude to take it and not do any work.'

'We need to visit that old guy, Tisdale, again,' said Slater. 'Maybe we can persuade him to let us look at the basement.'

'Let's give him until the morning,' said Norman.

'Okay. In the meantime, I'll go and speak with Duchess. Maybe she can give us a bit more background about Vernon Tisdale.'

* * *

As they walked through the rickety old gates onto the short driveway up to Vernon Tisdale's house, Norman stopped and stared up at the dismal grey house with its peeling paintwork. 'This house gives me the creeps.'

'It's not exactly warm and welcoming, is it?' agreed Slater. 'But maybe that's how we're supposed to feel.'

'And you're quite sure he doesn't have dementia or anything like that?'

'According to Duchess, Vernon's not exactly the warm, friendly type, but as far as his memory is concerned, she says he's as sharp as anyone at the afternoon club.'

This seemed to give Norman the resolve he needed. 'Right then,' he said, stepping forward with renewed purpose, 'let's see how sharp he is now he's had time to think about it.'

He strode up to the front door, rang the bell, knocked hard, and waited. After about thirty seconds he rang the bell again, but still there was no response. As he bent down to peer through the letterbox, Slater wandered over to the nearest window.

'No sign of life in here,' he said.

'There's a curtain over the letterbox so I can't see anything, but I'm sure I can hear a radio back there somewhere,' said Norman.

'Perhaps he went out and left it on.'

'I dunno,' said Norman, standing up straight. 'I have a bad feeling.'

'Are you sure it's not just this creepy house?'

Norman pulled a face. 'Maybe, but what if he's had a fall or something?'

Slater sighed. 'Okay, you stay here in case he comes to the door. I'll go have a look around the back.'

He walked around the side of the house, pushed open a creaky metal gate, and followed a path round to the back of the house. About halfway down the length of the house, a set of steps led down to a doorway. Slater thought that must be the basement and made a mental note to check it out before they left.

When he got to the back door he could see it was ajar, but, looking through the window, he could see no sign of anyone in the gloomy kitchen. Slater looked down the garden, but there was no one to be seen, and a feeling of déjà vu suddenly filled his head.

He turned back to the kitchen door and had just reached out to push it open when a voice suddenly whispered in his ear. 'Found anything?'

Slater jumped so hard he rapped his knuckles against the door handle. Hissing a curse, he spun round and glared at Norman. 'Bloody hell, Norm,' he said, shaking his painful hand. 'Did you have to creep up on me like that?'

'Jeez, are you in a crabby mood or what?' asked Norman.

'Of course I'm crabby. Some idiot just made me jump so hard I nearly broke my hand!'

'I just asked what was going on, that's all. Anyway, why are we whispering?'

Slater nodded towards the house. 'Because this isn't looking good. The back door is open, but there doesn't seem to be anyone around.'

Norman looked past Slater towards the kitchen. 'Gotcha. So, what do you want to do?'

'I think we'd better check it out, don't you? I mean, the door is open, and we know an elderly man lives here. Like you said, he could have had a fall or something.'

'That works for me,' said Norman. 'But you remember what happened last time we did this?'

'Yeah, I remember — we found a body and then got arrested.'

'I hope we're not going to find a body this time.'

'That's a risk I feel we have to take,' said Slater. 'I don't like this guy any more than you, but even so, if he's had an accident . . .'

'You don't have to convince me,' said Norman. 'I'm with you. I think we should do it, but first, have you touched anything?'

'Not yet.'

'Hang on a tick then,' said Norman, reaching into his jacket pocket. He produced two pairs of latex gloves and handed one to Slater. 'Better glove up, just in case.'

Quickly, they slipped the gloves on.

'Okay, let's go,' said Slater. He turned away from Norman and gently pushed the door open. The hinges creaked alarmingly as the door reluctantly swung open, and they both froze for a few seconds before finally easing their way into the kitchen.

Norman called out as soon as he walked on through the door into the hallway. 'He's out here, Dave.'

Slater rushed out to the hallway, where he found Norman kneeling beside the crumpled figure of Vernon Tisdale at the foot of the stairs.

'He's alive,' said Norman. 'And he's got a good, strong pulse.'

'I'll call an ambulance,' said Slater. 'D'you think I should call the police too?'

Tisdale's eyes snapped open. 'You'll do no such thing. There's no need to waste their time on an old man who simply fell down the stairs.'

'Are you sure that's what happened?' asked Norman.

'Of course, I'm sure,' said Tisdale testily. 'There's nothing wrong with my memory.'

'Oh, is that so?' asked Norman. 'Only yesterday you told us your memory was pretty hazy, but if it's better today, maybe you can answer our questions.'

'Is that how you two operate? Harassing an old man who's just fallen down the stairs? Perhaps you *should* call the police — so I can make a complaint against you!'

'That won't be necessary, Vernon,' said Slater. 'I'm about to call an ambulance, and we're not going to ask you any more questions right now.'

Norman looked at Slater. 'We're not?'

Slater winked at him. 'It's alright, Norm. I think Mr Tisdale's priority is to get to the hospital. We can visit him once he's comfortable in there, right?'

'Yeah,' said Norman. 'You're right. Hospital first.'

* * *

When the ambulance arrived, it didn't take the paramedics long to assess their patient.

'Is he always this touchy?' one asked Slater.

'Oh, he's in a good mood today,' Slater assured him. 'What's the prognosis? Is he going to be okay?'

'Well, there's not much wrong with him that a good mood wouldn't put right, but he's hit his head, so we'd better take him to the hospital and get him checked out.'

Before the ambulance took Tisdale off to hospital, Norman asked for his house keys.

'Why should I give them to you?'

'Because your house is going to be empty, and it's unlocked. We'll check it's secure, lock up for you, and bring the keys to you later,' he promised.

'How do I know I can trust you?'

'We can leave it unlocked if you prefer,' suggested Slater.

The old man thought about this for a moment. 'I suppose you have a point. The keys are in the kitchen drawer to the left of the cooker. If anything's missing when I get back, I'll know who to blame. I have two witnesses here who have seen you and heard the conversation.'

'We're doing you a favour here,' said Norman.

'Hmmph! Maybe you are, and maybe you aren't.'

'Mind you don't choke on those words,' said Slater.

'Which words?'

'I'm thinking of "thank you", but I suspect they're not words you're familiar with.'

The old man's face twisted into a grimace. 'You're a cheeky bastard, d'you know that?'

Slater grinned at him.

* * *

'Right,' said Norman, once the ambulance had driven off. He jangled the bunch of keys Tisdale had told him about. 'Let's have a quick look around and make sure it's all secure before we lock up.'

They had a quick scout around and met up in the hall five minutes later.

'Anything?' asked Norman.

'The guy seems to be some sort of hunting fan. There are fox heads and tails all over the place. There's even a bloody great stag's head in one room. I've never understood why people want to kill animals. I don't understand it at all.'

'I reckon it's a power thing. They do it just because they can, a bit like bullying. The fact the fox is outnumbered by about a hundred to one, and it takes hounds and horses to keep up with it, doesn't seem to enter into the equation. I think they should arm the foxes with machine guns — that would level the playing field quite a bit.'

Slater smiled his agreement. 'Before we go, if there's a key for the basement, maybe we can take a look down there.'

Norman looked hesitant. 'We didn't say anything to him about poking around—'

'He volunteered the keys,' insisted Slater. 'You told him we'd make sure it was secure. We wouldn't want to go off without making sure we didn't leave an intruder in the basement, now, would we?'

'Only if there's a key,' Norman said grudgingly. 'We're not breaking in, right?'

'What do you take me for? Of course we're not going to break in. I just think we should take a look while we have the chance.'

'He told us the place had been emptied and there was nothing to see.'

'And you didn't believe him any more than I did,' argued Slater. 'How come you're on his side all of a sudden?'

'It's not a question of sides. He's an old guy who's just been rushed off to hospital. I'm not convinced we should be taking advantage of his situation, that's all.'

'Look, we have a missing person to find, right?'

'Right.'

'And didn't we both agree this old guy was stalling when we spoke to him the other day?'

'I suppose so.'

'And he was adamant we shouldn't look in the basement, wasn't he?'

'Well . . . that's right,' said Norman. 'And that was when he asked us to leave.'

'Exactly!'

'You know, you're right. We need to take a look at that basement while we have the chance.'

* * *

'Well, that's a surprise,' said Norman, as he led the way into the basement. 'Looking at the crappy state of the steps and door, I was expecting a real dump, but it's actually quite clean down here.'

'And no damp smell,' said Slater. 'Basements often smell of damp, but this one doesn't.'

'It smells better down here than it does upstairs,' said Norman. He peered around the door into the first room. 'It looks like he was right about all her stuff being taken away,' he said, turning back. 'There's a couple of bits of furniture in there, but nothing personal.'

Slater turned through the next door, into the kitchen, and stopped in his tracks.

'Wow! Norm, get a load of this kitchen. It looks almost new.'

He walked into the kitchen and opened a couple of drawers as Norman peered around the door.

'Jeez,' said Norman, taking in the stylish kitchen. 'Why would he have a kitchen like that down here when his own kitchen looks like it's a hundred years old?'

'You'd better take a look at this,' said Slater. 'I think maybe your poor old friend Mr Tisdale may have been rather economical with the truth.'

As Slater moved off along the hallway to the next room, Norman took his place at the drawers.

'Crap,' he said. 'Do you think this is her stuff?'

'Can't be sure,' said Slater over his shoulder, 'but didn't he say it was all cleared away and it was empty down here?'

'I'll have a look through this. Maybe there'll be something useful in here.'

Slater disappeared down the hallway. 'This bathroom's pretty neat too,' he called a few seconds later. 'I think maybe I should move in here — it's much better than my place.'

He took a quick look around the tiny, but luxurious, bathroom. Something didn't seem quite right, but he couldn't put his finger on it, and after a few seconds he moved on.

'This is definitely a woman's bathroom,' he called, 'although I can't find anything to tell us who that woman is.'

Finally, he reached the last room down the hall. 'This must be the bedroom,' he said, pushing the door open. 'Aha! I think we might have something.'

Norman closed the kitchen drawers and hurried down the hallway. As he entered the bedroom, Slater was sitting on the edge of the bed, gingerly opening a small packing case that sat neatly in the centre of the bed.

'What have we got?' asked Norman.

'Not much,' Slater said, disappointed. 'Did you find anything in the kitchen?'

'It's all pretty nondescript. I can't find anything that confirms Martha lived here, but I did find an old envelope addressed to someone called Betty Glover.'

'Betty Glover?'

'Yeah, I know. Who the hell's Betty Glover, right? Do you think maybe Tisdale was telling the truth and he really didn't know who was living down here?'

Slater didn't reply as he looked through the contents of the packing case. After a few seconds, he sat back with a sigh and then looked up at Norman.

'Like you said about the kitchen, there's nothing that confirms Martha was ever here. These are women's clothes, but they don't tell us anything except whoever owns them is a size ten.'

Slater lay back on the bed and sighed again. 'Bollocks! I was really hoping we were going to find a clue here, but this tells us nothing.'

'It's frustrating, isn't it?' agreed Norman. 'I think I might even have preferred it if the place had been empty, like we were told.'

'I don't know what to suggest now,' said Slater. 'Any ideas, Norm?'

'Well, I think there are two possibilities. Either the old guy has let the basement to someone called Betty Glover, or this is Martha's stuff and it's as she left it.'

'And which do you think is more likely?'

Norman shrugged. 'There's no personal stuff here. No letters, cards, photos, or anything. We know Martha is supposed to be some sort of nomad, right? Now it figures that someone who's always on the move probably wouldn't have a lot of friends to write to them and quite possibly wouldn't have any photos and stuff.'

'There again, a nomad might well have a few treasured possessions they take everywhere with them,' said Slater.

'Have you got a better theory?' asked Norman.

'I'm just saying. It works both ways.'

'Yeah, I know. I guess we need to have another chat with Mr Ungrateful.'

'Yeah,' said Slater. 'We need to find out who the letting agent is.'

He let his head drop back so it hung back over the edge of the bed, and then he rolled over. He was now staring at the floor and was just about to push himself up when he noticed something poking out from under the bed. It appeared to be the corner of a wooden frame.

He reached down and carefully eased the frame from under the bed. It enclosed a six by four selfie photograph of two smiling women, their heads pressed close together. They weren't identical twins, but they could easily be sisters. He turned over and sat up.

'Could this be Martha?' he asked as he passed the photograph to Norman.

Norman studied the photograph, then pulled the photo of young Martha from his pocket and held it alongside. 'It could be her,' he said, 'but these two women are so similar she could be either one!'

'So Martha *was* here,' said Slater.

'That's a possibility, but not a cert. You're guessing. We have no way of knowing who these two women are, and as you said yourself, this photo we have of Martha was taken years ago. She could look quite different now.'

'But you have to admit it's a bit of a coincidence,' argued Slater, 'and we've got nothing else to go on.'

Norman considered for a moment. 'I tell you what. How about we agree it's a possibility one of these women is Martha?'

'There's a "but", isn't there?'

Norman nodded. 'But before we rush to conclusions, we speak to Tisdale again, and we need to show this photograph to Adrian Davies. If she's his sister, he must know what she looks like.'

'Well, that would be a good idea, but you seem to be forgetting that Stella says he's not her brother.'

'Jeez, for a minute there I forgot that. We'll just have to start with Tisdale. Maybe this photo will help jog his memory.'

They left the bedroom and headed along the passage. As they reached the bathroom, Slater stopped. 'Take a look in there, and tell me what you think,' he said to Norman.

'What am I looking for?'

'I'm not sure. It might just be my imagination. I just feel something isn't quite right.'

Norman raised an eyebrow. 'There's nothing like being vague, is there?'

'Just indulge me,' said Slater. 'Like I said, it's probably nothing.'

Norman walked into the small bathroom and looked around. 'You couldn't swing a cat in here. In fact, you probably couldn't get a cat in here, even if you did want to swing it. You wouldn't both fit in.'

'It's pretty luxurious, though,' said Slater. 'It's much better than my bathroom at home.'

'Yeah, well, that wouldn't be difficult to achieve.'

'I'll get around to tarting it up one day.'

'Yeah, right.' Slowly, Norman spun around, trying to see whatever it was Slater thought he had seen. 'Some sort of clue might help. Maybe something a little less vague this time.'

'If I knew what it was, I wouldn't be asking you to take a look,' said Slater. 'Maybe something that is there that shouldn't be, or something that should be there but isn't.'

'And that's supposed to be more helpful, is it?'

'Alright, forget it. As I said, it's probably just m—'

'Hang on a minute,' said Norman. 'Here. This mirror. Take a look for yourself.'

Slater poked his head around the door. 'What?'

'There's a screw in each corner—'

Slater could see what looked like four shiny chrome-plated screws. 'Yeah, four screws. That's what holds it to the wall.'

'Yes,' said Norman, patiently. 'But in this case, only three of those screws are holding the mirror to the wall. The other one is a camera lens.'

Slater looked again. 'Are you sure?'

Norman tapped the screw in the top right-hand corner. 'This is a lens,' he said. 'It looks just like all the others, only a bit more worn, like the chrome has been polished off. The thing is, it's not a screw, it's a lens, and I'll bet it's a wide-angle lens too.'

'Jesus,' said Slater. 'You mean someone has been spying on whoever uses this bathroom?'

'That's how it looks,' said Norman.

'Can we find out who?'

'That depends. If it's a wireless feed it could go anywhere, but if there's a wire it must be in the house somewhere.' He fiddled with the screw for a moment.

'The nearest house is too far away for wireless,' said Slater.

'You're right,' said Norman. He pulled the lens and a few inches of wire were revealed attached to it. 'It's almost certainly not wireless.'

'So it's got to be upstairs in the house then.'

'Eww,' said Norman. 'I hadn't thought about that. Does this mean we're dealing with a dirty old man?'

'It has to be a possibility, doesn't it? Let's go back upstairs and take a look.'

'Hang on. Let me put this back in place first.'

* * *

Back in the house, Slater stopped in the hall and looked around.

'What are you looking for?' asked Norman.

'I'm just trying to work out where we are in relation to the basement.'

Norman pointed at the stairs. 'The bathroom would be over there, under the staircase.'

'Are you sure?'

Norman stopped, stared at Slater, and folded his arms. 'I have to tell you, it really pisses me off when you do that.'

At first, Slater didn't quite catch on. 'Do wha— Oh, you mean the "are you sure" thing? Funnily enough, Robbins said the same thing.'

'Well, isn't that a coincidence? Trust me, she's right, and it's bloody annoying.'

'I'm sorry. I don't realise I'm doing it.'

'Well, it's time you did.'

Slater watched rather sheepishly as Norman unfolded his arms and walked across to the staircase. Tongue-and-groove panelling concealed what was beneath the stairs, and he slowly walked along, tapping.

'Here we go,' he said. He looked over his shoulder at Slater, who hadn't moved. 'You're not going to sulk, are you?'

'No, of course not. It's just that . . .'

'Look, it had to be said, okay?' said Norman. 'But I've said it now, and I'm sure you'll try not to do it in future, so can we just forget about it and carry on with our work?'

'Yes, sure,' said Slater. 'What have you got?'

'It's been very carefully made, and you can hardly see it, but there's a door here. If I can just figure out how it opens . . .'

Norman ran his hands around the edges of the door, then stepped back with a grin. 'Ha!' he said. 'Gotcha!' He pressed a hand against the panel. There was a soft, metallic click, and the door sprung open.

'Wow!' said Slater. 'I would never have guessed that was there.'

'I think that's the point. Whoever made it certainly knew how to conceal his work.' Norman swung the door open and looked inside. 'Well, would you look at that. A computer, a monitor, and a comfy seat. It's a voyeur's paradise.'

'That dirty old man,' said Slater. 'There could be recordings of Martha in her bathroom all over the internet.'

'I know how it looks, but we don't know for sure it's him,' said Norman.

'Well, I'm convinced. I mean, who else would it be?'

'I think we should keep this to ourselves for now. Let's see what Tisdale has to say before we start accusing him of anything.'

'You're not proposing we turn a blind eye to this, are you?'

'No way,' said Norman. 'Do you think I'm going soft? No, what I'm suggesting is we hold this back and use it as leverage if he's reluctant to talk to us.'

'Then what?'

‘Then we pass it on to the police and let them deal with it. Is that alright?’

‘Yeah, that works for me.’

‘Right, let’s close this creepy place up and get out of here,’ said Norman.

CHAPTER NINE

They had hardly been back in their office five minutes when the door opened and two men walked in. The older of the two was in his fifties. He wore an expensive overcoat, which was unbuttoned just enough to reveal a very stylish suit. Once inside, he stopped to peel off a pair of black leather gloves. As he did so, he glanced around the office and sniffed once or twice, his nose wrinkling with distaste.

'It's a shame,' he said. 'This place has so much potential, don't you think, Patrick?'

The younger man nodded his agreement. He was in his thirties, well over six feet tall, and sporting a pair of aviator sunglasses even though it was a dull, grey day. Something about him shouted ex-con to Slater. His physique was a testimony to the many hours he had spent in the gym, and he bore the confidence of a man who knew how to look after himself.

A once-broken nose suggested someone must have got the better of him somewhere along the line, and Slater wondered absently if this had happened in prison. He almost winced at the thought of what retribution might have been inflicted on the person who had broken it.

The giant was carrying a briefcase, which he handed to the older man before taking his place in front of the door, ensuring no one could come in — or escape. He stood with his hands behind his back, staring at a point somewhere above everyone's head. He didn't utter a single word the whole time he was there, but he didn't need to: no one was in any doubt what his purpose was.

It was the older man who was here to do the talking, and he didn't waste much time on introductions.

'Good morning,' said Norman.

'My card,' said the man, placing a card on Norman's desk.

Norman picked up the card and read it out loud. 'Samuel S. Shrivener, lawyer.' He smiled at the man. 'What can we do for you, Mr Shrivener?'

'I understand you've been harassing a Mr Vernon Tisdale.'

'I wouldn't say we've been harassing him,' said Norman. 'We're trying to find a missing woman and we heard Mr Tisdale might be able to help us.'

'He can't,' said Shrivener abruptly. 'You will cease with your campaign of harassment right now.'

'Are you his lawyer?' asked Slater. 'Only if you are, you need to understand there is no campaign of harassment.'

'Perhaps I'm not making myself clear,' said Shrivener. 'Mr Tisdale can't help you. He knows nothing about what happened to your missing woman.'

'Her name is Martha Dennis,' said Slater.

'Really? Well, in that case, he can't tell you what happened to Martha Dennis.'

'How can you be so sure?'

'You'll have to take my word for it. My client knows nothing about what happened to Martha Dennis, or anyone else.'

'You seem very sure something has happened to her,' said Norman. 'All we know is that she's missing. It seems you know a lot more than we do. Would you care to tell us what you know?'

Shrivener smiled indulgently at Norman but ignored the question. 'If you persist with your enquiries, you will regret it.'

'Is that a threat?' asked Slater. 'Is that why you brought your heavy along? To intimidate us?'

'You mean Patrick?' said Shrivener, indicating the giant standing in the doorway. 'He's my driver today, and a more pleasant young man you'd be hard-pressed to find. I'd hardly call him intimidating.'

'It's nice that you're happy with your driver,' said Norman, 'but we make our own decisions, and we don't take orders from people who just wander in off the street.'

'I'm not someone who "wandered in off the street", Mr Norman, and I'm not giving you orders. I'm simply suggesting it would be better if you left Mr Tisdale alone. He's an old man living on his own. It wouldn't look good if two so-called detectives were seen to be putting pressure on him.'

'Ah,' said Slater. 'Now I understand why you only have the one heavy riding shotgun — it's going to be intimidation by proposed litigation rather than violence, is that it?'

Shrivener's grin twisted his face into a humourless mask. 'I've done my homework on you two. It wouldn't need a very big lawsuit to put you out of business and bankrupt you both. But if you drop your case and leave Vernon Tisdale alone, we need say no more about it. I might even be able to put some work your way.'

Before they could speak, he turned on his heel and headed for the door. The heavy pushed the door open, stepped respectfully aside to let him pass, and then followed him out into the car park.

'Arsehole,' muttered Slater, as he and Norman watched the two men walk across the car park.

'He has a very nice car,' said Norman, as the two men climbed into a black, recently registered Mercedes.

'Yeah, top of the range by the look of it,' said Slater. 'They don't come cheap.'

'If he represents Vernon Tisdale, I'm a pink marshmallow,' said Norman. 'There's no way that old guy could afford someone like him.'

'This isn't about a little old man called Tisdale,' said Slater. 'Shrivener just said it — he wants us to drop the case. He's using Tisdale as an excuse.'

'I wonder who he's really looking out for.'

'Shall we find out?'

'What do you have in mind?' asked Norman.

'I hear there's a lonely old man down at the hospital. He had a fall earlier this morning, and there doesn't seem to be any family to visit him. Maybe he'd appreciate a couple of visitors.'

'Now that sounds like a plan. It would be the public-spirited thing to do, in line with our "giving back to the community" philosophy. And, as an added bonus, I'm sure we'll find out quite soon afterwards who Samuel S. Shrivener represents.'

'Exactly!' agreed Slater.

* * *

'I wonder what that Shrivener guy meant when he said he could put some work our way,' said Norman thoughtfully.

Slater took his eyes off the road for a moment to glance at his partner, but Norman was staring out through the side window. 'Who cares?' he said. 'We really don't want to be doing work for an arse like him, do we?'

'I thought you said earlier that we need to start making some money.'

'Well, yeah, I did.'

'The guy looks loaded.'

'I'm sure he is,' said Slater. 'I'm also sure his clients are the sort we should be working against, not for.'

'Yeah, I suppose you're right.'

Slater looked across at Norman again, but he was still staring out through the side window. 'You are joking, right?'

'What? Yeah, of course. I'm just curious, that's all.'

'Things are going to pick up, I know they are,' said Slater. 'We'll manage just fine without people like him, trust me.'

'Yeah, I'm sure you're right,' said Norman, but he didn't sound convinced.

* * *

'How are you, Mr Tisdale?' asked Norman.

'No better for seeing you two, that's for sure.'

'The nurse says they're going to keep you overnight for observation,' said Norman.

'This is all your fault,' said Tisdale. 'If you two hadn't come along—'

'You'd still be lying on the floor at the foot of your stairs,' said Slater. 'A "thank you" would be nice, but I won't hold my breath.'

'Thank you? Why should I thank you? Like I was saying, if you two hadn't been poking your noses in, he wouldn't ha—'

The old man suddenly stopped talking. Slater and Norman exchanged a look.

'He wouldn't have what?' asked Norman.

'I'm sorry?'

'You just said, "if we hadn't been poking our noses in, he wouldn't have", and then you stopped talking. Who's "he"?'

'And "he" wouldn't have what?' added Slater.

'You're making me confused again,' said Tisdale. 'I find the two of you very intimidating.'

'Yeah, so we've heard,' said Slater, 'but I don't think you're as fragile as you make out. I reckon it takes more than a couple of guys asking questions to intimidate someone like you.'

Tisdale glared malevolently at Slater.

'Look,' said Norman, 'we can see you're frightened of something, but it's not us, is it? Has someone been threatening you?'

The old man looked from Slater to Norman. Then he slowly raised a shaky hand and pointed at Slater.

'You have to leave me alone,' he said. 'It will be much worse than a fall down the stairs if I talk to you again.'

'You mean someone pushed you down the stairs?' asked Norman. 'Jesus, Vernon, what have you got yourself involved in?'

Tisdale stared at Norman and swallowed hard.

'We can help you, Vernon,' said Slater. 'But you need to tell us what's going on.'

'What I need is for you two to get out and leave me alone,' hissed Tisdale. 'You can't help me, and I can't help you.'

'We know about the hidden camera in the bathroom,' said Norman.

Tisdale looked puzzled. 'What are you talking about? What hidden camera?'

'Oh, come on, Vernon,' said Slater. 'You know exactly what we mean. The camera that you use to spy on your lodgers in their bathroom. The one that links to your little computer room.'

Now Tisdale looked totally confused. 'Computer room? Are you mad? I don't have a computer.'

Just then a nurse came over. 'Are you alright, Mr Tisdale?' she asked.

Tisdale didn't say anything, but his face told her all she needed to know.

'I think perhaps you two gentlemen had better leave,' she said. 'Vernon's still a little concussed from his fall.'

Slater was about to argue, but Norman beat him to it. 'Yes, nurse, you're probably right,' he said. 'C'mon, Dave, let's give Vernon time to recover.'

'When do you think he'll be okay for visitors?' Norman asked the nurse as she led them away.

'He'll probably be discharged tomorrow morning,' she said. 'Why don't you visit him when he's back at home?'

'Why don't we come and collect him tomorrow?' suggested Norman. 'We can give him a lift home and make sure he's settled in alright.'

* * *

'What was all that bollocks about not having a computer?' said Slater as they made their way back to the car.

'I'm not so sure. I thought he was pretty convincing.'

'Really? You bought that? So how do you explain the computer set-up in that little room under the stairs?'

'I'm not sure I *can* explain that. I just felt he really didn't know what you were talking about.'

'Yeah, but he's being evasive about the whole thing,' said Slater. 'He has been right from the start. He knows what's going on but he won't tell us.'

'I think he's too frightened to tell us anything. Don't forget — he was pushed down the stairs by someone.'

'If you hadn't been so quick to please the nurse, we might have found out who did it.'

'And if I hadn't stopped you, we probably would have been thrown out and maybe worse. You were frightening the man.'

'I was not,' argued Slater. 'Someone else had already frightened him. I was just trying to find out who it is!'

'And making him even more scared in the process,' added Norman. 'Look, it'll be alright. We'll pick him up in the morning, take him home, and get him settled. Then he'll talk to us.'

'I hope you're right.'

CHAPTER TEN

It was 9.30 a.m. Slater had just gone into the kitchen when his mobile phone began to ring.

'It's me,' hissed Robbins.

'Why are you speaking like that?'

'Because I've only got a couple of minutes, and I'm not supposed to be calling you.'

'I thought I told you not to take any risks.'

'I know, but I don't take orders from you, and before you say anything, we haven't got time for that argument right now. I just need you to listen. I've been looking into missing women aged between twenty-five and thirty-five.'

'I don't want you sticking your neck out for me.'

'I know, but it just so happens they have me looking at boring old crime figures and stuff. Missing people are just one of the things I've been asked to look at. So, you see, it's not really a risk.'

'I'd still prefer it if you didn't do it.'

'Well, tough, it's done now. Do you want to hear what I found or not?'

'Is it relevant?'

'Only you can decide that,' she said.

'Well, go on then. You obviously think it might be.'

'A young woman from Barking, in Essex, went missing eighteen months ago.'

'That's nowhere near here, and it's not in our time frame.'

'Let me finish. Her name is Betty Glover.'

Now she had Slater's interest. He reached for a piece of scrap paper and a pen. 'Did you say Betty Glover?'

'Yes, why? Do you know who she is?'

Slater thought before he replied. 'No,' he said. 'I'm just checking I've written it down correctly.'

'She's twenty-seven years old, blonde, slim, average height. She used to go jogging every day to keep fit.'

'Okay, so she's a physical match, and she likes jogging, but she still doesn't fit the time frame.'

'She is a freelance investigative journalist. The report says the last thing she told her boyfriend was that she was on the verge of something really big.'

'Hang on, not so fast,' said Slater, scribbling frantically. 'I'm trying to write and hold the paper at the same time.'

'Then write faster, I don't have much time. She was going undercover for a few weeks to get the full story. He never heard from her again.'

Slater stopped scribbling. 'What? You mean you think *she's* Martha?' he said, dismissively. 'You're kidding.'

'Now listen, David Slater. Don't get all shitty with me just because you have no clue and I have a plausible lead for you.'

'Plausible?'

'You can't deny it's a possibility, can you?'

'Well, anything's possible, I suppose,' he said, grudgingly.

He could almost feel her frustration coming over the airwaves. 'Alright, Clever Dick,' she snapped, 'have you got anything better?'

'I can't tell you about our case,' he said, trying to bluff his way out. 'You know how it is — client confidentiality and all that.'

He could hear her derisive snort. 'Client confidentiality, my arse,' she said. 'You're not even sure if your client exists, and if he does he's probably some sort of criminal.'

'Yeah, well,' he said.

'Ha!' She laughed. 'Admit it. You know I've found a lead worth following. That's another dinner you owe me.'

Slater wasn't quite sure he'd heard that right. 'Sorry?'

'Dinner,' she said. 'The deal, remember? I deliver information, you buy me dinner.'

'I didn't know that was an ongoing thing. I thought it only applied to last time.'

'Is there a problem with taking me to dinner?'

'A problem? No, of course not. I'd love to buy you dinner again, but you don't have to earn it by taking risks.'

'Should I take that as a yes?'

'When?'

'How about tomorrow evening?'

'Tomorrow evening?'

'Yes, you know. It's a part of what we call a day. We start with morning, then it's afternoon, the next bit is evening, and then it's night. I'm suggesting we use the evening part of tomorrow. Of course, if you don't want to have dinner with me . . .'

'Of course I do.'

'Well, then?'

'Same place?'

'Uh huh. Same place, same time.'

Slater's face was hurting, he was grinning so much. 'I'll be there.'

'Do you want the address?'

'I think I can remember where the restaurant is. It wasn't that long ago.'

'I'm not talking about the restaurant address, you idiot. Betty Glover had a boyfriend back in Barking. I assume you want to speak to him.'

'Oh, yeah, right. Of course we do.'

'Have you got that pen ready?'

* * *

'I think we might have something,' said Slater as he burst through the door.

Norman swung his chair round to face Slater. 'Does that hurt?'

'Does what hurt?'

'That grin. It looks like your face is going to burst. This must be good.'

'Remember that letter you found in the basement?'

'The one addressed to Betty Glover?'

Slater nodded. 'Stella just called. She's looking into missing persons. She's found a young woman called Betty Glover who went missing eighteen months ago.'

'So it's Stella now, is it? What happened to DI Robbins?'

Slater said nothing, but knew the colour of his face was giving him away.

'Why was she looking for Betty Glover?' Norman asked.

'She wasn't specifically, but she was looking for anyone who might fit the description of Martha Dennis, and Betty Glover does.'

Norman looked doubtful.

'She's a journalist,' continued Slater. 'Her boyfriend said she had gone undercover on a job, and then it seems she never came back.'

'I must admit it is a coincidence,' agreed Norman. 'But it's possible she just ran off with another guy and didn't have the guts to tell her boyfriend.'

'Maybe you're right, but even so, what else have we got? It's too much to ignore.'

Norman broke into a smile. 'Yeah, of course it is. So what do you suggest?'

'I have an address for the boyfriend. Maybe we could speak to him. If he knows what story she was working on, that might tell us something.'

'Have you got his phone number?'

'Yeah.'

'Then give him a call. See what he says.'

* * *

'We're on,' said Slater, a few minutes later. 'We're going to Barking this afternoon.'

'Do we need to leave yet?' asked Norman.

Slater shook his head. 'Her boyfriend says he will be at home all afternoon and evening, so there's no rush.'

'Right, get your jacket.'

'Why?'

'We have to collect Vernon Tisdale from the hospital, remember?'

'Ah, right.'

'You'd forgotten, hadn't you?'

'How could I forget that miserable so and so? Do we have to go now?'

'The nurse told me he would be released at eleven. We can sort him out and then head for Barking.'

Slater looked at the clock. It was just coming up to eleven o'clock. 'We're going to be late.'

'Yeah, well, I'm sure they'll keep him for us,' said Norman.

'Don't bank on it,' said Slater. 'After twenty-four hours of his bitching I'm sure they can't wait to get rid of him.'

'We'd better get going then,' said Norman, jangling his car keys.

'You driving? You're kidding? We're running late, and you know how slow you drive.'

Norman tossed his keys down on his desk.

'Okay, Speedy,' he said. 'You drive.'

* * *

'Hi, we've come to collect Mr Tisdale,' said Norman.

The nurse looked surprised. 'But he's already gone. His son collected him.'

'His son? Does he have a son?'

On the other side of the nurse, Slater was shaking his head.

'Of course he does,' said the nurse. 'He was here just a few minutes ago.'

'Can you describe this man?' asked Norman.

'I beg your pardon?'

'Is he good-looking, apart from the broken nose, about six feet four, wide shoulders, works out a lot?' asked Slater.

'That sounds like him,' said the nurse.

'And what about Mr Tisdale? Was he pleased to see his "son"?'

'He looked surprised when I told him his son had come to collect him,' said the nurse, 'but that's probably because he didn't know his son was in town.'

'I bet he didn't,' said Slater.

'He told me he'd rushed back from London when he heard about the accident.'

'Did he say who told him about the accident?' asked Norman.

'I never thought to ask.'

'How long ago did they leave?'

'About fifteen minutes. Is something wrong?'

'No, it's fine,' said Norman. 'We didn't know his son was back, that's all.'

* * *

'Damnit,' muttered Slater as they made their way back to the car park. 'I told you Tisdale knew what was going on.'

'Yeah, okay, don't rub it in,' said Norman gloomily. 'It's my fault. It was my idea to leave him until this morning.'

'Don't be an idiot, Norm. It's not your fault. We had no way of knowing this would happen.'

'How are we going to find him, though? With fifteen minutes' head start they could be anywhere by now. Where the hell do we begin?'

'Oh, that's easy enough,' said Slater, plipping the car door locks.

'It is?'

'Come on, Norm,' said Slater, as he climbed into the car. 'Stop blaming yourself and switch your brain back on.'

Norman looked puzzled as he climbed into the car. 'Am I missing something here?'

'Who was with Tisdale's "son" last time we saw him?'

Slater waited patiently as the connections whizzed around in Norman's head. Finally, he smiled and turned to Slater. 'Shrivener!'

'Exactly,' said Slater. 'And he very conveniently left us his card with his office address.'

* * *

Slater looked up at the imposing facade of the Georgian building. 'It must cost a fortune to maintain an office in this building,' he said. 'This easily has to be the most expensive part of Winchester.'

'It certainly goes with the car and the suit,' said Norman.

A brass plaque on the wall informed them they had found the correct building.

'C'mon, Norm, we're not going to be put off just because someone makes a lot of money, are we?'

'I'm not put off. I'm intrigued to know how these people do it. I mean, I wouldn't mind having some of that money for us.'

Slater looked at Norman curiously. 'Are you okay?'

'Don't you get fed up with scratching around for jobs, making do with whatever comes through the door?' asked Norman. 'We're better than that. I just think it's about time we got some of the cream.'

'Are you in some sort of trouble?'

'Trouble? What sort of trouble would I be in?'

'I dunno. You just seem to be talking about wanting money all of a sudden. It's not like you.'

'Since when has it been wrong to want a better lifestyle?'

'Whoa, easy tiger,' said Slater. 'I'm not looking for a fight here. It's just that you don't usually talk about money.'

'Well, maybe I'm just getting tired of not having any.'

Slater raised his hands. 'Okay, point taken. Why don't we see if we can't rustle up some better work?'

'Yeah, right,' said Norman derisively. 'And how do you suggest we do that?'

'Maybe it's time we went on a charm offensive around the Tinton area. Heck, maybe we should try our hand here in Winchester.'

'D'you really think it would work?'

'I can't promise, but what have we got to lose? We've tried sitting back waiting for the work to find us and it hasn't happened, has it?'

Norman was studying Slater's face, as if he wanted to believe him but couldn't quite manage it.

'So, what do you say, Norm?'

'I suppose, if we're being honest, we haven't *really* tried that hard, have we?'

'No, we haven't, and like I said, what have we got to lose? But before we start that, can we try and sort this Martha Dennis case?' He extended a hand towards Norman. 'Deal?'

Norman studied Slater's face a little longer, then grabbed his hand and shook it. 'Deal.'

* * *

The building was just as grand on the inside as it was on the outside. In the entrance hallway, they found themselves sinking into a powder-blue, thick-pile carpet, which immediately set the tone. Ornate curtains adorned the windows, and ancient-looking landscapes hung from the walls in gilded frames. They looked expensive, but art wasn't Slater's thing, and as he gazed at them he realised he had no idea if these were genuine or worthless fakes.

A portrait of a young woman caught his attention, and he moved for a closer look. The artist's name was inscribed in the right-hand corner, and he made a mental note of it before following Norman across the room.

A secretary was sitting at a huge oak desk, and she looked up with a smile as they approached. 'Can I help you, gentlemen?'

'We wanted to see Mr Shrivener,' said Slater.

'Do you have an appointment?'

'No, but it's important.'

'Could I have your names?'

'Slater and Norman.'

'Ah, yes, of course. Mr Shrivener is expecting you.'

Slater was sure he heard Norman's mouth drop open. 'He is?'

'Oh, yes. He's moved two meetings to fit you in,' she assured them. 'If you'd like to come this way.'

She led them through a door into another hallway and across to a second door, where she stopped and knocked.

'Come in,' called a faint voice.

She opened the door and led the way into Shrivener's office. He was sitting at another huge oak desk at the far end of the room, and Slater could understand why his voice had sounded so faint. The office must have been thirty feet from front to back, with the same thick carpet and curtains as the entrance hall.

As they walked in, Shrivener jumped to his feet and walked towards them, hand extended. 'Mr Slater and Mr Norman,' he said. 'What a pleasure to see you again.'

'Can I get you anything, Mr Shrivener?' asked the secretary.

'Coffee for three would be wonderful, thank you, Angela.'

'Yes, sir, of course,' she said, backing from the room and pulling the door closed behind her.

As far as Slater was concerned, he saw no reason to shake Shrivener's hand, but to his dismay, Norman grabbed the proffered hand and shook it vigorously. Shrivener offered the hand to Slater.

'I don't shake hands with people who threaten me,' said Slater.

'Very well, as you wish,' said Shrivener. He pointed to a settee. 'How about a seat? Will you sit and talk?'

'That's the reason we're here.'

'Good. Come and sit down.'

'This is quite a place you have here,' said Norman.

'Oh, I get by.'

'Get by? This place must cost a fortune to maintain,' gushed Norman.

'If you have the right clients, the sky's the limit.'

'Can we cut the crap and get to the point?' said Slater testily. 'We went to the hospital earlier to collect Mr Tisdale, and your heavy beat us to it.'

Norman looked daggers at Slater.

'It's alright, Norm. I've got this,' said Slater, then he turned back to Shrivener. 'We want to know what you've done with Tisdale.'

'What we've done with him?' echoed Shrivener. 'You seem to forget you're not supposed to go anywhere near Mr Tisdale.'

'Where have you taken him?' said Slater. 'And why?'

Shrivener smiled sympathetically at Slater. 'Have you been to his house?'

'His house?'

'His abode. The place where he resides,' said Shrivener patronisingly.

'I know what a bloody house is,' snapped Slater.

'Well, have you been there?'

'Of course not. We came straight here.'

'That's a pity, because if you *had* gone there, you would have found Mr Tisdale was there, safe and secure, with Patrick keeping an eye on him.'

Slater's mouth flapped silently. He hadn't been expecting this. 'What?'

'Patrick collected Vernon Tisdale from the hospital this morning, and he's now at home where he belongs.'

'If anything's happened to him—'

'I told you — he's safe and secure. Is that a problem?'

'Why's your gorilla there? Are you expecting that little old man to try and make a run for it?'

Shrivener did not look impressed.

'I think there may have been some sort of misunderstanding,' said Norman.

'Damned right there's been a misunderstanding,' said Slater. 'But I'm going to speak to Tisdale and find out what the hell's going on.'

'I don't think that's a good idea,' said Shrivener.

'No, of course you don't. That's because you don't want us to find out what's going on.'

'It's not a good idea because this morning, on behalf of Mr Tisdale, I have taken out an emergency injunction against each of you in the form of a trespass order.'

'What?' chorused Slater and Norman.

'I asked you to keep away from him yesterday, and as soon as I left you went to the hospital and began harassing him again.' He had been holding an envelope in his left hand, but now he held it aloft. 'In this envelope is a trespass order for each of you, stopping you from going within one hundred yards of Vernon Tisdale and his home. Patrick is there to make sure you don't.'

Slater was momentarily lost for words, but only momentarily. 'Now, wait a minute. You can't do that—'

'Already done it, I'm afraid,' said Shrivener, with a self-satisfied smirk. 'It appears you bothering Vernon in hospital yesterday was just too much for him. I was asked to arrange the injunction, and trust me, if you violate the terms by just one yard, you will first have Mr Patrick to deal with and then the police. Do I make myself clear?'

'This is bollocks,' said Slater. 'Tisdale can't afford your fees.'

'As you well know, client confidentiality forbids me from discussing my client's affairs with you, Mr Slater,' he said. 'It's a pity you want to fight me. I could use a good detective.'

'This isn't just about Tisdale, is it?' said Slater. 'So, who is really behind it all?'

Shrivener gave Slater another one of his condescending smiles. 'As I mentioned before, client confidentiality . . . Or perhaps you think I should ignore it?'

'I'm surprised you know about such things,' said Slater. 'Anyone can see you're as bent as a nine-pound note.'

'Careful now, Mr Slater. You know very well you have no proof to back up such an accusation. I'd hate to have to sue you for slander.'

'You can stick your slander where the sun doesn't shine, and while you're at it, why not shove your injunction up there with it?'

Shrivener sighed theatrically. 'Oh dear. I had rather hoped you would listen to reason, but it looks as if I was wrong. If you keep this up, I'll have no choice but to involve the police.'

There was a tense silence, finally broken by Norman. 'He's right, Dave — we have no proof he's done anything wrong, and if Mr Tisdale has a restraining order we have no choice.'

Slater looked at Norman, his eyes wide. He couldn't quite believe he was prepared to back down so easily. 'You're kidding, right? You're not going to let this scumbag push us around like this, are you?'

'But Mr Shrivener is right. What good will it do if we get locked up trying to speak to Vernon Tisdale? Who's that going to help?'

'I can't believe I'm hearing this,' said Slater.

Shrivener coughed quietly. 'I'm pleased to see that at least Mr Norman has some common sense, but I've no desire to listen to your little spat. Perhaps, if there's nothing else, we should call this meeting to a close.'

'You're right,' said Slater, jumping to his feet. 'We never should have wasted our time coming here in the first place. C'mon, Norm, let's get out of this place.'

By the time Norman had climbed to his feet, Slater was already on his way through the door. Norman turned to Shrivener and offered his hand.

'Don't mind Dave,' he told Shrivener. 'He's just having a bad day. He'll be okay. I'll make sure he's no bother.'

Shrivener took Norman's hand and shook it. 'I think you must be the sensible one of the two,' he said. 'Perhaps you should come back for a chat without your hot-headed colleague.'

'Really?' said Norman.

'Like I said, I could do with a good detective around here, someone who knows where his bread's buttered. I'm sure you understand what I mean.'

Norman grinned at Shrivener. 'Oh, yeah, Mr Shrivener. I understand perfectly.'

* * *

'What was all that "yes, sir, no, sir, Mr Shrivener, sir" crap in there?' demanded Slater when Norman climbed into the car.

'I don't know what you mean.'

'I've never seen you so happy to let someone push us around.'

'I was just being polite.'

'Being polite? You were licking his arse!'

'But he had a point,' said Norman. 'And he's got an injunction against us.'

'And you're going to let him win, just like that?'

'And what's *your* idea? Go to Vernon Tisdale's house, get beaten up by Patrick, and then get arrested? That's going to be a big help, isn't it?'

'But you're climbing in bed with the enemy!'

'I am not,' said Norman.

'That's what it looks like.'

'We don't even know, for sure, that he *is* the enemy.'

'What does that mean?'

'It means he might just be rather good at what he does.'

Slater thought about this for a minute. 'I don't get it. Whose side are you on?'

Norman looked disappointed. 'Do you really need to ask me that?'

Slater looked away.

'Oh great. Thank you for that vote of confidence. How about we say no more about this, and you just drive us to Barking?'

Slater started the car and put it in gear. He had a feeling this was going to be a long, quiet journey.

CHAPTER ELEVEN

When they had first planned the journey to Barking, they had agreed to stop for lunch along the way, and as he was driving, Slater made sure they stuck to the plan. It was a welcome break after an hour of what could best be described as a frosty journey. Anyone watching them climb from the car and walk across the car park would have had no problem recognising a couple who were in serious disagreement.

But Slater and Norman's relationship was made of stern stuff, and neither was prepared to let a situation like this fester. An hour later, as they made their way back to the car, it was clear an open and frank discussion had put paid to their dispute. The remaining hour of the journey passed in perfect harmony.

Now they were standing outside a house in Barking as the door opened to reveal a young man with wild hair, not unlike Norman's, Slater thought.

'Ryan Wilson? We spoke on the phone. My name's Dave Slater, and this is my colleague Norman Norman.'

Ryan Wilson did a momentary double take when Slater told him Norman's name, but he was quick to offer them a warm smile, shake hands, and welcome them into his home.

'You said I might be able to help you with a case, is that right?' he asked once they were settled.

'We've been asked to look for a young woman we're told has been missing for a few months,' Slater explained. 'During our enquiries, we came across a letter addressed to Betty Glover.'

'I really don't want to know if you've found her.'

'I'm sorry?'

'The police told me they believe she ran off with another guy. That's okay, I can live with that, but she didn't have the guts to tell me. Not even a note to say goodbye. I mean, who does that? Didn't I deserve an explanation?'

Slater didn't know what to say. This wasn't quite what he had been expecting.

'Anyway, it doesn't matter now,' said Wilson. 'She probably did me a favour. I'm over her, you see. That's why I don't want to know where she is.'

'And you're quite sure she ran off with another guy?' asked Norman.

'That's what the police told me.'

'And she didn't say anything to you? You had no idea?'

'She told me she was going undercover to investigate this big story and that she would be gone for a few weeks.'

'And that was it?' asked Slater.

'There was one more thing — she told me I wouldn't be able to contact her while she was gone.'

Norman raised his eyebrows.

'Yes, that was a nice touch, wasn't it?' said Wilson. 'And being a trusting sort of dummy, I believed her. By the time I woke up, she had been gone over six weeks. I never heard another word from her, and now I don't want to. If you've found her, tell her good riddance from me.'

He studied Slater for a moment. 'You *have* found her, right?'

'No, we haven't found her,' said Slater. 'The woman we're looking for calls herself Martha Dennis. Does that name mean anything to you?'

Wilson shook his head. 'I don't think so. Is there any reason why it *should* mean something to me?'

'We think we found where Martha was living before she disappeared. In a drawer, we found an envelope addressed to Betty Glover. We were hoping you might know of a connection.'

Wilson looked blankly from Slater to Norman and back again. 'You've come all the way here to tell me you found an envelope? Is this some sort of joke?'

Norman pulled a photograph from his pocket and handed it to Wilson. 'Is one of these women Betty?'

Wilson looked at the selfie photograph and then at Norman. 'It's possible, but it's not exactly a full-face portrait, is it?' He looked down at the photo again. 'This is a pretty weird angle to try and recognise someone.'

'Are you sure it's not her?'

Wilson studied the photo again. 'I can't say for sure. I suppose it could be. Who's the other girl?'

'We were rather hoping you might be able to tell us that,' said Slater.

'They look very close, don't they? Christ, you're not telling me she left me for another woman, are you?'

'We're not telling you anything, Ryan, because we don't know. We were hoping you could help us.'

'What makes you think I can help? Betty left me eighteen months ago. You said your woman went missing a few months ago. You also said your missing woman is called Martha. I don't get the connection.'

'Let me be honest with you, Ryan,' said Norman. 'We're struggling to get anywhere with our case. Every clue we've had so far has led us up a blind alley, and then we came across an envelope with Betty's name on it. That would have got us nowhere too, but we knew Betty had been reported missing, so we thought maybe there's some sort of connection, and we were hoping if we spoke to you, perhaps you could tell us something that might help.'

'Like what?'

'We heard Betty was some sort of journalist. Is that true?' asked Slater.

'I already told you — she does freelance investigative work.'

'What sort of things did she investigate?'

'It started off as local consumer stuff. She caught more than one builder who had conned some old person out of a fortune for shoddy work. Then she got some bloke down the market who was selling stolen goods. She saw herself as a sort of moral crusader.'

'So she worked for local newspapers?'

'That's how it started, but then she met this bloke who had taken the next step up. He said he was working for the national papers and magazines. She thought he was the bee's knees. He gave her some contacts and she thought she was going to make the big breakthrough, you know?'

'Do you have a name for this guy?'

Wilson stared thoughtfully at Slater.

'Does the name Adrian Davies ring a bell?' asked Norman.

'No, it definitely wasn't that. To be honest, she was quite secretive about her work and didn't really discuss it with me. I think his name is Eddie, that's all I know.'

'Are you sure it was Eddie and not Adie?'

'Eddie? Adie? To be honest, I don't give a damn whichever it was.'

'Have you any idea where we can find him?' asked Norman.

'If I knew where to find him, I would have kicked the crap out of him by now.'

'Ah,' said Slater. 'So you think Betty ran off with him?'

'The idea has crossed my mind. They seemed to be quite close.'

'You mean they worked together?'

'He let her help him once or twice, but I think she was star-struck and he was just using her to do the donkey work. She never got any credit for what she did, that's for sure. She would have shown me if there was a big story with her name on it.'

'She was proud of her work then?'

'Big-headed about it, more like,' said Wilson.

'Have you got any of her stuff?' asked Slater. 'Like a laptop?'

'You're kidding. Her laptop went everywhere she went.'

'What about notebooks?' asked Norman. 'All journalists use notebooks, don't they?'

'I burnt all that stuff months ago,' said Wilson. 'Everything in her notebooks was in some sort of weird code anyway.'

'You read them?'

'I looked through them hoping to find this Eddie bloke, but I couldn't understand any of it. As I said, it was all squiggles and weird code.'

'Shorthand,' said Slater.

'Whatever it was I couldn't read it,' said Wilson, 'so I made a bonfire out of it and had a party to celebrate.'

Slater muttered a soft curse under his breath. 'So you have nothing left of her work?'

'I have nothing left of hers full stop. No work stuff, no clothes, nothing. It made a nice fire, though.'

'What about the people she used to work for? Do you have any contact numbers?'

'All burnt.'

'Oh bloody hell! Any of that stuff would have been useful,' said Slater.

'Well, pardon me for clearing her out of my life and moving on,' said Wilson irritably. 'How was I supposed to know you guys would turn up over a year later? It's not as if any of her stuff would have helped you find someone down in Hampshire, is it?'

'We'll never know now, will we?' said Slater bitterly.

'Look, I'm sorry, but as far as I'm concerned, when someone walks out on me like that, they cease to exist. I'm not the one in the wrong here.'

Slater exhaled a sigh. He was frustrated and annoyed, but he knew there was no point in getting stroppy with Wilson for believing what the police had told him.

'I think we're done here, Norm,' he said.

'Yeah, I guess you're right,' said Norman.

'Is that it?' asked Wilson.

'I think so.'

Wilson opened the front door to let them out, Slater leading and Norman close behind.

'Well, if you see her,' Wilson said, when they were outside, 'you can tell the bitch I've burnt all her stuff. In fact, you can tell her I had a bonfire party, and it was a great night!'

CHAPTER TWELVE

It was 10 p.m. and Slater had just arrived home. Because they managed to catch the rush hour, what should have been an easy hour on the M25 became a two-hour crawl, and then to compound matters there was a multi-car pile-up on the M3 which caused a seemingly endless stop-start journey.

They finally reached a service station and decided they might just as well stop and eat. Unfortunately, they weren't the only ones to have this bright idea, and having escaped the queue on the road, they found themselves joining an even slower one for food. But now, at last, he was home.

As he reached to put his key in his front door, he could hear the phone ringing inside. He flung the door open and rushed to the phone.

'Hello?' he panted into the phone.

'Hello, David, it's your sister. I've been trying to get hold of you all day.'

Slater held his breath for a moment and wished he hadn't rushed to answer the phone. He'd had a shit day, what with the crappy journey home and feeling guilty about doubting Norm. The last person he needed to speak to now was his sister; he could vividly recall the heated argument that had ended their last phone call.

'Yes, I recognise your voice,' he said finally. 'I've been out at work all day. What d'you want?'

'If you sounded pleased to hear from me, it would be nice.'

'But I'm not pleased to hear from you. To pretend I was pleased would be a lie, and I think you know how I feel about family and lies.'

He heard the sharp intake of breath. 'Well, you *should* be pleased to hear from me,' she snapped. 'I'm your sister!'

'Half-sister,' he corrected her. 'And don't make out like we were ever close. I can't recall you ever being a part of my life before, and I certainly don't need you in it now.'

'It wasn't my fault you were nearly ten years younger than me.'

'That's true enough, but it was your choice to avoid me whenever you could. And you knew all about Mum and Dad but you never told me.'

'You found out, didn't you?'

'Yes, I did, no thanks to you, but it was just a couple of weeks before he died. I could have had years with him, but you let Mum spin me all that bullshit about it being his fault. You could have told me the truth.'

'Well, you won't have to worry about Mum telling you any more lies.'

'What?'

'She died this morning.'

He was stunned for a few seconds. It had never occurred to him she would die one day, and now she had, he wasn't sure how he felt. 'I didn't even know she was ill. No one told me.'

'That's your fault,' she said. 'You were the one who cut himself off and said he never wanted to hear from any of us again.'

'Yeah, but if she was ill—'

'Well, perhaps if I had your mobile number—'

'That's never going to happen, so you can forget it.'

'You might have managed to make me feel guilty about Dad, but don't you dare try to make me feel guilty about this,' she snapped. 'If you didn't know, you've only got yourself to blame. You disowned your whole family, remember?'

He wanted to argue, but he knew she was right. After the death of his father, he had made it very clear how he felt and how he never wanted to hear from either his mother or his sister again.

'What happened?'

'She died.'

'Yes, but how? I mean, what was it? Cancer or what?'

'It was a brain tumour, as if you care,' she hissed callously.

He was silent for a moment as he tried to figure out how he felt and what he should say. 'I don't know what to say,' he said. 'It's a shock. I wasn't expecting it.'

'That's what happens when you cut yourself off from your family.'

'Don't kid yourself, Sarah. I don't think I ever regarded you as family. You were more like a stranger.'

'I don't care about me,' she said. 'But how could you do that to Mum?'

This was the red rag to Slater's bull, and it took a huge effort not to shout down the phone. 'How could I do that to Mum? How could Mum lie to me about Dad for all those years?'

'She did what she thought was best for you.'

'No,' he said. 'She did what she thought was best for her. She conned me. Did you know she used to hide the cards and letters he sent?'

There was no reply, but Slater didn't care; he was in full flow now. 'You don't get it, do you? I had to listen to the other kids going on about their dads, and I couldn't join in. I could have gone to football matches with him, like the other boys did. We could have gone fishing and done all sorts of things together.

'When I was old enough we could have shared a pint together, but no, she made sure that didn't happen. D'you know what I finally got to do with him? By the time I met him, all I had left was time to hold his hand and watch him

die. After all those wasted years I found him, and then a few days later I lost him again, this time for good.'

He was close to tears now, so he stopped speaking before it was too late. He wasn't going to let her hear him cry. He could hear her, restless on the other end of the line, maybe not knowing what to say.

'We're not going to go through all this again,' she said finally. 'There's no point.'

'You're probably right,' he agreed reluctantly. 'What about a funeral? Do you need me to help—'

'I can manage the arrangements just fine. I don't need your help with anything. I can't imagine I ever will. I'll send you the details when I know them. It's up to you whether you choose to come.'

There was the softest of clicks as she ended the call, followed by silence. As if he were moving in slow motion, Slater put the phone down and then lowered himself into a chair.

He sat perfectly still for a couple of minutes and tried to figure out how he felt. He thought he should be feeling upset his mother had passed away, but he didn't feel upset at all; he didn't feel anything.

CHAPTER THIRTEEN

Next morning, which was Saturday and they'd both decided to come into the office, Norman was surprised to find Slater had beaten him to work, and, judging from the sounds emanating from the kitchen, it appeared he might even be making the tea. This was almost unheard of at this time of the morning, so, not wishing to interfere, Norman went to his desk to check his emails.

A couple of minutes later, Slater emerged from the kitchen carrying two mugs of tea.

'D'you think I'm normal?' he asked, as he placed one of the mugs on Norman's desk.

Norman looked up, mouth open. 'Presenting me with a cup of tea as soon as I arrive at the office isn't normal.'

'I'm serious,' said Slater, taking a seat next to his friend.

Norman studied his face. 'What's brought this on?'

'I'm just wondering — do I react like other people or do you think I'm somehow different?'

'Okay . . .' Norman said. 'I'm not sure where you're going with this, but if you really want to know.' He thought for a few seconds. 'I recall the time you spent several minutes looking down the barrel of a gun. Afterwards you said it scared the crap out of you. I think most people would say much the same thing, so that seems normal enough.'

'That's not what I mean,' said Slater.

Norman spread his arms. 'What exactly *do* you mean? You're going to have to help me out here, because I'm not sure what I'm supposed to say.'

'What about when Jenny Radstock died? I mean, she was living with me for months, sharing my bed, but did I get upset when I found out she was dead?'

'Ah, right, now I see where this is going. We're talking about your relationships with women. Don't forget you had already split up from her. You were no longer a couple.'

'Yeah, okay, but I wasn't even upset when it ended, was I?'

Norman studied Slater's face. 'D'you really want to do this?'

Slater nodded.

'Why?'

'Does it matter?' He didn't give Norman a chance to answer before he spoke again. 'Then there was Watson. We had a good thing going — she even went away with me — but that was about as far as it went, and then that was over. Again, was I upset when it ended?'

Norman assumed this was another rhetorical question, so he picked up his mug of tea, took a sip, and kept quiet. Sure enough, Slater started talking again.

'It's the same every time I get in a relationship, and I never seem to get upset when it ends like other people do. That's not normal, is it?'

Slater stared expectantly at Norman, who was sipping his tea and staring into space. 'Well?'

Norman turned his stare towards him. 'You want me to speak?'

'Of course I do.'

'Then you need to leave a little space here and there to allow me to fit a few words in.'

'I'm sorry,' said Slater sheepishly.

Norman placed his mug carefully down on his desk. 'Right, I'm going to be honest, but I'm not promising you're going to like what I have to say. Don't forget we have to work together, and that's not going to be easy if I piss you off.'

'You will not piss me off, Norm,' said Slater. 'Now stop beating about the bush and get to the point.'

Norman sighed. 'Okay. You're not normal.'

Slater looked disappointed.

'But there are mitigating circumstances.'

'What circumstances?'

'I think, deep down, you're scared of making a commitment.'

'That's bollocks,' said Slater. 'I'd love to be in a committed relationship.'

'On the surface, yeah, sure you would,' said Norman. 'But I'm talking about deep down in your subconscious. That's where the issue lies.'

'Cobblers.'

'Is it? Let's take a look at your parents. Didn't their marriage break up?'

'You know it did. So what? Loads of marriages break up.'

'Yeah, and lots of kids have issues as a result. Your mother cheated on your father, right? That's a trust issue. Your mother then compounded that by telling you it was your father who cheated. That's another trust issue. Then, later, you were engaged to be married, only to find your future wife had been cheating on you. Yet another trust issue.'

'Are you saying I don't trust women?'

'I'm saying why would you?' asked Norman. 'The two women you loved most both broke your trust. Maybe, deep inside, you aren't prepared to take the risk that it might happen again.'

'Yeah, but your wife did the same, and it hasn't stopped you and Jane getting together.'

'I was over fifty when that happened. I had plenty of life experience to help me deal with it. You were just a kid when your parents split up, and you weren't much older when all your hopes and dreams were shattered by your girlfriend.'

'But that was a long time ago.'

'Sure it was, but how did you face up to it and deal with it at the time? You quit your job, left Winchester, and started again in Tinton.'

'I thought a clean slate was the best thing for me.'

'I'm not saying it wasn't, but you didn't face up to the situation and deal with the issue — you ran away from it. It's the same with your mother. When you found out the truth about your father, you didn't confront the issue, did you? You cut yourself off from her. I still think you should go and see her to talk about it.'

Slater was studying the tea in his mug, and it was a few seconds before he spoke. 'That's going to be a bit difficult. She died yesterday.'

Norman was horrified. 'Oh no! I'm sorry. Why didn't you say? I had no idea. Do you need to take a few days off?'

'Why would I do that?' asked Slater.

'Aren't you upset?'

'Well, that's the thing, you see. I'm not upset at all. I don't seem to feel anything.'

'Maybe you're in shock. Sometimes it takes a while—'

'I'm not in shock, Norm, honestly. I briefly felt a bit numb when I heard, but that was it. It's not normal, is it?'

'So that's what's *really* triggered this idea you're not normal.'

'Well, I'm not, am I?'

'I think it's this trust thing, honestly. It's still there, deep inside. That's why you feel nothing now your mother has died, and it's why you always contrive to get your girlfriends to give you the boot before you get too close to making a commitment.'

Slater continued to stare at his mug but didn't say anything.

'I'll tell you something else,' continued Norman. 'You're not stupid. I reckon you already worked all this out for yourself. I mean, it's not rocket science, is it?'

Now Slater looked at Norman, a wry smile on his face. 'You know me too well. How did that happen?'

'It happened because you tell me things, and d'you know why that is?'

'Because I confide in you.'

'Yeah, but why do you do that?'

Slater looked puzzled.

'Because you trust me, of course,' said Norman.

'Look, about yesterday . . .'

'You were angry,' said Norman. 'I get that. Anyway, it doesn't matter. We sorted that out, didn't we? Underneath it all, you trust me. I know you do, and you know I'm right.'

'Yeah, you're always right,' admitted Slater. 'Maybe I should marry you.'

Norman chuckled. 'I don't think so,' he said. 'I know how loud you snore, and I'm sure I'm not the right one for you. You could do much better.'

They shared a laugh.

'Are you sure you're okay?'

'I'm okay about my mother passing,' said Slater. 'But what do I do? How do I get over this trust thing?'

'Has it occurred to you there could be another reason you don't want to commit?' asked Norman.

'Another reason? Isn't one issue enough?'

'What I mean is — maybe you just haven't met the right person yet.'

'You think so, after all these years? That makes me think I never will.'

'Sure you will.'

'How will I know, if I can't trust?'

'Maybe the right one will be the one you feel you *can* trust. Perhaps that's how you'll know she's the right one.'

'So, basically, you're saying I just have to keep on testing the water, and eventually I'll find someone I can trust?'

'It's either that or you could go and talk to someone who can help you sort your issues out.'

'You mean a psychiatrist?'

Norman shrugged. 'It's an option.'

'No,' said Slater firmly. 'It isn't.'

The conversation was obviously over, so Norman turned his attention back to the email he had been about to open. He clicked the email and started to read.

'Changing the subject,' he said to Slater, 'have you thought any more about this idea that Betty Glover could be Martha?'

'I have to admit that finding that envelope was one hell of a coincidence, and I can't explain how it got there, but I'm still not convinced.'

Norman pointed to the screen before him. 'Well, maybe this will help convince you.'

Slater looked across at the monitor, but he couldn't see what Norman was talking about. 'What's that?'

'Betty's bank debit card was being used for six months after she left Barking.'

'How did you . . . Have you been speaking to Vinnie again?'

Norman grinned at Slater and winked. 'You haven't heard the best bit yet. The last time it was used was right here in Tinton!'

CHAPTER FOURTEEN

'So, how is your case going?' Robbins asked Slater once they were settled at their table.

'Well, despite your best efforts to help us, we're not getting anywhere fast.'

'Have you found Betty Glover, or should I say Martha?'

'We don't know for sure that Betty Glover *is* Martha.'

'But your face says you think she could be.'

'Let's just say the odds have definitely improved.'

'Does that mean her boyfriend was helpful?'

'Her boyfriend is an idiot. The local plod told him they thought she had probably left him for another bloke, but she didn't have the nerve to tell him. And he believes them! In fact, he's so convinced she was cheating on him, he had a bonfire party and burnt all her stuff.'

'And what do you think?'

'I think it would have been good if he hadn't had the bonfire.'

She smiled indulgently. 'That's not what I meant, and you know it.'

Slater nodded — of course he knew it. 'I just don't see it,' he said. 'It doesn't add up. He told us she was some sort of crusading journalist. People like that tend to have courage in their convictions and say it how they see it. Does it seem likely she wouldn't have the guts to tell him she thought he was a twat and that she was leaving him?'

'Does this mean you think she was telling the truth about going undercover for a job?'

'It means I think she would have told him if she was leaving him.'

She gave him a disapproving look.

'And yes,' he added, 'it's quite possible she was going undercover.'

Now she smiled. 'You haven't told me why the odds are improving.'

'Her bank card was being used for six months after she left Barking, and the last time it was used was in Tinton.'

She sat back in surprise. 'How do you know that?' she asked, and Slater froze as he realised what he'd just done. Then, as quickly as she seemed to have trapped him, she gave him an escape route. 'Has this come from Norman's friend up in London again?'

'What? Oh, yeah, that's right.'

She pulled a face. 'I bet Norman's not telling *him* he shouldn't take risks for you two.'

'He's not the sort of guy you can tell what to do,' Slater said honestly.

She smiled. 'And I'm not the sort of girl you can tell what to do.'

'I'm not planning on telling you what to do.'

'Yes, you are. You keep telling me not to help you.'

'Trust me, your help and the guy in London . . . it's not the same thing,' said Slater.

'It's fine,' she argued. 'The research I'm doing means I can look at stuff for you, and no one will ever know.'

'I don't want you putting your career on the line.'

'Look, I'm a bloody good detective who's been shunted into a siding. I'm saddled with the dullest job in the world, which is probably designed to make me resign. If it wasn't for your case I'm sure I would go mad or die of boredom.'

Slater studied her face. It was a picture of determination. 'Okay. I can see you're not going to listen, but for God's sake be careful or they won't need to make you resign.'

'I will be careful. I promise.' She grinned, impishly. 'So, what else have you got?'

'Are you trying to solve my case for me?'

She laughed. 'Now that would be good, wouldn't it? Police one, private eyes nil.'

'It's not going to happen,' said Slater. 'Slater and Norman are a damned good team.'

'Did this other journalist have a name?'

'The boyfriend didn't know the guy's surname, but his first name might be Eddie, and before you say it, yes, we do realise there's not much difference between Eddie and Adie.'

'It all seems to tie in, don't you think?'

'There are a lot of "mights",' said Slater. 'I'd much rather have just one piece of definite proof.'

Robbins pulled a face. 'I can't help you with a definite,' she said, 'but I can give you another "might be".'

Now it was Slater's turn to sit back with surprise. She fished a thin folder from her bag and placed it on the table before him. 'Like I said, it's a "might be".'

Slater looked at the folder as if it might bite him, then he looked around the room to make sure they weren't being watched. 'Jesus, Stella, you can't go handing me police files.'

'Don't be such a drama queen. It's not a police file, it's a photocopy.'

'That's just as bad!'

Even so, Slater couldn't resist opening the folder as Robbins filled him in.

'This girl has been dead for weeks, and everyone has forgotten about her. And when I say everyone, I'm talking about the whole UK, not just Hampshire. No one's going to know I've copied the file.'

'And how does it help us?' he asked as he scanned the report.

'Her body was found in a lay-by near Southampton, so it's not a million miles from here.'

'Right.' Slater wasn't convinced.

'She was hit by a truck or something similar.'

'Was there a bloke with her?'

'Sorry?'

'We think she probably took off with a bloke called Alex.'

'There's no mention of anyone else being involved.'

'Why do you think this is relevant to us? It says here there's no DNA, fingerprint or dental record match. Even if her prints and DNA weren't on file, surely Betty Glover would have dental records?'

'Yes,' said Robbins, 'but on the other hand, she matches the description, and she was wearing red jogging gear.'

'Hmm. It's a bit tenuous, isn't it?' said Slater. He looked at Robbins and registered her disappointment. 'I'll show it to Norm on Monday morning and see what he thinks. Thank you.'

He closed the folder and slipped it into his jacket pocket. 'That's enough about my case. What about you? How's your week going?'

'Crap is probably a good word for it,' she said. 'My life is so boring right now. I'd much rather talk about your week. It must be much more colourful than mine.'

'I'm not sure colourful is the word I would use, but it's certainly not been dull.'

'Go on, then, give me the highlights.'

'Let me see, we found an old man lying at the foot of the stairs, and the ungrateful old sod did nothing but complain when we called an ambulance.'

Robbins grinned. 'It just proves you can't help some people.'

'He wasn't just ungrateful,' said Slater. 'The next thing we knew there was some smart-arsed lawyer marching into our office, laying down the law about harassing helpless old men!'

'And were you?'

'If it wasn't for us, he would still be lying on the floor.'

'Does this lawyer have a name?'

'Samuel S. Shrivener.'

She had been raising her drink to her lips, but she stopped halfway. 'Really? You've had a visit from Slimy Sam? You must be stirring some serious shit.'

'Who is this guy?'

'Slimy Sam Shrivener. Acts as lawyer to one Jools Hanover. Ever heard of him?'

'Isn't he some sort of property tycoon down on the coast?'

'On the face of it he owns a couple of casinos, three nightclubs and lots of property in the Portsmouth area, but what interests us is what's under the surface.'

'I see. Got his fingers in lots of pies, has he?'

'Our vice unit believes so. When it comes to Jools Hanover, what you see on the surface is just the tip of a very big iceberg.'

'You said "they believe" he's into other stuff. What exactly does that mean?'

'It means they think he's into illegal gambling, money laundering, pornography, prostitutes, extortion. You name it, he's probably got his dirty little mitts in it. The problem is, we've never been able to prove anything.'

'That means he's either very good—'

'Or we're crap at what we do,' she finished.

Slater smiled. 'Actually, that's not what I was going to say. I meant he's either very good or perhaps there's nothing to find.'

She pulled a disapproving face. 'I can't believe that!'

'No, you're probably right.'

She studied Slater's face for a few seconds. 'So, Shrivener, what did he really want?'

'He came to warn us off.'

'Did he succeed?'

'What do you think?'

'Be careful. These people don't mess around. We're sure Hanover is behind more than one unpleasant death. I don't want to be scraping you off the pavement at the foot of a tall building.'

He winked at her. 'I'll be sure to say no if they invite me onto a roof.'

She gave him a sharp look. 'I'm not joking,' she said. 'If you've had a warning you should take note and keep your wits about you. And if you do find something that we can use against Hanover, hand it over to us. Please don't try to be a hero.'

'Don't worry, me and Norm don't do hero. We'll be fine.'

She gave him an unhappy smile. She obviously wasn't convinced he was taking her seriously.

'Look, Stella, I appreciate the warning, but we already know the people involved in this are bad news, and we realise we have to be careful. We have dealt with people like this before, you know.'

She didn't look any happier for his reassurance.

'Okay,' he said. 'I think it's time to change the subject. Is that okay?'

She sighed and nodded. 'That's probably a good idea.'

'Okay, where shall we start?'

If Slater had been expecting her to reveal something of herself now, he was quickly disappointed.

'What else has happened in the world of David Slater this week?' she asked.

'Not much, really.'

'What's not much?'

'I mostly work, and when I'm not at work, I tend to stay at home and watch TV or listen to music. It's all pretty dull and boring. What about you?'

'About the same,' she said.

Slater studied her face. 'You don't give much away, do you?'

'We do similar jobs, and it sounds like we do the same things when we're not at work. As you said, it's pretty dull and boring.'

'You've got your mother's dog to walk.'

'That tends to be a weekend pursuit, and no I haven't, not since I walked with you.'

'Where does your mother live?'

'In Winchester. What about yours?'

Slater was about to tell her his mother lived in the area too, and then he remembered and stopped himself.

'She, ah, actually she died yesterday.'

A mixture of shock and panic filled her face. 'Oh my God. Why didn't you say? I had no idea. Are you sure you want to be here tonight?'

Slater raised his hands. 'Honestly, Stella, I'm fine. I didn't say anything about it because I didn't feel the need, and there's nowhere else I would rather be right now.'

'But you must be upset?'

'Well, there's the thing, you see. This is going to sound weird, and I'm almost ashamed to say it, but I'm not upset.'

'That'll be shock,' she assured him. 'It will catch up with you.'

He shook his head. 'No, I don't think it will. I've lost plenty of people who were close to me, and the only one I got upset about was my father.'

'Why him?'

'It's a long story.'

'Do you want to talk about it?'

'You're kidding, right? We've done nothing but talk about me, and my case, since we got here.'

'But you've just lost your mother. Bereavement's a big deal, and you obviously have some sort of issue. Sometimes it helps to talk about it.'

'I think we should talk about you.'

'Listen to me,' she said earnestly. 'I saw it in your eyes when we met this evening, and I can see it now. You need to talk to someone, and I'm willing to listen. We can talk about me another time.'

At the mention of there being another time, Slater felt himself relax, and his spirits lifted. He hadn't realised just how badly he had wanted her to suggest they should see each other again.

'Come on, talk to me,' she said, encouragingly.

'On one condition.'

'What's that?'

'Next time we only talk about you.'

'You'll find it very boring.'

'That's for me to decide,' said Slater. 'Anyway, that's the deal.'

She studied his face as she thought about his offer. 'Okay, it's a deal.'

* * *

And so, over dinner, Slater told her all about his early years. About how his father had left home, his nearly marriage, and then about how he had finally learned the truth about his father only to find he was dying. And then, finally, about the phone call from his sister just last night.

Now they were enjoying a coffee to end their evening.

'Norm thinks it's a trust thing,' he said. 'He reckons I'm unable to trust women.'

'I can't say I disagree with his logic,' she said, 'but maybe it's just that you haven't met the right one yet.'

'He said that too.'

'What is he, your life guide?'

Slater smiled fondly.

'You're very close to him, aren't you?' she asked.

'Who, Norm? Yeah, I am. If I could choose a big brother, it would be Norm. I can tell him anything, or ask his opinion about anything, and he always tells me what he thinks, even when it's not what I want to hear. I've come a long way since I met him, and I'm a much better person because of him.'

'Wow! That's quite a testimonial.'

Slater hadn't thought of it that way, but now she had said it, he thought she was right. It was a testimonial, and he'd nailed it.

'Yeah, well, he's quite a bloke,' he said.

She was studying his face.

'What?' he asked.

'You get quite emotional when you talk about him. I think that's really something.'

'Look, I'm not in love with him or anything, it's just that he's the best friend I've ever had. He's always got my back.'

'And I think that's wonderful,' she said. 'You're very lucky.'

'Yes, I believe I am.'

'So, what's going to happen about this funeral?'

'My sister insists she's making the arrangements and that she doesn't want my help.'

'I didn't mean that. I mean are you going?'

'What? To the funeral? I don't know. Probably not.'

'But she is your mother.'

'I'd be about as welcome as a flea infestation.'

'But they're your family.'

'You know what they say; you can choose your friends . . .'

'I'm sure it can't be that bad.'

He sighed. 'The thing is, I was always the outsider, and then, not long ago, I told them to stick it. It wasn't exactly the way to win them over and show them what a nice guy I am, was it?'

'Whatever she did, she's still your mother. If you don't go, you could end up regretting it for the rest of your life.'

'And if I do go, I might end up regretting it for the rest of my life. It would be like me against the world. I'm not sure I care enough to go through that sort of hassle.'

'When is it?'

'I don't know yet. Sarah's going to let me know, and then she says it's up to me if I want to go.'

'Perhaps you need someone to go with you.'

'You mean Norm? No, I don't think so. He does enough for me already.'

'Actually, I wasn't thinking of Norm.'

Slater looked at her. 'Well, who then?'

She smiled back at him.

'No, Stella. Honestly, I couldn't ask you to do that.'

'You didn't ask. I'm volunteering.'

'But that's like volunteering for a suicide mission. I mean, you hardly know me, and you certainly don't know any of my family. You have no idea what it will be like.'

'I think it might be fun.'

'No. Really, you—'

'Look, we're not arguing about this. Let me know when it is, and I'll take a day off and come with you. Then you won't be on your own.'

'Yeah, but—'

'That's settled then,' she said. 'Now, are you going to take me home, or am I walking?'

* * *

Once again, the mood of the evening changed as soon as they left the restaurant. Slater had been very mindful of last time and had made sure he didn't crowd her or say anything that could be misconstrued. By the time they were in his car, Robbins was positively distant, but at least this time he was confident it wasn't because of anything he had done. Even so, he felt he was walking on eggshells.

He pulled up outside her house and switched the engine off, making sure his hands were on the steering wheel where she could see them. Now what happens? he thought, keeping his eyes to the front. Alongside him, Robbins was looking to the front, but he felt she was also watching him out of the corner of her eye.

'I'm sorry, but I can't invite you in,' she said, her voice almost a whisper.

'That's okay,' he said.

'I'm sorry, really.'

'It's okay. There's no need to be sorry.'

'You asked me where my mother lives.'

This seemed a rather random statement, and he couldn't help but turn to look at her. 'I did?'

'You were asking about the dog, and then you—'

'Oh, yeah, that's right, I did.'

'Well, she lives here.'

'With you?'

'It's more the case that I live with her.'

'Oh, right. You must get on with her better than I got on with my mother.'

'My dad lives here, too. It's their house. I grew up here.'

Slater wasn't quite sure what he was supposed to say to this so, as a diversion, he leaned forward to look at the house through the windscreen. Of course, it was dark, and there was a tall hedge in the way, so he couldn't possibly see any detail. As he stared upwards, a sudden triangle of light indicated that the corner of a bedroom curtain had been pulled aside. A face appeared to be looking straight at him and then was gone again, reminding Slater of an irate father years ago who didn't approve of him canoodling with his daughter.

'It looks nice,' he said, leaning back. 'Like a proper home.'

'Yes, it is.'

There was an awkward silence. Slater was confused. His instincts told him making any sort of move would be the wrong thing to do. The issue was obviously something to do with being alone in the car with him. Or maybe it was just being alone with any man. He realised he was holding his breath.

'I'm not sure this is a good idea,' she said, finally.

'Sitting here?' he asked. 'Yes, you're probably right—'

'No. I mean you seeing me. It's not a good idea.'

Slater felt crushed. 'What about earlier, when you said about next time? I thought you meant you'd like to see me again.'

'I did mean it,' she said, 'and I do enjoy your company, but it's not fair on you when an evening ends like this.'

'Ends like what?'

'Like this. I know what's supposed to happen now, but I just can't do that sort of thing.'

'What exactly do you mean when you say "that sort of thing"?'

'I can't get physical. I thought I could, but I can't, not anymore.'

'Now wait a minute,' said Slater. 'I assume you're talking about sex, right? Who said every date has to end with us in bed?'

Now she turned to stare at him. 'Isn't that what you want?'

Slater's immediate thought was that he was caught in a trap. If he said he didn't want her, would it look like he thought she was undesirable? On the other hand, if he said yes, would she think that really was all he wanted? Then the mature Slater took control of his mind. This wasn't about him, was it? It was about a frightened woman. A frightened woman he suddenly realised how much he cared about.

'Look,' he said, 'I have no idea why you're frightened, and I'm not going to demand you tell me. But—'

'Who said I'm frightened?'

'Maybe that's the wrong choice of word, I'm sorry. What I'm trying to say is I want to help you.'

'Who says I need help? Why would you do that?'

'How about because I care about you?'

'You hardly know me.'

Slater nodded. 'That's true, but maybe it's because you never tell me anything about yourself. But, if I see you again, you said *you* would be doing the talking, so I'll get to know you better, won't I?'

'Did I really say that?'

'Yes, you did. Anyway, didn't you listen to me earlier? Didn't you volunteer to come to my mother's funeral?'

'I'm happy to help.'

'And I'm happy to help you! You did say talking helps, didn't you?'

He seemed to be considering the idea. 'It's difficult.'

'I won't push. I'll wait until you're ready. I just want to be there when that time arrives.'

'I don't know if I can.'

'You'll never find out if you don't try,' he countered.

'It will probably be a waste of your time.'

He turned a wry smile in her direction. 'Yeah, maybe, but it's my time, and I get to choose how I waste it.'

'I'm not sure.'

'So why don't you sleep on it?' said Slater.

She stared into his face, her anguish clear to see. He felt she was looking right into his soul, as if she was trying to work out if she dared to trust him.

'Just think about it,' he said. 'Take as long as you want. You've got my number.'

'I should go,' she said. 'Thank you for a lovely evening.'

'The pleasure's mine, Stella, trust me.'

She hesitated, and, for just the briefest moment, he thought she was going to offer her cheek, or maybe even kiss him, but then she turned away, eased the door open, and slipped from her seat. Before she closed the door, she turned back to speak to him.

'I nearly forgot. Make sure you call the mortuary in the morning. I told them to expect a call from two detectives who might be able to identify their Jane Doe.'

She closed the car door and walked over to the gate. As she opened it, she looked back and waved. He raised a hand, watched as she disappeared through the metal gate, and then let out a long sigh.

At the sound of the gate shutting, the triangle of light showed on the side of the house again for a few seconds and then was gone. As he started the car and began the journey home, Slater was shocked to realise how badly he wanted her to agree to see him again.

CHAPTER FIFTEEN

'I told Stella about our encounter with Shrivener,' Slater told Norman on Monday morning. 'She says he only has one major client. He's a guy named Jools Hanover.'

'Should I know that name?'

'You wouldn't know him from your old stomping ground, but apparently he's very big down on the south coast, especially in Portsmouth and the surrounding area.'

'Big in what way?'

'On paper he's a property developer, but the police think that's just a front. According to Stella, his tentacles spread far and wide, and it's all pretty sordid stuff.'

'My, my, isn't that a coincidence?' said Norman. 'He sounds like just the sort of guy who might catch the attention of an investigative journalist.'

'That's exactly what I thought.'

'Where do we find him?'

'She didn't tell me, but she did say we need to be really careful.'

'Got a reputation, has he?'

'They think he's responsible for more than one murder, although they have no proof.'

'So, he's clever with it.'

'So it seems,' said Slater.

'In that case, we'll just have to be a bit more clever,' said Norman.

'Let's just keep him in mind until we have a good reason to think he's involved.'

'I think the fact his brief is interfering seems a pretty good reason.'

'Yeah, I know,' said Slater. 'I feel exactly the same, but let's not poke the dragon until we know what it's done, right?'

Norman nodded. 'Yeah, you're probably right.'

'Anyway, I have a treat for you this morning.'

'What treat?'

Slater gave him a wicked smile. 'You're going to love it.'

'Love what?'

'I just have to make a phone call to arrange the visit.'

'What visit? Where are we going?'

Slater reached for his phone. 'Let me make this call and I'll tell you all about it.'

* * *

Ten minutes later, they were sitting in Slater's car.

'You're kidding me, right?' asked Norman.

Slater grinned as he started the car.

'This is a joke, isn't it? I mean, a mortuary? Really? You know how much I hate those places.'

'Look, we're not going to witness an autopsy. It's just a dead body, and it's been dead for weeks. There won't be any blood and guts or anything like that.'

Norman sighed. 'Jeez, I thought we were finished with those places years ago.'

'It won't be that bad, Norm. I'll buy you lunch on the way back.'

'Eww. Don't talk to me about food and a mortuary in the same breath. How could you do that?'

* * *

It didn't take much more than an hour to reach the mortuary. Having been detectives in the police service, they had both spent their fair share of time in mortuaries, so even though Norman hated these places, they expected to be familiar with the surroundings — but they were in for a surprise or two.

The first surprise came in the form of the young pathologist who greeted them. Norman thought the guy could have been a resurrected corpse judging by his colour. Slater recognised his style as goth. This was confirmed by the pounding music that greeted their arrival in the viewing room.

'Can you turn that down a bit?' asked Norman.

'What?' called the pathologist.

'The music. Can you turn the music down?' Norman shouted.

'I'm sorry, I can't hear you.'

Meanwhile, as Norman engaged in his futile conversation, Slater decided he wasn't prepared to risk his eardrums or waste his breath. He took matters into his own hands and strode across to the music system, where he quickly located the 'off' switch.

In the sudden silence, Norman could clearly be heard making an observation as to why the pathologist couldn't hear him. 'Maybe it's because of that bloody din.' He looked around guiltily. 'I'm sorry,' he said. 'That's just not quite my kind of music, and it's a little loud for my old ears.'

'No worries, man,' said the pathologist with a pale smile. 'It's cool. No offence taken.' He extended a hand. 'My name's Bill Bridger.'

Having made the introductions, Bridger wasted no time in leading them through to what he called 'the viewing room'. Once there, he pulled out a drawer to reveal a body in a bag. 'Here's my Jane Doe. DI Robbins said you guys could help me identify her.'

'*Your* Jane Doe?' asked Norman.

'No one else has claimed her,' replied Bridger, 'so I feel like it's down to me to care about what happens to her. The poor girl was left for dead in a lay-by, run over by an HGV or truck of some sort. There's no dignity in that, is there? I think everyone deserves a bit of dignity in death, don't you?'

'Well, yeah, I do, actually,' said Norman.

'There's probably a family out there somewhere missing a daughter, or a husband wondering where his wife is. If I can identify her, maybe I can then find her family and make sure she at least gets a decent funeral. To my mind that's just as important as finding out what killed her.'

Norman nodded his approval, and the young pathologist rose a long way in his esteem. 'We're on the same side, then,' he said. 'You've got a body that needs a name, and we've got a name that needs a body. Obviously, we were hoping to find a live one, but it is what it is.'

'DI Robbins said you've been through all the databases,' said Slater.

'Not exactly. I've done DNA and fingerprints. They both drew blanks. I didn't bother with dental records.'

'Why not?'

'You've gotta have teeth.'

'What?'

'You can't do a dental comparison if there's no teeth to compare.'

'She had no teeth? Was that because of some sort of disease?'

Bridger shook his head. 'Oh, no, you don't understand. They were extracted.'

'There must be a dentist, somewhere, with a record of an operation like that.'

'If there is such a record, I haven't found it, but then I'm not surprised. I'm confident these teeth weren't removed by a dentist; the jaws have been too badly damaged. Her teeth weren't extracted in the normal manner. They may even have been knocked out.'

Norman winced. 'Jesus, that's brutal.'

'I would suggest this girl had a pretty brutal life,' said Bridger. 'She's also had both arms broken at some stage.'

'Any idea how?' asked Norman.

'I couldn't say *how* they were broken with any certainty, but the way the breaks have healed suggests she didn't get the best medical care after they were broken.'

'You think someone broke them on purpose?'

Bridger pulled a face. 'Again, I can't be sure, but . . .'

'Bloody hell, poor kid,' muttered Norman.

'It gets worse. She was covered in mud and her clothes were torn and scratched. The police said they thought she was out running and got lost.'

'You don't believe that?'

'I think she was running, alright, but she wasn't running for pleasure — she was running for her life.'

'What?'

'If you look beyond the major trauma she suffered from colliding with a massive truck and look at the more superficial cuts and scratches on her arms and legs, I would suggest she was being hunted and was running through trees and brambles and that sort of stuff. She may well have run under the truck in blind panic.'

'Holy shit!' muttered Norman.

There was an awkward silence.

Bridger began to unzip the bag. 'Her face is a bit disfigured, I'm afraid, but that's what happens when you get hit by a truck.'

He flipped the cover back to reveal her face. Her nose was broken, and something about her left eye didn't look quite right. Slater looked at the face and then at Bridger.

'If you think she looks bad now, you should have seen the state of her when she was found. We cleaned her up as best we could and found some false teeth to make her face look the right shape, but I can't do much about the fractured eye socket or the broken nose.'

Norman produced the photograph of the young 'Martha' and they compared them. Then they did the same with the photo of the two women taken from Vernon Tisdale's basement.

'You must do this all the time, Bill,' said Slater. 'Do you think one of these women is her?'

Bridger compared the photograph to the dead woman. 'Are these two women in this photograph sisters?' he asked after a minute or so.

'That's what we want to know,' said Slater.

Bridger twisted the photo around to get various views for comparison. After about five minutes, he turned to Slater. 'If I had to decide, I'd say the face I have here is more of a match for the one on the left in the photograph.'

'I'll agree with that,' said Norman.

'At last! Now, if you can just tell me her name . . .'

'The thing is, we have two names . . .'

'Which figures, as there are two girls.'

'If only it were that simple,' said Slater.

'But I thought—'

'We have two names,' said Norman. 'Martha Dennis and Betty Glover.'

'So which one is this?' asked Bridger.

'This is where the problems begin. You see, we think Martha and Betty are the same person, but we don't know which one of these women she is. So, even if we *can* identify one, if it's not yours, we don't know who the other one is.'

Bridger's shoulders slumped. 'You're kidding. Robbins told me you were going to tell me who she is.'

'Yeah, I'm sorry about that,' said Norman.

Bridger's face suddenly brightened. 'But it's not all bad news! If we have names, I can maybe do more specific tests and searches.'

'But I thought you said you'd done the searches,' said Slater.

'Yes, but now I have a name. If I'm searching for a specific person, I might find something that helps identify her.'

'Or not,' added Slater.

'Or not,' agreed Bridger, 'but even if we eliminate her, and I'm left still not knowing who my body is, at least you'll know it's not your missing woman.'

Slater wasn't convinced it would necessarily move them forward, but it couldn't hurt, could it? 'What do you think, Norm?'

'I think it's worth a try, but I think we should tell Bill about Martha, just so he doesn't waste a load of his time.'

'Tell me *what* about Martha?'

'The real Martha Dennis died years ago. We think Betty stole her identity.'

'Why would she do that?'

'As far as we can make out, she's an investigative journalist, and she's gone undercover to get a story.'

'And she stole a dead person's ID to do that?' said Bridger. 'That's a bit extreme, isn't it? Couldn't she just invent a new ID?'

Slater shrugged. 'Trust me, we're as intrigued as you are.'

'What if it's not her?'

'Let's cross that bridge when we get to it,' Slater suggested. He hadn't meant it as a hint, but Bridger obviously thought he had.

'Oh, right. I'll get on with it then.' He looked down at the face in the body bag. 'Sorry, love, not this time,' he said as he slowly pulled at the zip. 'Maybe later.' Then, looking at Norman, he asked, 'Have you got a number where I can contact you?'

Norman fumbled in his pocket and drew out a business card. 'You can always reach me on this number.'

CHAPTER SIXTEEN

Norman had been in his office since 7 a.m. Slater wasn't due in until eleven thirty that morning, so Norman had decided to pursue a line of enquiry he had dreamed up overnight. It was a long shot, and he had no idea if it was just a crazy idea that would come to nothing, but as he had a free morning he didn't think it would do any harm to find out.

He had been so engrossed in his research he was quite unaware how much time had passed until his phone began to ring. As he reached for the phone, he was surprised to find it was nine thirty.

'Yo!' he said into the phone.

'Is that Norman Norman?'

'That's me.'

'It's Bill Bridger from the mortuary.'

'Oh, hi, Bill, how are you?'

'I'm fine, but can I say something?'

'Yeah, go ahead.'

'It's none of my business, of course, but I don't think shouting "Yo!" down the phone is a very professional way of greeting a potential client.'

'But you're not a client.'

'I could have been, and I have to say I wouldn't have been impressed.'

Norman could feel his face turning red. He had spent years answering internal calls that way and often answered his mobile phone in the same, casual way, but he knew there was no place for such informality if they wanted their business to be taken seriously.

'Yeah, you're right,' he admitted. 'I was so engrossed in what I was doing I'd gone back ten years in my head.'

'A nice friendly receptionist, that's what you need. Someone with a smile in their voice.'

Norman felt himself bristling. Bridger was definitely pushing his luck now. If he wanted business advice, he wouldn't go to a goth pathologist, any more than Bridger would seek advice about cause of death from a detective.

'Okay, Bill,' he said frostily. 'I take your point about the greeting, but there's no need to get carried away. What have you got for us?' Even as he spoke, Norman regretted biting Bridger's head off.

'I can confirm it's definitely not Betty Glover lying in that body bag.'

'Well, I suppose that's good for us, but I don't suppose it helps you, right?'

'Oh well, that's just how it goes, isn't it?' said Bridger. 'You win some, you lose some.'

'How did you find out it wasn't Betty?' asked Norman.

'Dental records. It's much easier to find one person's record than it is to find a match across millions. I found Betty Glover's dentist quite easily, and he confirms she had a full, healthy set of teeth just eighteen months ago. There's no way she can be the same person.'

'But you still think it's the woman in that photograph we showed you?'

'The face is too badly damaged to say with total confidence.'

'So, what are you thinking? Seventy-five, eighty percent?'

'I'd go as far as ninety percent,' said Bridger.

'That's pretty confident in my book,' said Norman.

'It doesn't help me know her name, though, does it?'

'No, but if we're right about Betty Glover being the other woman in the photograph, we now know what she looks like, which gives us more than we had yesterday. Maybe that will help us find Betty and she can identify the other woman.'

'I suppose some good might come from it then.'

'Listen, Bill, I promise you, if we find out who your girl is, you'll be the first to know.'

'I would really appreciate that,' said Bridger, 'and if there's anything else I can do to help you, just let me know.'

'Sure thing, Bill.'

As he put the phone down, Norman felt guilty about the way he had reacted to Bridger's comments. He had been right about the greeting, and he was right about them needing a receptionist.

He rose stiffly from his chair, stretched his back for a couple of minutes, then made his way to the kitchen. He needed a cup of tea and then he should have another hour or two before Slater arrived. With any luck, he might even have something to show for his efforts by then.

An hour later, he leaned forward in his chair and stared open-mouthed at his monitor. 'Oh, wow!' he said out loud. 'Norman Norman, you are a genius.'

He pushed his chair back, got to his feet, and danced a little jig over to the kitchen.

CHAPTER SEVENTEEN

'Did you get any response to your newspaper ad?' asked Slater when he arrived an hour later.

'Not a squeak,' said Norman gloomily. 'It's been out two days now, so I'm sure that was a waste of time.'

'Oh well, never mind. It was worth a try.'

'The pathologist called. He confirmed it's definitely not Betty Glover.'

'I think we more or less knew that anyway,' said Slater.

'Yeah, I guess so, but at least it's confirmed now.'

'It would have been an unfortunate coincidence if "Martha Dennis" had been killed in a traffic accident for a second time,' said Slater dejectedly.

'But it's not all bad news,' said Norman, rising from his desk. 'Here, sit down while I make the tea and take a look at this.'

'What is it?' Slater asked, as he slipped into the vacant chair and looked at the monitor.

'Read it and you'll see.'

Five minutes later, a beaming Norman placed two mugs of tea down on the desk.

'I don't get it,' said Slater, looking up at him. 'How is this relevant? Is it a new case?'

'No, it's not a new case, but if I'm right, this could be very relevant to our current case.'

Slater looked at the monitor and then back to Norman. 'Maybe I'm being even more thick than usual, but I don't understand.'

'Last night I was thinking what I would do if I was a truck driver and I ran over a young woman.'

'You'd call the police,' said Slater. 'You know you would.'

'Well, yeah, of course I would, but suppose I wasn't me, and suppose I had reason to want to avoid getting found out.'

'Then you'd drive off and leave her, but you'd have to be a callous bastard to do that.'

'But what if I was in a situation where I felt I had no choice?'

'Like what?'

'Jeez, I don't know,' said Norman. 'Just bear with me for a minute and stop trying to destroy my idea before I've even explained it.'

Slater raised his hands. 'Sorry. I'll keep quiet.'

'Okay, now just suppose I'm a truck driver. I have a wife and two kids I love. I'm the major earner, so I can't afford to lose my job.'

Slater nodded. He was with Norman so far.

'And then, somehow, I accidentally run this woman over. Who knows, maybe it was her fault and she stepped out in front of me, or perhaps she was behind me and I didn't see her. It's a terrible accident, but if I report it I could end up getting convicted and I could lose my job. I can't let that happen — my wife and kids depend on me, right?'

Slater pointed to the monitor. 'And you think this guy—'

'He's not a bad guy,' said Norman. 'It was an unfortunate accident, but he panicked and left the scene. Then it's not long before it starts to play on his conscience, and eventually the guilt becomes so great . . .'

'He commits suicide,' finished Slater.

'What do you think?' asked Norman.

'Where did this idea come from?'

'I dunno, really. I just got to thinking someone must have run her down, right? Now, it's possible whoever was driving had no idea what they had done. I mean, big truck, small woman, would you notice the impact if you were driving?'

'If the driver didn't even know he'd done it, we have no chance of finding who it was,' said Slater.

'That's what I thought at first,' said Norman, 'but that's the negative way of looking at it. I decided to take the opposite view and then it became a case of what if the driver *did* know what they'd done? Or, if he didn't know at the time, he saw the story and realised he could be the driver in question.

'Now it becomes a very different scenario. Now it means whoever was responsible didn't just run her down but also drove off and left her for dead. I don't doubt there are some guys out there who could do that without a second glance, but what if our guy wasn't that thick-skinned? What if he had a conscience?'

'And you figured you'd start by looking for truck driver suicides?' asked Slater. 'That's a bit out of left field, isn't it?'

'It must have been stewing away in my head while I was asleep. I woke up at six this morning, and it was my first thought.'

'You didn't think he might have gone to the police?'

'Sure, I considered that idea, but I'm assuming the police would have linked his story with the dead body we saw yesterday. As far as we know from what Robbins has told you, they haven't, so . . .'

Slater nodded thoughtfully. He could see where Norm was coming from, even if it was a bit of a radical idea.

'It's going to be a bit difficult to question a dead man,' he said.

'Yeah, but it's possible his widow will have some ideas. Heck, maybe he even left a note.'

'Is there anything to suggest he did?'

'Not in the newspaper reports, but she could have kept it quiet. Maybe he confessed, but she didn't want anyone to know.'

'There are a lot of ifs and maybes,' said Slater, 'and that's assuming she'll be prepared to speak to us. Have you thought about how you would start that conversation?'

'I admit I haven't got that far yet, but give me time. I'll think of something.'

'Yeah, well, good luck with that,' said Slater dubiously.

'You sound doubtful,' said Norman. 'D'you think I'm wasting my time?'

Slater smiled. 'It's not that, Norm. I think it's a very imaginative theory. In fact, it's so far out of the box I'm rather envious that I didn't think of it. I just don't know how you're going to start that particular conversation with the widow.'

Norman crinkled his brow. 'Yeah, I know, it's a tricky one. I'm going to have to give this a lot of thought.'

'Well, I'll leave you to it,' said Slater, heading for his own office. 'I have an idea I want to explore too.'

'What's that?'

'I'll tell you if it's worth following up,' said Slater mysteriously.

* * *

When they had gone to Shrivener's office, Slater had been drawn towards a portrait hanging on the wall. He had taken a mental note of the artist's name and then promptly forgotten it, but the image had stuck with him, lurking on the edge of his consciousness.

He had been drawn to the portrait but at the time he hadn't realised why. Then, last night, he realised it was because the face bore more than a passing resemblance to the two women in their photograph. It was neither one nor the other, but somehow managed to be an amalgamation of both. Or perhaps he was just seeing what he wanted to see.

Either way, it had been quietly driving him crazy, because without the artist's name it was unlikely he would be able to investigate further, but then this morning he had seen a painting in a shop window and he had remembered: the artist's name was Guy Jefferson.

He made himself comfortable at his desk and fired up his laptop.

* * *

'How do you feel about art?' he asked Norman an hour later.

'Any particular sort of art?'

'Yeah, paintings.'

'You're not going all arty-farty, are you? Because if you're looking for advice on what to buy—'

'No, it's not that. Do you remember when we were at Shrivener's there were paintings everywhere?'

'Yeah, mostly landscapes,' said Norman. 'They all looked pretty old, but I would imagine they were fakes. Why are you suddenly interested in them?'

'It wasn't the landscapes that caught my eye,' said Slater. 'There was also a portrait of a woman.'

'I didn't get a good look at it,' said Norman.

'But I did. There was something about it that drew me to it.'

'Did it show bare shoulders? I always have to look twice at bare shoulders. There's just something about them.'

Slater smiled. 'No, it wasn't that. It was only last night I realised — the face was just like the girls in our photograph.'

'Which one?' asked Norman.

'Well, that's the weird thing. It was neither one nor the other, and yet it was both of them.'

Norman stared at Slater. 'You're joking, right? I mean how could it be both of them?'

'I can't explain it,' said Slater. 'It's just the impression I got, but you said yourself they could be sisters.'

Norman smiled indulgently. 'Go on then, I'll buy it.'

'Buy what?'

'You mean this isn't some sort of joke?'

'No, Norm, I'm serious. It was like someone had used two models and combined them into one face.'

'Okay,' said Norman, sitting back in his chair. 'I assume there's a point to this?'

'What if the artist actually did use the two girls in our photograph as his models?'

Norman seemed unable to comprehend, so Slater thought maybe he should clarify. 'Look, I understand it seems a pretty wild theory—'

'A wild theory? You think?' said Norman. 'I don't want to sound negative, but didn't you say my suicidal truck driver was way outside the box?'

Slater nodded. 'Well, yeah, bu—'

'So where does that put this idea of yours?'

'Is my idea really so much more radical? Let's be honest, they're both pretty wild theories when you think about it.'

Norman studied Slater's face. He certainly seemed to believe what he was saying. 'Okay, let's say you're right, and they both modelled for the portrait. That would only help us if—'

Slater beamed as he finished Norman's sentence. 'We knew who the artist was. Yes, that's right.'

'You know who it is, don't you?'

'The name was right there in the corner of the canvas, but I couldn't recall it, and then this morning I was walking past a shop with a couple of portraits in the window and the name just came to me. His name is Guy Jefferson.'

'And I assume you've spent the last hour tracking him down, right?' said Norman.

'He works out of a studio at his home.'

'Which is where?'

'Well, that's the thing. He only lives a few miles outside Tinton.'

'So how come we've never heard of him before?'

'Probably because we're not into art, and from what I can make out, he's a retired businessman who paints for a hobby, so he's not exactly well known in the art world.'

'Not making megabucks then?' asked Norman.

'Just topping up his pension, I think.'

'And you really think he used our two girls in his painting?'

Slater sighed. 'I couldn't say for sure, Norm, but he's local and they were local. Maybe they hooked up somehow. But perhaps I just see them because that's what we're focused on right now.'

'But it wouldn't hurt to ask the question, would it?' said Norman with a wry smile. 'Okay, I'll indulge your wild idea, but only if you're still prepared to do the same for me.'

'That sounds like a fair deal,' said Slater. 'Where shall we start?'

'You can start by buying lunch. After that, we'd better head off to see your artist guy. I haven't worked out the best way to approach my widow yet.'

'You haven't? Maybe you need to sleep on it.'

CHAPTER EIGHTEEN

Guy Jefferson lived in a small village half a mile from a busy dual carriageway. It hardly sounded like an idyllic setting, but a wall of dense trees screened the road, reducing its noise to a barely perceptible background shushing sound.

'I'd love to live in a place like this,' said Norman as they drove past a mixture of quaint cottages broken up by the occasional bigger, grander, old house.

'I dunno,' said Slater. 'The trouble with villages like this is there's nothing to do. I mean, there's not even a pub, is there?'

'Well, yeah, but look how pretty it is.'

'And you need loads of money,' continued Slater. 'Houses like these cost a fortune. Even one of these tiny cottages would cost an arm and a leg. And there's usually some crusty old duffer who seems to think he's entitled to tell everyone else how they should live their life. Anyway, you're a city boy, right? That's what you always used to say when you first came down here.'

'But, I've been away from the city for quite a while now . . .'

'This is where the other half live, Norm, it's not for people like us.'

Norman turned to look at Slater. 'Was there something wrong with your lunch?'

'Huh?'

'I thought perhaps you ate something bitter.'

'What? Why would you think that?'

Norman rolled his eyes. 'I really can't imagine,' he said, as he turned his attention back to the passing houses.

They drove on in silence for a minute or two.

'Here we go,' said Slater. 'The Haywain. This is the place.'

'I think that house name is just a tad pretentious for an artist,' said Norman.

Slater turned the car off the road and onto a gravel drive. They could see a large imposing house a short way ahead on the right, but there was a left fork in the drive before they got to the house.

'He told me to take the left fork to get to his studio,' said Slater.

They turned left and followed the drive until they saw a sleek, modern-looking building ahead.

As they took in the building, Norman let out a long, low whistle. 'Jeez, is this his studio? I thought you said this guy painted for a hobby.'

'That's what it said online.'

'This building looks as if it would have cost a fortune to build,' said Norman.

'He was some sort of businessman before he retired.'

'Wow! What did he do? Because he must have been pretty good at whatever he did if it's paid for this house and this studio.'

'I don't know,' said Slater. 'I didn't look into his background — I just wanted to discover where we could find him.'

* * *

The building proved to be much more than just a simple art studio. They could see they were being monitored by CCTV, and as they reached the front of the building, a pair of sliding doors glided open and a disembodied, slightly mechanical female voice bade them welcome.

'That's pretty cool,' said Norman, as they crossed the threshold and the doors eased closed behind them.

'Please state your names,' requested the voice.

'Dave Slater and Norman Norman,' announced Slater.

'Ah, yes,' said the voice. 'Mr Jefferson is expecting you. Please wait here — he will be with you shortly.'

'Jeez,' said Norman quietly. 'It's like science fiction. I'm half expecting a robot to come and escort us inside.'

'Yeah, it's pretty weird,' agreed Slater, looking around the small reception area.

There was a sudden hiss, and a hidden door in the wall opposite them slid open to reveal a tall, smiling, silver-haired man. He gave them a little bow in greeting.

'Mr Slater and Mr Norman? My name is Guy Jefferson. Welcome to my studio. Please come through.'

He extended a hand, which they both shook as they joined him.

'This is quite a place you have here, Mr Jefferson,' said Norman. 'I didn't expect to find something like this in the middle of a sleepy little village.'

'Welcome to the future. This place is my little indulgence,' he said, smiling warmly. 'I'm not as young as I used to be, and when I'm painting at the other end of the building it can take me a while to get to the door. This way I'm warned in advance and visitors are ushered inside instead of waiting on the step.'

He led them through to the next room. The wall facing them consisted of folding glass doors, and beyond a deck outside, a lake stretched away before them. Jefferson pointed to a seating area that overlooked the lake.

'Please, take a seat,' he said.

'Is the whole place high tech?' asked Norman.

'I can show you around, if you like.' Jefferson looked at Slater. 'But I'm sure you didn't come here just because you wanted to take a look around, did you?'

‘As I told you when we spoke earlier,’ said Slater, ‘we came across a painting of yours the other day. It’s a portrait of a young woman who looks similar to someone we’re looking for. I was wondering who the model was.’

‘I don’t use a model, unless someone comes specifically asking me to paint them. Most of my work is done from photographs.’

‘Is there any particular reason for that?’

‘Models cost money.’

Slater looked around.

‘Ah,’ said Jefferson with a smile. ‘You think that’s out of character when I’m obviously not short of money?’

‘It had crossed my mind,’ admitted Slater.

‘There’s the risk factor too. An old man with money, a young woman with ambition. Who knows what he might be accused of if she wanted to make a fast buck.’

‘That’s a pretty cynical point of view.’

‘I’m afraid the world is a pretty cynical place.’

While Slater and Jefferson were talking, Norman was finding it hard not to keep looking at their surroundings. It seemed there were futuristic gadgets everywhere. Jefferson had noticed Norman’s roving eye, and now he addressed him.

‘Would you like to take a look around while I talk to Mr Slater?’ He looked at Slater. ‘Unless you both need to be here?’

‘No, that’s fine,’ said Slater. ‘I only have a few questions, anyway.’

‘Are you sure you don’t mind?’ asked Norman.

‘Not at all,’ said Jefferson. ‘Please carry on.’

Looking like a child set free in a toyshop, Norman got to his feet and headed for the nearest door, which quietly hissed open as he approached.

‘Don’t get lost,’ called Slater as Norman disappeared through the door. ‘Sorry about him,’ he said, turning back to Jefferson. ‘He’s fascinated by anything that’s a bit high tech or futuristic.’

'It's no problem, he won't come to any harm,' said Jefferson indulgently. 'Now then, where were we?'

'I was asking about this portrait I saw.'

'I've done more than one, you know.'

'Would it help if I told you I saw it at the office of a Mr Shrivener? He's a lawyer, based in Winchester.'

There was just a momentary hesitation before Jefferson answered. 'No,' he said, looking thoughtful. 'I don't think I know him. Are you sure it's one of mine?'

'It has your signature in the corner.'

'Oh, I see, well then I suppose it must be one of mine. Perhaps this lawyer bought it from someone else.'

'Does that happen often? Do your paintings sell for much?'

Jefferson laughed. 'Oh, I wish. I'm afraid I barely cover my costs. It's just a hobby, you see. It was something I always wanted to do, but life, and the need to earn a living, always managed to get in the way. I only have the time now because I'm retired.'

Slater was disappointed. He had been hoping Jefferson was going to be a bit more forthcoming.

'As I said, I've done lots of portraits. Maybe if you could describe it to me,' suggested Jefferson.

'It's just a woman, from about here up,' Slater indicated a point just below his own shoulders. 'She appears to be naked.'

'Most of them are, so I'm afraid that's not much help.'

Slater produced a photograph. 'The face in the portrait looked like an amalgamation of these two young women.'

He laid the photo down in front of Jefferson and watched the colour drain from his face. 'Do you know these two?'

Jefferson stared at the photograph but didn't answer.

'Mr Jefferson?'

When Jefferson looked up at Slater, his colour had returned. 'No, sorry. They would make excellent models, but I've never set eyes on them before. Are they who you're looking for?'

Slater nodded.

'Well, I hope you find them. I'm only sorry I can't help you.'

'Maybe you *can* help.'

'Really? I don't see how.'

Slater produced a photo of the face from the mortuary. 'Can you do a portrait of this woman for me?'

'Good God,' said Jefferson, as he looked at the photograph and then up at Slater. 'Is she . . .'

'Dead? Yes, she is,' said Slater.

Jefferson's face was ashen as he stared at the dead face. Slater couldn't decide if it was because he had recognised her or if it was because he'd never seen a dead face before.

'I'm thinking that if you could paint her face and make her look alive, we could show it around and maybe someone will recognise her.'

'I'm not sure I can,' said Jefferson. 'This girl is dead. That makes it hard to know what she would have looked like when she was alive.'

Behind Jefferson, the doors hissed open. Norman had returned from his explorations. 'This is a fascinating place, Mr Jefferson.'

Slater looked up at his colleague, who nodded and winked at him over Jefferson's shoulder.

'What?' Jefferson looked confused.

'It's a great place,' repeated Norman. 'Very futuristic.'

'Oh, yes, thank you.' Jefferson looked up at Slater. 'D'you know, I think I need to call a halt to this now. I'm not feeling at all well.'

'I understand,' said Slater. 'It must be the dead face. I'm sorry I had to show it to you.'

'Yes, I'm not used to that sort of thing. Would you mind . . .'

'Of course,' said Slater. 'But you'll think about painting that portrait? It would really help.'

'Err, yes, I suppose . . .'

'We'll come back in a day or so,' said Slater. 'I hope you feel better real soon.'

'Don't you worry. We'll see ourselves out,' said Norman.

* * *

'What do you think?' asked Norman as they made their way back up the drive to the road.

'He knows something,' said Slater. 'He tried to hide it behind the sweet, innocent, little old man thing, but he's not a very convincing liar.'

'Did you challenge him about it?'

'I let him think I believed him.'

'What about the painting? Does he make any money out of it?' asked Norman.

'He says he barely covers his costs and that's why he paints from photos and doesn't use models. He says it's just a hobby.'

'That's a damned expensive hobby room, don't you think?'

Slater stopped at the road to let a car pass before he pulled out, but the car slowed and the driver flashed his lights angrily. At the last minute, he indicated he intended to turn into the drive they were currently blocking.

'Well, why didn't you indicate earlier?' said Slater out loud as he put his car into gear. 'If I had known you were coming in here . . .'

'Arsehole,' muttered Slater, as he pulled out. 'Just because he's got a bloody Mercedes . . .' He tried to stare at the driver as he pulled out, but heavily tinted windows made it impossible to see. 'Are they allowed to have windows tinted that dark?'

Norman grabbed his mobile phone, and as the car swung into Jefferson's drive, he leaned over the back of his seat, took a photograph, and then settled back in his seat.

'You think he's important?' asked Slater.

Norman shrugged. 'I have no idea. I mean, we can't even see who it is, but with what I've just discovered, I don't think we should ignore anyone heading up this drive.'

'So, you *did* find something interesting. I guessed you must have from the nod and the wink.'

'I certainly did,' said Norman. 'I just hope I've done the right thing by not confronting Jefferson back there.'

'Well, come on then, let's hear it.'

'We're not supposed to know it, but he's actually got two studios in that building. One of them has a few unfinished portraits lying around, and there are even a couple of landscapes. I have to say, he's pretty good at painting that lake out there. The thing is, I don't think he uses that studio very often.'

'What do you mean?'

'If he was painting in there when we arrived, there would be some evidence, wouldn't there? A half-finished canvas, maybe a few brushes, or even some paints lying around, but there was nothing like that.'

'So? Maybe he wasn't painting.'

'Oh, he was,' said Norman, 'but he was painting in the second studio — the one I wasn't supposed to find.'

'How did you find it?'

'Sheer fluke. I was just wandering around and the door opened right in front of me. I'm sure it wasn't meant to. Maybe he forgot to lock it. Anyway, that's where I found it.'

'Found what?'

'Treasure.'

'Can you stop speaking in riddles?'

'Jefferson told you he barely breaks even on portraits, and that's probably right, but I can tell you what he has there is more than just a hobby. I wouldn't be at all surprised if that whole building has been paid for by his paintings.'

For a few seconds, Slater took his eyes off the road and stared at Norman. 'How does that work if he barely breaks even? It doesn't make sense.'

'He doesn't make any money on the stuff he showed you, but what he didn't tell you is that he paints pornography. He's halfway through one right now.'

'He what?'

'He paints pornography.'

'I knew the old sod was up to something! He was lying all the time.'

'He was telling the truth about not using models — he really does paint from photographs. I found hundreds of them. Young women in all sorts of poses and doing all sorts of things.'

'Any of our two girls?'

'Oh yeah, dozens.'

'What, posed?'

'Oh no, these were taken in the bathroom in Vernon Tisdale's basement — being naked, getting in and out of the shower, drying herself, that sort of thing. I'm sure the poor kid had no idea she was being photographed.'

'Are they both in the photos?'

'That's where it gets interesting. All the nude photos feature our dead girl.'

'So it's not Betty Glover?'

'Definitely not.'

'That explains why Jefferson turned a funny colour when I showed him her face from the morgue. He's seen her before. I thought he had.'

'What do you want to do now?' asked Norman.

'Do you think he'll know you've been in that studio?'

'I was careful. I don't think he'd know.'

'Let's assume he doesn't know we're on to him. I promised him we'd be back, so why don't we keep that promise . . . but before we do that, we'll do our homework and find out all about Mr Jefferson.'

'Part of me says we should tell the police, but another part tells me they would be more interested in the porn ring and our dead woman would probably be forgotten about.'

'Yeah, I agree, but let me speak to Stella. I'll call her tonight. Maybe, with her being on the inside, we can make sure our girl's not forgotten.'

'You know what's happening tomorrow morning, don't you?' asked Norman.

'What's that?'

'Adrian Davies is supposed to be coming to see us for his first update.'

'Oh, yes. I'd almost forgotten about that. Of course, he might not turn up.'

'Yeah, I realise that,' said Norman, 'but we need to speak to him, so let's think positive about this. He will be there — I can feel it in my water.'

CHAPTER NINETEEN

Much to Slater's surprise, Adrian Davies arrived, as arranged, at 10.30 a.m.

'Ah, Mr Davies, come on in,' said Norman. He led Davies towards their small informal seating area and invited him to sit down. Slater joined them just a moment later.

'You'll be pleased to know we're making progress in locating your sister,' began Norman.

'Really? Oh, that is good news. Have you actually found her?'

'Not yet, but we think we're on the right trail. We might even have found where she was living, but before we get to that, we're hoping you might be able to provide us with a bit more information.'

'I'll certainly try,' said Davies.

Norman handed the photograph of the dead girl to Davies. 'Can you confirm this isn't Martha?'

Davies studied the photo and began to turn a little pale. 'I don't understand. Is this woman dead?' he asked.

'I'm afraid she is,' said Norman. 'You see, we had to explore the possibility Martha might be dead. Now we're pretty sure this *isn't* Martha, but she does fit the description, so we need you to confirm it's not her.'

Davies handed the photo back to Norman as if it was a hot potato. 'No. That's definitely not her.'

'Okay, thank you,' said Norman. 'Now I want you to take a look at this photograph.'

He handed the photograph of the two women to Davies. 'We found this photograph. We're hoping you can identify these two women.'

Davies studied the photograph. 'Where did you get this?'

'We found it in a flat in Tinton. We believe one, or both, of the women in that photograph were living in the flat.'

'Did you find Martha's belongings? Her laptop?'

'I'm afraid the flat was empty and we didn't find anything like that, but can we get back to the photograph?'

Davies looked at the photo again. 'The one on the left is Martha, but I have no idea who the other one is.' He looked a bit closer. 'Hang on, the other one looks a bit like the dead girl you just showed me. Is it her?'

'Yes, it is,' said Norman. 'But this photo was taken before she got hit by a truck, so her face is a little different. You're quite sure that's Martha on the left?'

'Definitely. I'd know my sister anywhere.'

'Really?' said Slater. 'And you're quite sure this is your sister?'

'What?' Davies licked his lips. 'Yes, of course I'm sure.' He tapped the photo and handed it back to Norman. 'I'm certain that's her, right there.'

'Well, that's rather odd,' said Norman. 'Maybe your sister has a double. They say everyone has one somewhere.'

Davies frowned. 'A double? I'm not following you.'

'Then let me explain,' said Slater. 'You see, the real Martha Dennis died years ago. We believe the woman in the photo is using the name Martha Dennis, but her real name is Betty Glover.'

Davies' mouth flopped open.

Norman smiled at his discomfort. 'Just to demonstrate we're not quite as dumb as you think, you should be aware we also know your real name isn't Adrian Davies, but we'll come to that later. Now, Betty is an investigative journalist, and according to her ex-boyfriend, she knew another journalist called Eddie — or possibly Adie.'

'Isn't that a coincidence?' added Slater. 'Her boyfriend also told us that the last time he saw her, she told him she was going undercover for a story.'

'Now,' said Norman, 'how about you tell us what's really going on?'

Davies cast a sideways glance at the door.

'I wouldn't try it,' said Slater. 'Even if you managed to get away, we'd soon track you down.'

Now Davies' eyes were darting back and forth from Slater to Norman.

'You look surprised, Adie,' said Norman. 'Like I said, we're not quite as stupid as you thought we were, huh?'

Davies swallowed a couple of times then rubbed his hands across his face. 'I admit I stretched the truth a little,' he said.

'No, you didn't stretch anything. You lied,' said Slater, 'and we've caught you out. Now we want to know what's going on.'

'And don't give us any more bullshit,' said Norman.

Davies sighed, and his shoulders slumped. 'Okay, okay, you guys win. Me and Betty were on to a story. She went undercover. At first it was okay, but then I lost contact with her. I waited and waited for her to get in touch, but she never did. That's when I came to you.'

'So, what's the story?' asked Norman.

'It all involves exploitation of desperate young women who are smuggled into this country thinking they're going to have a fantastic new life, but when they get here, they find they have no choice but to become slaves, working as prostitutes, drug mules, and who knows what else.'

'Who's behind it all?'

'That's what we've been trying to find out.'

'You mean you have no idea?'

'None at all.'

'And you've been investigating this for how long?'

'About two years, maybe a little more.'

'And Betty was undercover for how long?'

'A year.'

Slater and Norman exchanged a glance. 'Why did Betty decide to use Martha's ID?' asked Slater.

'I don't know.'

'I thought you were working together.'

'As far as I knew, it was just a name. I didn't know she'd stolen a dead girl's ID.'

There was a silent stand-off as Slater and Norman contemplated Davies' story. It was Slater who broke the silence. 'I have to confess I'm having trouble believing your story.'

'Look, I did lie before, but I can see how stupid that was. I'm telling you the truth.'

'The thing is, it's all a bit vague,' said Norman, 'and Dave here doesn't like vague.'

'What do you mean?'

'You say you were working this story with Betty for about two years, which is vague enough, but then you tell us you have no idea why she chose to steal Martha's ID. That doesn't sound like you were working closely together. You also said Betty went undercover a year ago. Her boyfriend says it was eighteen months.'

Davies shifted in his seat.

'I'm not even sure you're a journalist,' said Norman. 'You see, if Betty was on to someone, and that someone knew, maybe you were sent to find Betty and stop her.'

Davies frowned. 'Stop her? What do you mean, *stop her*? You mean kill her? Jesus, that's crazy. I don't want to kill anyone.'

'So, what do you want? Why are we really looking for her?'

Davies sighed and shrugged. 'I *am* a journalist,' he said. 'Look, I can prove it. I have an NUJ card.' He produced the card and showed it to them.

'Adrian Reynolds,' said Norman, reading from the card. 'Your name really is Adrian. At least that much is true.'

'I met Betty three or four years ago. She wanted to advance her career and I said I could help.'

'So, you're the guy Betty's ex was telling us about,' said Slater. 'He said she did a lot of legwork for you but didn't get the credit she deserved.'

'That's crap,' snapped Reynolds. 'I looked after her. He just doesn't understand how the system works.'

'Or perhaps he understood exactly how the system worked and how you were using her,' suggested Slater. 'Whose idea was it for her to go undercover?'

'That was her idea. I didn't even know about it until she disappeared.'

'How did you find out?'

'She sent me an email telling me I wouldn't be able to see her again for as long as it took.'

'Had you been "seeing" her? Her boyfriend certainly seems to think there was something going on.'

Reynolds blushed. 'I didn't plan it, it just sort of happened. You know how it is.'

'Jesus, you really *were* using her, weren't you?' said Slater, shaking his head.

'Look, I've had enough of this,' said Reynolds angrily. 'I didn't come here to have my integrity called into question.'

'I'm not sure you have any integrity to call into question.'

'And, now you come to mention it, we still haven't established what exactly you *did* come here for,' added Norman.

'I want you to find Betty.'

'You know, I'm not so sure that's true,' said Norman. 'I'm beginning to think you knew nothing about this story of Betty's until she went undercover. I think she maybe told you enough for you to realise she might be on to something really big, and you want a slice of the action.'

'How can you think that?'

'Because you've done it before, and because the first thing you asked about wasn't Betty — it was her laptop. You also gave us a whole heap of crap when you first came to us. I don't think you want us to find Betty at all. I think you just want her story!'

Davies — or rather Reynolds — jumped to his feet and pointed a finger at Norman. 'This is all bullshit! First you accuse me of trying to murder her, and now you say I'm after her story. I should have known when I first came here I was dealing with idiots. Well, you can call an end to this whole thing, right now. You won't get another penny out of me.'

He strode across to the door, let himself out, and slammed it hard behind him.

* * *

Norman watched Adrian Reynolds leave and then turned to a grinning Slater. 'Was it something I said?'

'My guess is he just doesn't like the fact you've sussed him out,' said Slater.

'Yeah, but did I get it right? What if I'm wrong and he *has* been sent to stop her?'

'Even so, he has no more idea where she is than we do, and we didn't tell him most of what we know, so we're way ahead of him. Anyway, I think you're spot on. I don't see him as a killer, but it is easy to see him as the sort of guy who uses people and steals their stories.'

'Where does it leave us, though? We still have no idea where Betty is.'

'But if we're right about him, and Betty really was working on a story, then we have another clue, and it might just fit in with what we know so far,' said Slater. 'What if Betty's friend in the photograph was actually part of the story? We know Jefferson is making arty pornography, and we know he was using Betty's friend as an unwitting model.'

'Do you think that's the story? Some old guy painting artistic pornography?'

'I'm not convinced Jefferson can be making that much money. I think it's got to be something bigger than that. Reynolds was on about people smuggling and sex slaves. I think that would be a much bigger story.'

'Yeah, but our girl doesn't quite fit in with the idea of being a sex slave, does she?' asked Norman. 'I mean, yeah, she was being photographed, but I've seen some of those photos. If you had seen them you would agree she was innocent and had no idea she was being photographed. She wasn't posing in any way. And another thing — she was allowed to come and go from that basement. Every time she went jogging she could have gone to the police or made a break for it. That doesn't sound much like slavery to me.'

'But what if her innocence in those photos was the whole point? Let's face it, she was a pretty girl who looked like butter wouldn't melt in her mouth. Maybe that's where these people get their kicks. I guess it's a form of artificial voyeurism. Think about it — looking at a painting of a pretty young woman towelling herself dry would be like looking at her through the eyes of a peeping Tom.'

Norman was thinking. 'You know, you could be right. I hadn't thought of it like that. But I still don't see how she's a sex slave.'

'Maybe not in the conventional meaning, but perhaps they had something on her that made her stay. Lots of these women and girls come from Eastern Europe and get smuggled here by gangs. What if she was lured here with the promise of being able to send money back to her family? Then, when she gets here, they tell her if she doesn't do what they say, her family will suffer. She's come from a close-knit family, and she knows only too well the gang is quite capable of causing her family a lot of grief. She feels she has no choice, so she does whatever they say.'

'It makes sense when you put it like that,' said Norman. 'And, of course, she could just be the tip of a very large iceberg. I wonder how Betty found her.'

'I have no idea,' said Slater, 'but meeting through jogging was a clever idea.'

'Or it could have made someone suspicious enough to want to find out what Betty was up to.'

'Good point, Norm. Maybe it wasn't such a clever idea after all.'

'Good point or not, what do we do now?'

'I feel like we're making progress,' said Slater.

'Yeah, me too.'

'And it's not as if we've got anything else to do.'

'I can't argue with that.'

'There's always an outside chance we're wrong about Reynolds, and he's looking for Betty and not the story.'

'I hope you're wrong about that,' Norman said.

'So do I, but if I'm right, it would be a lot better for her if we found her first.'

'We're not going to get paid if we carry on, and we agreed we weren't going to do any more unpaid work.'

'That's true,' said Slater, 'but then with no work we're not going to get paid anyway. At least this way we won't get bored.'

'That's settled then,' said Norman. 'I'll see if the vehicle search I started has come up with anything.'

'And I'll see what I can dig up about Guy Jefferson.'

* * *

'That solicitor guy, Shrivener,' said Norman, half an hour later. 'Didn't you say he had one big client?'

Slater looked up from his laptop. 'That's what Stella told me. He's a guy called Jools Hanover. Why?'

'Remember there was a guy flashing his lights at you when we were leaving Jefferson's place?'

'You mean the arsehole with the Mercedes who could have saved all the light-flashing if he'd just used his indicators a bit sooner?'

'That's the one,' said Norman. 'I've just got a response to my licence plate enquiry. Guess who owns that car?'

'Who? Jools Hanover? You're kidding!'

'Interesting, right?'

'That means Hanover is now linked to Vernon Tisdale *and* Guy Jefferson.'

'In which case, I think it would be one hell of a coincidence if he isn't involved in whatever's going on here.'

'Stella told me they suspect Hanover is into prostitution and porn, among other things.'

'Do you think this is the story Betty was investigating?' asked Norman. 'All Jefferson is doing is painting soft porn. I would have expected her to be after something much bigger.'

'Maybe it *is* much bigger,' said Slater. 'Perhaps what we've stumbled upon is on the fringes.'

Norman pursed his lips thoughtfully. 'You're right. Tinton isn't exactly the sort of place where there's a lot of demand for prostitutes, but it would be a good place to hide someone who's frightened to step out of line and doesn't even know they're being exploited. Perhaps Betty had figured out a lot more than we have and decided it would be easier to find a contact out here in the sticks. I can't imagine there would be many slaves who are allowed to come and go in a bigger town.'

'We need to speak to Jefferson again,' said Slater.

'I'm pretty sure Vernon Tisdale knows a lot more than he makes out. I think we should try him again.'

'Don't forget he has a bodyguard now.'

'That's true. We'll have to think of a way past him.'

'Yeah, well, good luck with that,' said Slater, returning to his laptop.

'How are you getting on with that?' asked Norman.

'Gimme half an hour. I was just getting to some interesting stuff when you came in.'

* * *

'Okay, here's what I've got so far,' said Slater a little while later. 'Guy Jefferson was managing director of a modelling agency. It seems he started out as a photographer and then worked his way to the top.'

'I suppose that sort of thing pays pretty well if you know what you're doing,' said Norman. 'Ten percent of a top model's fees would probably be a substantial amount.'

'From what I can see, this agency wasn't that big, and they're not credited with finding any stars. The accounts they filed don't show enough income to be paying big salaries.'

'That house wasn't cheap. Maybe he married into money.'

'Never married,' Slater read from his screen. 'Never been in trouble either from what I can see.'

'He must have been into some sort of fiddle then.'

'He's a photographer who likes to paint. Maybe he's been painting his soft porn for years.'

'Or maybe he keeps the really hard stuff hidden away where no one can stumble upon it,' suggested Norman.

'Definitely a person of interest,' said Slater.

Norman looked at his watch. 'I have things to do this evening. How about we sleep on all this information and then tomorrow morning we'll decide how to move forward.'

'That suits me,' said Slater, 'and I'll call Stella later on. Maybe I can pick her brains and learn a bit more about Jools Hanover.'

'Right. That sounds like a plan.'

CHAPTER TWENTY

'What did Robbins say last night?' asked Norman the next morning.

'It's got a bit awkward. It seems someone has noticed she's getting quite specific about some of the stuff she's looking into.'

'Oh, crap. She's not in trouble, is she?'

'Fortunately it hasn't come to that yet, but I feel really bad about it. I told her not to get involved and then let her persuade me it would be okay.'

'Don't beat yourself up too much. No one made her help — she chose to get involved.'

'Yeah, but even so. She's still being held back since the last time our paths crossed.'

'I thought that was just going to be a slap on the wrist. How come she's still grounded?'

'She says they haven't reached a decision yet.'

'That's one long slap on the wrist,' said Norman. 'Are you sure there isn't more to it than that?'

'She doesn't exactly give much away, so I can't be sure about anything.'

Norman raised an eyebrow. 'Do you have doubts about her?'

Slater shook his head vehemently. 'God, no. She's great, but there's something going on with her that I haven't figured out yet.'

'What sort of something?'

'She gets really edgy when we're alone together, like in the car. I think it's possible she's been attacked, and she hasn't got over it yet.'

'Oh, wow. That isn't good.'

'I'm just guessing, but I think I might even be the first guy she's been alone with since it happened.'

'Have you spoken to her about it?'

'She says she's not ready to talk, but I told her I was willing to wait until she *is* ready.'

'That's some commitment,' said Norman. 'It could take months, years even.'

Slater avoided eye contact. 'Yeah, well, I'm in no hurry.'

Norman nodded slowly but said nothing. He had known Slater through several relationships, and he knew his friend well enough to understand this thing with Stella Robbins was different, so it was no real surprise to find he had offered to be there for her. 'Well, whatever it is, I hope she gets through it.'

'Yeah, thanks.'

'I take it we're none the wiser when it comes to Jools Hanover?'

Slater sighed. 'Not really, no.'

'No problem,' said Norman. 'I think we have plenty of other leads to follow, and we're aware Hanover could be behind them all. We also know we need to be wary of the guy, so I think we're covered.'

'Stella wants us to call in the police.'

Norman frowned. 'You told her what we found out?'

'She's stuck her neck out for us, so I thought it was only fair.'

'Is she going to blow the whistle?'

'I made her promise not to. She's worried about Hanover getting to us, but she also understands we want to find our missing girl.'

'And she agreed to keep quiet?'

'She admits the police might see different priorities to us. They've been after Hanover for years, but as far as they're concerned, Martha isn't even missing. On the other hand, they've never been able to build a case against Hanover. She knows we don't have enough evidence yet, but she thinks we might just be able to do it, so she's holding off for now.'

'What does, "holding off for now" mean?'

'It means I have to check in with her at set times. If I don't, she's going to assume we've been sussed by Hanover and we're in big trouble. If that happens she's going to call the cavalry.'

Norman's frown slowly turned to a smile. 'So, she likes you as much as you like her.'

'What? No, it's not that. She believes that if she gives them cause to arrest Hanover, they'll have no choice but to put her back on active duty.'

Norman grinned. 'Yeah, right, whatever. So, where are we going to start today?'

'I told Jefferson we'd call back about him painting a portrait of our dead girl. How about we go over there now unannounced?'

'You still want him to do a portrait?'

'I don't think that will be necessary. You said he had plenty of photographs of her. Why don't we ask him for a couple of them?'

'I like this idea,' said Norman. 'Let's turn over a few stones and see what crawls out!'

* * *

'With all the technology in this building, I can't believe there isn't CCTV monitoring who comes and goes up this drive,' said Norman as they drove up to Guy Jefferson's art studio.

'Yeah, it's hard to think he doesn't know we're here,' said Slater. 'But even so, as we're not expected, it could take him a while to hide everything away. Let's see how long it takes before he lets us in.'

'You think he *will* let us in?'

'We're just about to find out.'

As before, when they approached the studio the sliding doors glided open and the artificial voice welcomed them.

'Please state your names,' said the voice.

'Dave Slater and Norman Norman.'

'I'm sorry, gentlemen, Mr Jefferson isn't expecting you this morning. However, if you would like to sit down and wait, he will be with you in a few minutes.'

Slater wasn't sure he should respond to the voice but found he couldn't help himself. 'Thank you,' he said, rather self-consciously.

It had been almost exactly five minutes to the second when the interior door slid open, but it was a quite different Guy Jefferson today. The warm, welcoming smile he wore yesterday was nowhere to be seen.

'Visitors are supposed to call first,' he said. 'I don't like it when people arrive unannounced. It disturbs my concentration.'

'I thought I said I would be coming back,' said Slater.

'But you didn't say when. You should have called to make an appointment.'

'We were just passing,' said Norman cheerfully. 'As you had been so helpful we didn't think you'd mind—'

'Helpful?'

'Oh, yes. We learnt a lot when we were here yesterday.'

'I couldn't answer most of your questions. How could I have been helpful? I'm not prepared to paint a portrait of a dead girl.'

'That's okay,' said Norman. 'We don't think we need it anyway.'

'You don't?'

'No. You see, we know where we can get our hands on some photographs of her, taken when she was alive.'

Jefferson's face had turned pale.

'The thing is, you invited me to take a look around yesterday, remember? You have a really neat place here. I mean, that studio, with the view over the lake. Wow! What a place that is.

Anyway, I was in there looking around, admiring your landscapes, when this hidden door suddenly opened in front of me.'

'How dare you!' snapped Jefferson. 'I didn't give you permission to—'

'I think your exact words were, "Would you like to take a look around while I talk to Mr Slater?",' said Slater. 'To me, that sounds like granting permission.'

'Yes, but—'

'I was invited to look around, and I didn't break in,' said Norman. 'I assume you have some way of locking that door, but you must have forgotten. It opened automatically when I approached it. Heck, I didn't even know it was there until it opened.'

'And you went inside?'

'What do you think? I already said we learnt a lot.'

'There's no law against it,' spluttered Jefferson.

'No law against what, Mr Jefferson?'

'I paint for my own pleasure. What I paint is my own business.'

'We think what you paint is probably a very lucrative business,' said Slater. 'But that's not really what we're interested in.'

'You're not?'

Slater shook his head. 'What we're interested in is one of your models. You know who we mean. I showed you her morgue photograph yesterday.'

'You've been photographing that young woman without her knowledge,' said Norman. 'I bet you have video footage too. That's a criminal offence, even if you do paint for your own pleasure.'

'I didn't take those photographs. I don't take any photographs any more. They were all given to me.'

'But you would have known she was an innocent,' said Norman. 'Granted, most of your photos are posed and the girls involved know exactly what they're doing. I'm sure they get well paid for it too, but you would have known this one was different.'

'It's the innocence,' he said. 'That's what makes it so special.'

'She's dead, Jefferson,' snapped Slater. 'Doesn't that bother you?'

'Of course it bothers me. Why do you think I was taken ill when you were here yesterday? But you can't blame me — I didn't even know the girl!'

'You might not have killed her,' said Norman, 'and you might not have known her, but even so, you were still exploiting her.'

'I'm not responsible—'

'I'm not sure the police would see it that way,' said Slater.

'What? The police? But you can't tell them.'

'Why not?'

'You just can't! It's more than my life's worth.'

'I admit the view wouldn't be the same, but I believe you can still paint in prison,' said Norman.

'You can't tell them. Please. I'll do anything!'

Slater and Norman exchanged a glance. This wasn't quite what they had been expecting. Jefferson seemed genuinely terrified.

'It sounds like you've got yourself into a bit of a mess, Mr Jefferson,' said Slater. 'Who are you so frightened of?'

'I can't tell you.'

'The name Jools Hanover doesn't mean anything to you then?'

'Who?'

'Jools Hanover.'

'I've never heard that name before.'

'Oh, come on, Jefferson. He was here yesterday.'

'I assure you, I don't know that man.'

'Okay, have it your way,' said Norman. 'So, who *did* come here just after we left yesterday?'

'No one.'

'C'mon! We saw him. We nearly collided with his damned Mercedes.'

'That would have been a friend of my wife. She came to deliver a present.'

'That wouldn't have been more photographs by any chance?'

'If you must know, it was her birthday. The present was flowers.'

'And her friend just happened to be driving Hanover's car?'

'I have no idea whose car she was driving. I didn't even see her — she's my wife's friend, not mine.'

'Maybe we can call in and check with your wife.'

'I'm afraid you'll have to take my word for it. My wife has gone away for a few days on a cruise with some of her friends.'

'My, my, isn't that convenient?' said Slater.

'You can be as sarcastic as you want,' said Jefferson. 'It's the truth. I can give you the details of the ship and its route, if you wish.'

'Yeah, I think that's probably a good idea,' said Norman.

'It's in the house. I'll email it to you.'

'Make sure you do.' Norman handed Jefferson one of his cards. 'Or I'm going to be here again first thing tomorrow morning, and I won't go away until I've got what I want.'

'Let's forget Jools Hanover for a minute and get back to the photographs,' said Slater. 'Where do you get them from?'

'They're sent to me.'

'Sent to you?'

'That's right. By post, or sometimes in a parcel by courier.'

'Which courier?'

'It's never the same one twice.'

'And you don't know who sends them.'

Jefferson looked away. 'I have no idea.'

'You might be quite good with a paintbrush, Jefferson,' said Norman, 'but you're hopeless with a lie.'

'I beg your pardon?'

'Why don't you stop pretending you're the victim here and start thinking about the *real* victim? There's an innocent young woman dead, and you've been painting pictures of her. I think the police would be very happy to put two and two together, don't you?'

'I'm telling you the truth.' Jefferson was pleading now. 'The photographs arrive by post. I don't know who sends them, or where they come from.'

'But why would someone send photographs to you anonymously? What would be the point? What's in it for them?'

'I don't know. How many more times do I have to say it?'

'We don't believe you.'

'Believe what you like. It won't make any difference. I can't tell you what I don't know.'

'What do you do with the pornographic paintings?' asked Slater.

'I've told you I paint for my own pleasure. There's no law ag—'

'Yeah, yeah, there's no law against it. We heard you the first time,' said Norman. 'The thing is, we know what you're up to, and we're going to prove it. It would just be a lot easier if you come clean now.'

Jefferson seemed to have regained his composure. 'I've said all I'm going to say. If you think you should call the police, then so be it. Do your worst, but I won't tell them any more than I've told you.'

Norman and Slater were taken aback by this sudden about turn. 'You really don't want them crawling all over this place,' said Norman.

'Why not? I've got nothing to hide.'

There was a brief stand-off.

'Not quite so full of yourselves now, are you?' snapped Jefferson. 'Why's that, d'you think? I'll tell you why, shall I? Because this is a fishing trip, isn't it? You're just guessing. You have no real evidence of anything, have you?'

Neither Slater nor Norman had a response ready, and they didn't get a chance to speak anyway.

'I'll tell you what you should do next,' said Jefferson. 'You should get back in your car and bugger off out of my life before I call the police and have you arrested for trespass and harassment.'

'You haven't seen the last of us,' said Norman.

'Oh, I think I have,' said Jefferson. 'I'll make sure you won't be able to come anywhere near me or my property!'

Slater looked at Norman and shrugged. 'Come on, Norm,' he said, heading for the door. 'Let's not waste any more of our time. I don't think this guy would care if it was his own daughter who had been murdered.'

As Norman began to follow Slater, Jefferson's mouth flapped soundlessly a couple of times. Finally, he spoke, just as they stepped outside. 'Murdered? What do you mean murdered?'

Slater slowed and looked over his shoulder. 'Oh, didn't I say? The young woman you've been so happily exploiting was chased under a truck and run down. She didn't have a chance.'

Jefferson watched wordlessly as they walked to their car, a look of horror on his face.

* * *

'That was weird,' said Norman as Slater turned the car around. 'Look, he's still standing there looking horrified. He didn't know, did he?'

'He knew she was dead,' said Slater. 'He knew that yesterday, but he didn't seem to give a damn then.'

'Well, yeah, he knew she was dead, but he didn't know she'd been murdered. That stopped him in his tracks, just as he thought he was getting the upper hand. I think that came as a complete shock.'

'But what does it mean?'

'Well, forget all that bullshit about just painting for his own pleasure,' said Norman. 'I saw how many different canvases he has on the go. If he's been painting like that for the

last five years, his house must be full of the damned things. He's definitely selling them. He has to be.'

'You agree with me that he's part of something organised?'

'Sure. No question. Even if he's telling the truth about the photos coming by post, it makes no difference, does it? He's still using them.'

'I've been thinking about that,' said Slater. 'It's possible he really doesn't know who sends the photos.'

'Why d'you think that?'

'If he doesn't know who's sending them, he can't give us a name even if he wants to.'

'You think?'

'Maybe the whole thing is set up like that,' said Slater. 'Say, for argument's sake, there are half a dozen different parts, run by half a dozen different people, yet no one knows who any of the other people are?'

'I hope you're wrong about that,' said Norman, 'because without a name for the dead girl, this was hard enough already.'

Slater sighed. 'Yeah, I know, but let's not lose sight of the fact we're not trying to break up a porn ring. We're only looking for Betty Glover, although I'd like to find out who the dead girl was too. We can hand over what we know to the police and let them unravel the dirty picture thing.'

'Yeah, you're right,' said Norman. 'We need to focus on the two young women. The rest of it is a distraction. So where to next?'

'I think it's time for lunch, and then I think we need to revisit Vernon Tisdale.'

'What about the gorilla?'

'You mean that nice Mr Patrick? I dunno. I haven't figured that out yet.'

'We should play it by ear,' said Norman. 'We could spend ages coming upon with a plan now and then find he's not even there.'

'You're probably right there,' agreed Slater.

'Can we call in at the office on the way?'

'Are you expecting something?'

'I just wanna check my emails and stuff.'

'Sure, why not?'

* * *

Back at the office, Norman quickly took his place at his desk and checked his emails. 'Are you doing anything tonight, Dave?' he asked a minute later.

'Like most nights lately, I have nothing planned.'

'Keep it that way, will you? Pam Bristow would like to have a chat with us.'

'Pam Bristow? Wait, isn't that the truck driver's wife? You contacted her by email?'

Norman shrugged. 'Look, I tried phoning a dozen times, but she refuses to answer the phone. I didn't think turning up unannounced would be right, so I left a message with my email address. What else could I do?'

Slater nodded. 'I suppose when you put it like that it was good thinking. Did you tell her what we want to talk about?'

'Not in so many words. I told her we were looking for information about a truck driver, but it seems from her reply that she actually *wants* to talk to us anyway.'

'Really? Did she say why?'

'No. Just that she wants to talk, and she would prefer it if we go to her place this evening at about eight o'clock, when her kids are in bed.'

'Okay, that seems fair enough,' said Slater. 'Let's grab some lunch and then head off to Tisdale's house.'

CHAPTER TWENTY-ONE

'I don't see the car out on the road,' said Norman as they approached Tisdale's house. 'Just drive past real slow and let me see if it's on his drive.'

Slater did as Norman suggested. 'It's all clear,' said Norman. 'No sign of it anywhere.'

'That's no guarantee Patrick's not here,' said Slater. 'And it's quite possible he's taken Tisdale somewhere, in which case this is a waste of time.'

'Only one way to find out,' said Norman. 'Park here and we can walk back to the house.'

Slater parked the car, and they made their way back to the house. As before, the building seemed like a dark and forbidding place as they approached the front door.

'It doesn't seem the sort of place a young woman would choose to live,' said Slater. 'It's not exactly a happy-clappy atmosphere, is it?'

'Yeah, but if our theory about her being coerced into staying there is right, she didn't choose to live here, did she?'

'That theory seems even more likely now,' said Slater. 'I can't see any other reason for her to be here.'

'How d'you want to do this?' asked Norman. 'Should we make sure Patrick's not here or just assume he's not?'

As he spoke, Slater banged on the door and pressed the doorbell. Norman aimed a frown at his partner. 'Or we could just charge in without a second thought, knock on the door, and see what happens.'

Slater grinned. 'Now, that sounds like my sort of plan.'

'Yeah, well, let's hope we don't regret it,' muttered Norman.

They waited a couple of minutes, and then Slater banged on the door again.

'You don't think maybe we need to go around to the back door again?' suggested Norman.

'No way,' said Slater.

'But what if—'

'If you're going to say "what if he's fallen down the stairs again", then he can stay there until Patrick comes back.'

'You don't mean that.'

'Oh, yes, I do.'

'If you recall, he didn't fall last time — someone pushed him. You'll feel really bad if—'

'No, I won't, and that's because the crabby old git didn't appreciate our help last time, did he? Anyway, how come you're so keen to defend him? Right now he's on their side, against us.'

'It's not a question of sides,' said Norman. 'He's a frail old man. Let's face it, none of us are getting any younger, are we? I guess I'm just thinking that if I was his age and I was pushed down the stairs, I'd hope someone might care enough to help me.'

'Look, if I knew he was in trouble I'd be there, but I'm not going around there on the off chance. It could be a trap, with Patrick waiting to ambush us, and if it is, I'm not walking into it.' He gestured towards the side of the house. 'If you're not happy with that, be my guest.'

Norman was trying to think of a smart reply, but he was interrupted by the sound of a door being unlocked, followed by a bolt being slid across. Then the door opened just enough for them to see a taut chain and, just below it, an angry, beady eye glared out at them.

'What the hell do you two want? Don't you know there's an injunction? You shouldn't be within a hundred yards of this house.'

'Hi, Mr Tisdale,' said Norman. 'Yeah, I know we're not supposed to be here, but we were worried about you, and we didn't know how else we could find out how you are.'

'Worried? Why would you be worried about me?'

'Don't you remember? You fell down the stairs, and we called an ambulance—'

'And I ended up wasting a day in the damned hospital. Of course I remember, you idiot.'

Slater was going to speak, but Norman grabbed his arm. 'We came to see you in the hospital,' he said. 'We brought your keys back. We just wanted to see you were okay.'

'It wouldn't hurt you to say thank you, would it?' asked Slater. 'Isn't that what people normally do?'

There was a lot of harrumphing from behind the door and then it closed. They could hear the sound of a chain being taken off the door. Slater looked at Norman and raised his eyebrows as the door swung slowly open.

'You can come in for five minutes,' said the old man, 'but if you think I'm going to thank you for getting me dragged off to that hospital, you're wasting your time.'

'Well, there's a surprise,' muttered Slater as he followed Norman into the house.

'What's that?' asked Tisdale.

'I said this is a nice surprise,' said Slater. 'Being let in to see you, I mean.'

Tisdale didn't look convinced, but Slater really didn't give a damn what he thought. The old man turned and closed the door, then swung round to face them. It was obvious they weren't going to be invited any further into the house.

'Now, what d'you want?' asked Tisdale.

'It's about your basement flat,' said Norman.

'I thought you said you wanted to see how I am?'

'I can see you're just fine,' said Norman. 'Where's your bodyguard?'

'Who?'

'Patrick. The guy who bought you home from the hospital,' said Slater.

'I don't know who you mean. The hospital arranged a driver for me. He brought me home and I haven't seen him since.'

Slater smiled. 'Hospitals don't have patients driven home in a Mercedes, Mr Tisdale.'

'I think you'll find they do.'

'That was arranged privately,' said Slater, 'as you well know. Does the name Jools Hanover mean anything to you?'

'Who's she?'

'Actually, she is a he, but if you don't know *him*, how about Samuel Shrivener?'

Tisdale thought about this one. 'Nope. I can't say I know that name either.'

'So, you don't know the solicitor who arranged the injunction for you?'

'No, I don't.'

'I find that hard to believe.'

Tisdale's lips curled into a sickly smile. 'Believe what you like, sonny. I'm telling you I don't know anything about it. The man who drove me home told me about it.'

'Look, you obstinate old g—'

Norman could see Slater's frustration was starting to get the better of him. 'Maybe it would be better if I spoke to Mr Tisdale,' he suggested.

'Yeah. That's probably a good idea,' said Slater through gritted teeth.

'Tell us how you came to fall down the stairs,' Norman asked.

'I didn't fall. I was pushed.'

'Really?' said Norman, surprised. 'You remember that much then. So you were pushed by whom?'

'I don't know. I didn't see him. Look, I think you should leave now. I should never have let you in.'

'Do you have any idea who might want to hurt you like that?'

'I'm not supposed to talk to you two.'

'Who told you that?'

'The man who drove me home. That's why I have the injunction. If they find out I let you in, I'll be in serious trouble.'

'Why are you being threatened?'

'Because of you two. Everything was quiet and peaceful until you two came along. Now I'm being pushed down stairs and threatened . . .'

'Why don't you call the police?' asked Slater.

Tisdale was wringing his hands. His earlier aggression had been replaced by anguish. 'That's the last thing I want to do. I was told not to speak to the police and not to speak to you.'

'Why?'

'I don't know. Maybe it's got something to do with that damned basement. I never really wanted them to let it in the first place.'

'You never wanted "them" to let it? Who are they?'

'I was told it was a way I could make the most of my house and make a bit of extra money. All I had to do was allow them to clean up the basement, and they would handle everything else. I was greedy. I regret it now.'

Slater was watching Tisdale. He seemed to be getting more and more stressed. 'And you got paid for this?'

'That's right. I got the rent money. Now, please will you leave? That man comes back two or three times a day. If he finds you here I don't know what will happen!'

'I think we'd better go, Dave,' said Norman. 'Mr Tisdale's getting upset.'

'Yeah, we've probably got all we're going to get.'

'I'm sorry if we've upset you, Mr Tisdale,' said Norman. 'We'll get out of your hair now and leave you in peace, but you really should think about calling the police.'

'Maybe you're right. I'll think about it,' said Tisdale.

The door was closed so quickly behind them that it caught Slater's heel, but he didn't bother trying to complain. He could already hear the bolt being slid across, quickly followed by the rattling of the chain.

'I didn't think he'd get quite so upset,' said Norman as they walked away. 'I didn't mean for us to do that.'

'Come on, Norm, wake up,' said Slater. 'He was acting. He's playing us for fools.'

'I'm not so sure.'

'Trust me, I'm right. He knows a lot more than he's letting on. Didn't you notice? First off, he claimed he hadn't seen Patrick since he came home, and then he said the guy checks in two or three times a day.'

'You didn't pick him up on that.'

'That's because you let him off the hook before I could.'

'How?'

'By saying we should leave.'

'That was the right thing to do. He was getting upset,' protested Norman.

'He's a good actor.'

'No. I think he's just a frightened and confused old man.'

'I'm afraid we're just going to have to disagree about that,' said Slater. 'I wouldn't trust him as far as I could throw him.'

'We'll see,' said Norman. 'If he goes to the police we'll know I'm right.'

'He won't go to the police. He'll want them as far away as possible.'

'Wanna bet? A tenner says he does.'

'Okay. I'll take your money,' said Slater as he plipped the car locks.

* * *

It was 3 p.m. when they got back to their office. 'I'll put the kettle on,' said Slater, as Norman let them in. 'I'm gasping for a cup of tea.'

'Really?' said Norman.

'What?'

'Oh, nothing. If you want to make the tea, I'm not going to stop you. Should I mark it down on the calendar?'

'Sarcasm really doesn't become you,' said Slater from the kitchen.

A few minutes later, he emerged with two mugs of tea, just as the front door opened and the now familiar figure of Samuel Shrivener entered the room.

'What? Again?' said Slater.

Shrivener gave him an ice-cold smile.

'Where's your goon?' asked Slater.

'If you mean Mr Patrick, I have no idea where he is.'

'So, what can we do for you?' asked Norman.

Shrivener's smile widened and there was even a hint of warmth about it. 'Actually, it's a case of what I can do for you,' he said.

'Yeah, go on,' said Slater. 'I'll buy it if it means you clear off and leave us alone.'

Shrivener slapped an envelope on Norman's desk. 'It looks as if it's your lucky day,' he said. 'Here's emergency injunction number two.'

'What do you mean, injunction number two?' said Norman.

'A Mr Guy Jefferson contacted me. Apparently, you've been terrorising him just like you did Mr Tisdale. He asked me if I could help, and of course I was delighted to do so.'

'This is a joke, right?' said Slater.

'You think so?' said Shrivener. 'I suggest you take a look. I don't think you'll find anything to laugh at in there.'

'I don't understand; how can you get these things arranged so quickly?'

'It's called expertise. It's what my clients pay for, Mr Slater. Anyway, that's my job done, so I must get on. Places to be, people to see, you know how it is.'

'This just shows you're all in it together,' said Slater.

'I don't know what you mean.'

'Sure you do, and we'll prove it — you see if we don't.'

'Goodbye,' said Shrivener. 'Let's hope I don't have to drop in again.' He smiled genially as he stepped through the door and pulled it closed behind him.

Slater banged the mugs of tea he was still holding down on Norman's desk, slopping tea everywhere. 'How the hell can he get these things put together so bloody quickly?'

'Like he said, he's an expert. That's why these people go to him,' said Norman. He pointed at his desk. 'I hope you're going to clean up this mess.'

* * *

'There's a police car just pulled up outside,' called Norman an hour later from the front office.

'Maybe they need the help of some good detectives,' joked Slater from his own office.

'Funny you should say that — they're heading this way.'

'Tell them they couldn't afford us,' said Slater. He heard the outside door open, followed by the murmur of voices.

'Dave?' called Norman. 'I think you'd better come out here.'

Slater got to his feet and walked through to the front office. A uniformed police sergeant and a constable stood waiting.

'You owe me a tenner,' said Norman.

'What?'

'Tisdale *did* call the police.'

Slater was confused. 'Why are the uniforms here? Where are CID?'

'They haven't come for a consult,' said Norman.

'You are David Slater?' asked the sergeant.

'That's me,' said Slater.

The sergeant turned his attention to Norman. 'And you must be Norman Norman.'

'I can't deny it,' said Norman.

'I took a call this afternoon from a Mr Vernon Tisdale. Mr Tisdale claims you went to his house earlier this afternoon. Is this correct?'

'Er, yeah,' said Norman.

'You admit you were there?' asked the sergeant, surprised.

'Yes, we were there,' said Slater, beginning to realise this wasn't a friendly visit. 'Is there a problem?'

'Mr Tisdale claims you forced entry into his house and were harassing him despite the emergency trespass order that was taken out against you.'

'That injunction is a bloody joke,' said Slater. 'Anyway, have you been to his house? It's like Fort Knox. You couldn't possibly get in there without an invitation. We didn't force our way in — he let us in.'

'He's a frail old man.' The sergeant's implication was clear. 'Anyway, you're missing the point. There's a trespass order against you, and yet you still went there. That seems a pretty stupid thing for two ex-police officers to do.'

'Yeah, you're probably right,' said Norman. 'But we only went to enquire after his health.'

'He says you had him dragged off in an ambulance.'

'That was the other day. We found him lying at the foot of his stairs. He'd fallen so we called an ambulance. Isn't that what we're supposed to do?' argued Norman. 'Perhaps you would have preferred it if we'd left him there on the floor and he had died.'

For a few seconds, the sergeant didn't seem quite so sure of himself.

'He didn't tell us about that, did he?' he asked the constable.

'No, he didn't.'

'You can check with the ambulance crew and the hospital,' said Slater. 'Just ask them about the ungrateful old sod who fell down the stairs. They'll remember him.'

'We're getting away from the point,' said the sergeant. 'Whatever your excuse, you defied the injunction. It's lucky for you I took his call.'

'It is?'

'Yes, it is. It's why I've come over here personally. I've heard of you guys. You both worked at Tinton, didn't you?'

Slater and Norman both nodded.

'Well, because of that, I'm going to cut you a bit of slack. I'm going to let you off with a warning, but if you do it again, I won't be able to help. There will be serious consequences. Do I make myself clear?'

Slater felt himself squirming like a naughty little boy, but he knew things could be a lot worse. He looked across at Norman, whose face was glowing a nice shade of cherry red.

'Message understood,' said Slater. 'We'll make sure we don't do it again.'

'Please don't.'

'Right, got it,' said Norman.

To their surprise, the sergeant stepped forward and extended a hand, which they both shook. 'We'll be off, then,' said the sergeant. 'Nice meeting you.'

He turned and led the constable from the office and across the car park to their car.

'Wow! That was embarrassing,' said Norman.

'D'you still think Tisdale is frightened and confused?' asked Slater.

'Yeah, well. It was your idea he should call the police,' said Norman. 'Maybe he got confused and—'

'Oh, come on, Norm, that's bollocks and you know it. He's no more confused than I am.'

'So you mean you're *not* confused?' asked Norman. 'Because I have to say, I don't think I've ever been more confused by a case.'

Slater sighed. 'Yeah, you're right about that. I feel as if I haven't got a bloody clue what's going on, and now we can't even go near two of our biggest suspects.'

'Maybe we'll have some luck later. Why don't we call it a day now and I'll pick you up later?'

CHAPTER TWENTY-TWO

Despite Slater moaning non-stop about Norman's pedestrian driving, they arrived at Pam Bristow's house at 8 p.m. as arranged. It was a small house, about the same size as Slater's. It looked cosy enough, but as they walked up to the door, Slater wondered how on earth two adults and two small children could possibly have enough room to move. In his opinion, his own house was barely even big enough for him.

Norman checked his watch as he rang the doorbell. 'See? Right on time,' he said smugly.

'We're just lucky the roads were empty,' said Slater grudgingly.

Before Norman could reply, the door suddenly opened. They knew Pam Bristow was in her mid-thirties, but the small, weary-looking woman who opened the door could easily have been twenty years older.

'Mrs Bristow? My name's Norman Norman, and this is my colleague Dave Slater.'

'Of course, please, come in,' she said. 'I hope you don't mind me asking you to come this late. It's just that I'm at work all day, and the boys are in bed now . . .'

'It's not a problem,' said Norman. 'We're just grateful you were prepared to speak to us. It must be a very difficult time for you.'

'Yes, you could say that,' she said. 'It's been weeks now, but I still can't quite get my head around the fact he's never going to be coming home again.'

'I'm really sorry,' said Norman. 'I only wish there was something we could do.'

'Well, perhaps there is,' she said, as she ushered them through to a small living/dining room. 'I'll just make some tea.'

As she clattered around in the kitchen, Slater looked quizzically at Norman, but Norman just shrugged.

'I'm so glad you contacted me,' she said as she carried a tray and placed it on the small dining table. 'I know you came here to ask me some questions about a missing woman, but I need some help with a problem of my own, and I don't know what to do.'

'If there's something we can do to help, we'd be happy to, Mrs Bristow,' said Norman.

For the first time, a real smile broke through. It transformed her face. 'Please call me Pam. Mrs Bristow doesn't seem right now.'

'Okay, Pam. I'm Norm.' He pointed at Slater. 'And he's Dave.'

There were smiles all round at this declaration of informality, then she continued. 'I hope I'm wrong, but this problem might even be something to do with your missing woman.'

'Really?' Slater's surprise was loud and clear. 'What makes you think that?'

'Let me start at the beginning, and you see what you think.'

'Please, go ahead.'

'My husband was a lovely fella. He adored me and the kids. He used to work his arse off to make sure we had the best he could possibly give us.'

She stopped to take a sip of the glass of water she had brought in for herself. Slater felt sure there was a 'but' coming up.

She put the water carefully on the table in front of her. 'The thing is, he had a problem. He kept it hidden for a long time after we first met, but eventually he told me. I convinced him to get help, and he did. By the time the kids came along, he was as good as gold, but then about a year ago, I don't know why, but it started again.'

'What started again, Pam?' asked Norman, gently.

She looked embarrassed. 'He liked a bet,' she said. 'The trouble is, once he got started he couldn't stop. And he'd bet on anything.'

'Did he run up debts?'

'Just the one, I think, but it was twenty thousand pounds!'

'Jeez,' said Norman. 'Who did he owe that much?'

'I don't know. I didn't know anything about it until I found the note he left us. He said suicide was the only way and that he didn't deserve to be alive.'

'I didn't realise there was a suicide note,' said Norman. 'There was no mention of it.'

'I didn't tell anyone,' she said. 'He had worked so hard to get himself straight before, I didn't want people to know. It would have killed his mum to think he'd slipped back into his old ways.'

'Did you keep the note, Pam?' asked Slater.

She shook her head and stared off into nowhere for a few seconds until Norman spoke and broke her trance.

'I'm really sorry,' he said. 'Addiction is like that. You think you've got it beat, but it's always there, waiting for a chance. One moment of weakness and it's got you all over again. Have you any idea how he ran up the debt? We might be able to work out who was responsible—'

'Oh, *he* was responsible,' she said. 'I can't blame anyone else for Pete's weakness. You can blame the people who own betting shops and casinos, but no one makes you go in and place a bet, do they?'

'I suppose that's one way of looking at it,' said Norman awkwardly. He didn't quite see it like that, but he wasn't going to argue with a widow.

'Anyway, I was just beginning to get myself together when this parcel arrived.'

'Parcel?'

'I came home one day last week and there it was, sitting on my doorstep. I had no idea who it was from, but I've had so many gifts and bunches of flowers left at the house, I thought it was another one, so I brought it inside and opened it. Look, I'll show you.'

She disappeared into the kitchen and re-emerged carrying a package wrapped in brown paper. It had been half opened.

'You haven't opened it yet?' asked Norman.

'I started to, but when I saw what was inside, I stopped.'

She placed the package on the table, and they could clearly see what was contained within.

'Wow!' said Slater. 'That's a lot of money.'

'Yes. According to the note that was inside, there's ten thousand pounds, all in used ten- and twenty-pound notes.'

'Jeez,' said Norman. 'Do you still have the note that was inside?'

She pulled a folded note from her pocket and placed it on the table.

'May I?' asked Norman, reaching for the note.

She nodded her assent. Norman unfolded the note, read it, and passed it to Slater. 'It says here his debt has been cleared and the cash is a bonus to help you out. Have you any idea how Pete could have earned all this money, or why he should keep quiet about it?'

She swallowed hard, reached for the water, and took another sip. 'In his suicide note, Pete said he was sorry for what happened to the girl in red. He said it was all his fault for being such a coward and agreeing to do what they said. He said he only agreed to do it to clear the debt, but he didn't realise exactly what he had done until afterwards.'

'He didn't say what he'd actually done?'

'No, that was it, but I'm sure he was talking about the girl who was run down in a lay-by a couple of months back. I remember seeing the story in the newspaper, and I know Pete was never the same after that. It was only a couple of weeks later that he . . .'

Norman reached across and placed a hand on her shoulder. She turned to stare sadly into his eyes. 'Did he kill that girl?' she asked.

'I can't say for sure, Pam, but I think it's a possibility.'

'Do you know who she was? Is she the girl you're looking for?'

'She's not who we're looking for, but we believe they were friends.'

'Oh, Pete,' she said sadly. 'What on earth did you do?'

There was an awkward silence as Slater and Norman waited patiently for her to regain her composure. Finally, she took another sip of water, gently shook her head, and then managed a half-hearted smile. 'Sorry about that. I'm alright now.'

'No problem,' said Norman. 'You have nothing to apologise for.'

'But what do I do about this money? I don't want it, and it can't be right to keep it, can it? That would be like saying it was alright to kill that girl. I'd give it to the police, but then everyone will know what Pete did.'

'You should really give it to the police,' said Slater. 'I understand why you're reluctant, but it's the right thing to do. If you think she was deliberately run down, they have to be told.'

'I suppose you're right,' she said. 'Well, I *know* you are really. I'm going to have to tell his mum first, though. It has to come from me. Will that be alright?'

'When will you tell her?' asked Norman.

'I'll go and see her on Saturday. My neighbour will have the kids for the day. Will it be okay to wait until then?'

Norman gave her a sad little smile. 'Yeah, I should think so. Are you sure you're going to be okay going to the police on your own?'

'I don't have anyone to go with.'

'I'll come with you. I know how these things work. I can guide you through it. Don't lose that note, though. They'll want that too.'

'Are you sure?'

'Here's my card,' said Norman. 'You can reach me on that mobile number any time. Just let me know when you're ready to go, and I'll come and get you.'

* * *

'That must be so tough,' said Norman, as he drove away from Pam Bristow's house. 'It must be bad enough knowing your husband killed himself, but now she finds he probably killed a young woman as well.'

'And got paid for it,' said Slater. 'That makes him a contract killer, doesn't it?'

'On paper, yeah, I guess it does. But I hope the police are going to be a bit more charitable about it than you are.'

'Just saying it as it is, Norm. It looks like the guy got paid for killing someone. I can't see how you can interpret that any other way.'

'Yeah, I suppose you're right. I just think Pam Bristow's been through enough already.'

'I know, mate, but that's unlikely to be a consideration for the police, is it?'

'And where's this guy Alex? We haven't come across a single mention of him anywhere. It's almost like he's invisible. You don't think he was working against Betty, do you? And, of course, is Hanover involved?'

Slater sighed. 'Honestly? I have no idea, Norm. It's difficult to work out who was doing what, or even who is who! I mean, no one seems to be who they first appear to be, do they? I'm beginning to think we're being led a merry dance. Someone's playing with us. I only wish I knew who it was. Someone's got to be pulling the strings.'

'Maybe we've got it all wrong, and we need to start over,' said Norman. 'Go back to square one and see what we've missed.'

They drove on in moody silence for a few minutes.

‘What if we’re focusing on the wrong girl?’ said Slater suddenly.

‘How d’you mean?’

‘We’ve let the dead girl become the focus, don’t you think?’

‘I suppose we have, yeah.’

‘But what if that’s what we’re supposed to do? I mean, as far as we know, this girl was an innocent, right? She didn’t really know what she was part of. She just did as she was told and lived in that basement because she thought her parents were in danger.’

‘We don’t know about the parents for sure,’ said Norman.

‘Fair enough, but we know it’s a distinct possibility.’

‘Go on, I’m listening.’

‘So, our mystery girl wasn’t a threat to anyone, but Betty, the investigative journalist posing as Martha, *was* a threat. Now, we know they both look similar, and they both wear red jogging gear, right?’

‘Right, so?’

‘I see two possibilities. First, the innocent girl was deliberately chased under the truck to distract us. Maybe whoever did the dirty work was supposed to make sure everyone thought she was Martha.’

Norman didn’t look convinced. ‘What’s the second possibility?’

‘What if someone was sent to get rid of Martha, the jogger in the red suit, but they killed the wrong girl?’

‘But wouldn’t they have realised their mistake by now?’ said Norman.

‘You’re right,’ said Slater gloomily. ‘I didn’t think that through, did I? They could have realised their mistake and come back and killed Betty, but we haven’t found her body yet.’

‘There is another possibility,’ suggested Norman. ‘Perhaps we were supposed to follow the trail to girl one while Betty’s being held somewhere?’

'You really think she's being held captive somewhere? Why would they do that?'

'Heck, I don't know, but it makes as much sense as anything else in this case.'

Slater thought about what Norman had said. 'Now you say it, it does make sense, Norm. Besides we've got nowhere so far, so why not?'

'Yeah, it's a great idea,' said Norman cynically, 'but we still have no idea who might want to hold her captive, or why they would want to hold her when we know they have no qualms about killing people. And I don't even want to start thinking about where she might be.'

'I think it's safe to say the person holding her is the person behind the pornography and sex trafficking.'

'And who's that then, Sherlock?'

'There's that sarcasm again,' said Slater. 'It's not like you at all.'

'Maybe this case is starting to get to me. I mean look at that poor woman we've just been to see. Her whole world has been turned upside down. Is it any wonder I'm getting cynical?'

Slater wasn't prepared to go down that particular road, so he steered the conversation back where he wanted it to go. 'Okay. Suspects. I think first we've got to consider Jools Hanover, who seems to be at the end of every trail. Then there's Sam Shrivener, who appears every time we question anyone. It's almost as if he knows our every move.'

'Maybe we've been bugged,' suggested Norman.

Slater pulled a face. 'Frankly, it wouldn't surprise me, but let's get back to my list.'

'There's more?'

'In my opinion there are two more suspects, or persons of interest, who, at the very least, know what's going on and therefore know who's in charge. The first of these is Guy Jefferson.'

'You really think he's got it in him?'

'He was so quick with that injunction. He must be seriously rattled.'

Norman couldn't argue with that. 'Okay, who else?'

'None other than your friend — and mine — Vernon Tisdale.'

Norman laughed out loud. 'I'm sorry,' he scoffed, 'but I think you're way off the mark there. Tisdale isn't even sure what day it is. How could he possibly be behind something like this?'

'You don't have to agree with me, Norm, I'm just saying what I think.'

'Well, I think we should focus on Jools Hanover. He sounds like the sort of guy who would have the money to set up something like this, and didn't Stella say his business is something of a mystery?'

'Okay,' said Slater, 'so why don't we start with him? But instead of creeping around on the internet, why don't we stop wasting time, take the bull by the horns, and visit him?'

'You really think it'll be that easy to get to speak to him?'

'I have no idea, but I'll let you know after I've called his office in the morning.'

CHAPTER TWENTY-THREE

'Hi, it's Stella. I'm sorry to call you so late.'

'Don't apologise,' said Slater. 'I was still awake, and it's nice to hear a friendly voice. You *are* friendly, aren't you? You're not calling to slap another injunction on us.'

'Injunction? What have you done now?'

'Another one of our suspects has run to Shrivener to ask him to slap a trespass order against us.'

'My, you must be rattling some cages.'

'They seem to be trying to make it impossible for us even to go near our suspects, never mind speak to them.'

'You could always hand it all over to us, you know,' she said.

'We'll only do that when we've got evidence of a murder, or something serious enough to warrant your intervention.'

'You're full of big words this evening.'

'They must be rising to the surface as a result of banging my head against a brick wall.'

'Not getting anywhere then?'

'We're riding a very confusing merry-go-round. At least, that's how it seems. We're definitely going around in circles.'

'Then I have something that may help you.'

'Jesus, Stella, not again. You've got to stop doing this!'

'I didn't go looking for this. It came across my desk and I thought of you. I was going to wait until tomorrow morning to call you, but I thought it would be nice to hear your voice now.'

'That's very sweet of you, but I've told you before, you really shouldn't take risks for me.'

'Yes, but as I've told you before, I make my own decisions.'

Slater sighed. She sounded so confident tonight he could imagine the raised finger pointed his way. This woman was a real conundrum. 'Go on then, let's hear it.'

'As I said, this communication arrived this afternoon from Europol. They're looking for a young woman who has been reported missing. The picture shows a very sweet, innocent-looking Ukrainian woman, blonde with blue eyes, aged twenty-two. Last known whereabouts — the south of England.'

Now she had Slater's full attention. 'Have you got a name?' he asked.

'Her name is Alexandra Kobevko. Her parents say she came to England over a year ago. At first, they were hearing from her regularly, but that stopped four months ago, and they've heard nothing since. I thought she sounded a bit like—'

'The girl we're trying to identify. Yes, she does,' said Slater. 'She sounds a lot like her.'

'I think she looks quite like her too, although I've only seen the original mortuary photos and her face is rather disfigured in those.'

'Can you email me the photograph in the morning?'

'I've got it here. I'll do it right now.'

'Thanks, Stella, I really appreciate this.'

'And now you owe me,' she said.

'Dinner?'

'I thought we might walk the dog on Sunday, if that's alright?'

'That would be great,' he said. 'But we could do dinner too, couldn't we? Tomorrow?'

'I've got no information to exchange for that.'

'That's too bad,' he said. 'I suppose I'll just have to make do with your company. I'll book a table, and how about this time I pick you up from home? Say about seven thirty?'

He could sense her uncertainty; the suspense was killing him, but eventually she spoke. 'Okay. I'll see you tomorrow.'

* * *

It was after midnight, and down on the floor by Norman's side of the bed, something was buzzing loudly like a demented wasp. In his half-awake state, Norman wasn't quite sure if he was dreaming, but then a sharp elbow dug into his ribs and an irritated voice suggested he probably wasn't.

'Will you answer that phone?'

'Oh, crap. Sorry, Jane. Is it real? I thought I was dreaming.'

Jane was normally good-natured, but she had difficulty sleeping and was never at her best when woken unexpectedly. 'Well, I can assure you you're not, but I should be.'

Norman leaned over the side of the bed.

'For God's sake, Norm, don't take all the quilt with you. It's freezing!'

'Sorry, sorry,' mumbled Norman, fumbling the quilt back over Jane's side of the bed. He sat up and started arranging it around her.

'I can do that myself,' she hissed, slapping at his hands. 'Just get the damned phone.'

Norman leaned back over the side of the bed. It took him a while to locate the phone under the pile of clothes he had abandoned earlier, which prompted a barrage of further mutterings and angry tutting, but eventually he discovered it in his trouser pocket. As he sat up again, he looked at the caller ID.

'It's Dave,' he said, staring at the screen.

'Wonderful,' she said bitterly. 'Ask him if he realises what time it is!'

'Yo, Dave!' said Norman into his phone. 'This had better be good. Jane doesn't take kindly to be woken in the middle of the night.'

'You won't believe this, Norm,' said Slater.

'What? What won't I believe?'

'I can't believe we've been so stupid.'

'Why have we been stupid? What are you talking about?'

'The answer was under our noses all the time.'

'Have you been drinking?'

'Drinking? Of course I haven't been drinking. Why would you ask that?'

'Whoa, whoa,' said Norman. 'Let's just stop for a minute, can we? Do you know what time it is?'

'Er, yeah, it's a quarter to one.'

'That's right, it's a quarter to one in the morning,' said Norman. 'Jane and I were fast asleep, then my phone starts ringing, waking her, which is never a good idea, and then you start babbling away like an idiot. Is this the sort of thing we normally do?'

'No, I suppose not.'

'Then I think it's quite reasonable to assume you've either been drinking, or doing drugs, and I know you wouldn't take drugs—'

'Alright, alright, I take your point,' said Slater. 'I'm sorry, but this is important.'

Norman put his hand over his phone and turned to Jane. 'He says it's important.'

'Oh, good. I'm so pleased. Tell him so is my sleep.'

Norman took the not-very-thinly-veiled hint, climbed from the bed, and made his way out of the bedroom. 'Right, I'm awake now,' he said to Slater. 'What's so important it couldn't wait until the morning?'

'I spoke to Stella earlier. A Europol notice has come across her desk about a missing girl. She sent me a copy of the photograph attached to it. I'm sure it's the girl we saw in the mortuary.'

'Oh, right, that's good, but why didn't you call earlier?'

'Because I've only just realised how stupid we've been.'

'How does this make us stupid? And how was it under our noses all the time if it's only just come from Europol?'

'Her name is Alexandra Kobevko.'

'Yeah, so now we know her name. It's sad, but couldn't it have waited?'

'We've been looking for a woman who is with a man called Alex.'

'Yeah, and?'

'We never considered Alex might be a woman!'

'Well, why would we? Davies told us it was a guy.'

'But did he?' asked Slater. 'I seem to recall what he actually said was, "Alex is just a name".'

Norman stared into the darkness and then, finally, he was wide awake. 'Jeez. I just realised what you mean. Alexandra *is* Alex.'

'Exactly,' said Slater. 'Betty was never with a man — she was with another young woman.'

'You're saying this poor kid was smuggled in from Russia just so someone could take photos of her, and then, when they had enough photos, they chased her under a truck? Jesus, what a sick, twisted world we live in.'

'Yeah, you're not wrong about that,' said Slater. 'The thing is, was Betty with Alexandra when she died?'

'You think there could be another body near that lay-by? I wouldn't want to have to search that area. There's miles and miles of forest and fields. You'd need an army — and a couple of years.'

'You're right. Maybe we should carry on as we were for a few more days, and then if we're getting nowhere we can always come back to that lay-by.'

'Let's sleep on it and speak in the morning.'

'Okay. Tell Jane I'm sorry I woke her up.'

'She won't thank me for waking her again. I'll tell her in the morning.'

'I'm sorry, mate. I didn't think. I forgot she doesn't sleep so well.'

'It's okay, don't worry. I'm sure she'll understand when I tell her why you called. When I get into the office in the morning, I'll get in touch with Bill at the mortuary,' said

Norman. 'At least we can make sure Alexandra's parents get the chance to give her a decent burial.'

'Goodnight, Norm.'

'Goodnight.'

CHAPTER TWENTY-FOUR

'Jools Hanover is happy to speak to us,' announced Slater.

'Is there a reason why you look disappointed about that?' asked Norman.

'It's not that I'm disappointed. I mean, I'm happy he'll speak to us, but I wasn't expecting him to be quite so amenable. I thought he'd tell us to go take a hike, not welcome us.'

'Did you actually get to speak to him?'

'Yeah. I didn't think he would, but his secretary put me straight through.'

'Did you tell him what we want?'

'He says he doesn't see how he can help, but he's happy to speak to us.'

'Sounds like he's been expecting us to call, if you ask me. I bet he's had his story ready for months, just in case.'

'I don't know — I would have expected him to know what was going on, but I got the impression he had no idea who I was.'

'It's easy to act dumb over the phone,' said Norman. 'Let's see what happens when we're face to face. I bet it'll be different then.'

'I expect you're right.'

'When do we go?'

Slater looked at his watch. 'In about an hour. Apparently he's just bought a golf course and they have an amazing chef. He's invited us to join him for lunch. I said we'd be there around midday.'

'Are you okay with that?' asked Norman. 'If he's behind all this, we really shouldn't be socialising with him.'

'I didn't want to put his back up before we even met, so I compromised and said we'd join him for a drink, but we were pushed for time and I wasn't sure we'd have time for lunch.'

'Very diplomatic,' said Norman.

'Not bad for thinking on my feet, right?'

* * *

Tinterberry Golf Course was less than an hour's drive, and after a pleasant journey in warm autumnal sunshine, they pulled into the car park, comfortably on time, just before midday. As Slater picked his parking space behind the clubhouse, Norman took a good look around.

'Are you sure this is the right place?' he asked.

'Of course. Why else would there be signs saying Tinterberry Golf Course everywhere?'

'It doesn't look much, that's all. Rundown is the expression that comes to mind when I look around.'

'Maybe he has plans for it.'

'Yeah, demolition, probably,' said Norman. 'That's if it doesn't fall down first. Does this look like the sort of place where you'd find a top-quality chef?'

'It's good to see you have an open mind,' said Slater as he opened his car door. 'I thought you were the optimist in this partnership.'

'I just think it looks like a dump, that's all.'

The signs directing them to the main entrance indicated a path that led round the side of the building and then up a long flight of steps.

'If I played golf, I wouldn't want to have to carry a bag of clubs up these steps before I even got out on the course,' puffed Norman as they neared the top.

'It's not exactly user-friendly so far,' agreed Slater. As he was a few steps in front, he reached the top first. As he did, and took in the view, he couldn't quite believe his eyes.

'Oh, wow. Just look at this view,' he said.

A couple of seconds later, Norman joined him. 'Holy smoke! I didn't expect anything like that. Who would have guessed?'

They were on a wide paved area that stretched almost a hundred feet across the front of the clubhouse and must have been thirty feet deep. The entire front of the building consisted of huge windows, and the paved area had numerous tables and chairs set out at intervals. Everything was designed to make the most of the view.

From their vantage point, they were looking down a gently sloping hillside, which housed the golf course, and then beyond across acres and acres of fields resembling a patchwork quilt in shades of amber and yellow. On the far side of the fields, autumn had painted a distant forest in shades of yellow, orange and brown.

It was a scene of rare beauty that only nature could produce and, mouths open, they stared in silent wonder at this amazing sight.

'Do you like the view?' asked a voice behind them.

They swung round to see the owner of the voice, a handsome man in his forties, dressed in dark blue trousers, a pale blue shirt, and a cream blazer, emblazoned with a crest on the pocket which bore the legend *Tinterberry Golf Club*.

'It takes your breath away,' said Slater.

'I'm afraid those stairs had already taken my breath away,' said Norman, 'but I have to agree — it's one hell of a view!'

'A view worth buying, don't you agree?'

'Are you Mr Hanover?' asked Slater.

The man extended a hand. 'I certainly am, and you must be Mr Slater and Mr Norman?' They shook hands all round, and Hanover indicated a table. 'Shall we sit out here? It's such a beautiful day it seems a shame to be inside.'

'What do you think of my purchase?' he asked as they took their seats.

'I don't know much about golf courses,' said Slater diplomatically.

'It's a long haul up those steps,' said Norman, 'especially if you had to drag a bag of clubs up here.'

Hanover smiled. 'It's definitely a bit rough around the edges, and you're right, it's a long way from the car park to the clubhouse. I plan to install lifts, a ramp, and maybe an escalator to get past that one. The clubhouse is going to be demolished and rebuilt and the course upgraded. That should satisfy the golfers, and then on top of that, the kitchens are going to be the best money can buy. Can you imagine coming to dine out here with that view? With the right chef, there's a goldmine just in the restaurant.'

'Those are big plans,' said Norman suspiciously. 'That sort of thing costs a lot of money.'

'I have millions in the bank,' said Hanover, 'but it earns very little these days. This is a much better investment. I'll see a real return this way. Besides, you can't take it with you, can you?'

'I thought casinos and nightclubs were more your thing?'

'That's where I *made* my money, and it's allowed me to buy a lot of property, but now I want to do something different. This is something I've always wanted to do.'

'You're lucky you can afford to do it,' said Norman.

Hanover bristled. 'I can assure you there's no luck about it. I've worked bloody hard to get where I am. Businesses don't become successful on their own, you know. Someone has to make decisions, and one wrong one can mean disaster. I'm very good at making the right decisions, and that's definitely not down to luck!'

Inwardly, Slater was cursing Norman's lack of tact. He had fully expected the atmosphere to go downhill at some stage, but already?

'I understood you wanted to ask me some questions, not cast aspersions about my business acumen,' said Hanover, his good humour now gone.

'Yes, that's right,' said Slater.

'Then perhaps you'd like to get on with it. I'm a busy man.'

'Of course. We're actually trying to locate a missing woman called Betty Glover, who also sometimes uses the name Martha Dennis.'

'And why would this concern me?'

'How about a girl called Alexandra Kobevko?' asked Norman. 'Maybe you know her.'

'What is she, Russian?'

'Ukrainian,' said Norman.

'I'm confused,' said Hanover slowly. 'Why would you think I would know this girl? And why does the other girl use two names?'

'Betty Glover is an investigative journalist,' said Slater. 'She uses the name Martha Dennis as a cover.'

'An investigative journalist? And you think she's investigating me?'

'We have reason to believe it's a possibility.'

'So where does the Ukrainian girl come into this?'

'We think Betty had been in contact with her.'

'And why would this be relevant, if she was investigating me? I don't see the link.'

'The link,' Norman said, slowly and clearly, 'is your car — and your gorilla driver.'

Hanover looked genuinely surprised. Slater was aghast. What was Norm trying to do?

'I beg your pardon? My driver?'

'Yeah. The big guy, Patrick. Drives your black Mercedes.'

Hanover frowned. 'I have no idea what you're talking about. I don't have a black Mercedes, and my driver is downstairs having his lunch. When I'm ready to go, he will drive me home — in my Bentley.'

'Bullshit,' said Norman, fumbling in his pocket. 'I'll show you. I have a photograph of the car right here on my phone. It's a black Mercedes registered to Jools Hanover.'

'You do realise Jools Hanover is also the name of my company, don't you? The company owns a fleet of black Mercs. We lease them out to numerous people.'

Norman was momentarily lost for words. Slater, who had been thrown by Norman's abrupt change of tack, tried to salvage something from this interview. 'Mr Hanover, do you know Samuel Shrivener?'

'Sam? Yes, of course I do. He's my lawyer.'

'Does he have one of your cars?'

'Yes, I believe he does, but I couldn't tell you what the registration number is. It's not something I deal with. I can tell you we lease it to him at a preferential rate, and in exchange I have access to his expertise whenever I need it.'

'Now it makes sense,' said Norman. 'I guess he advises on all your dodgy dealings, right?'

Hanover stared at Norman and then his face slowly broke into a smile. 'Now I get it. You've been talking to the police, haven't you? Have they sent you here to see if you can do what they can't? They've made a big mistake if they have. You two are quite hopeless, aren't you?'

'I'm sorry, but you've lost me,' said Slater. 'You think we've been sent by the police?'

'There are several officers working for Hampshire Police who have been trying, for several years, to find some dirt on me. They seem to think my business is a cover for something much darker. The thing is, they've never found a single shred of evidence, and the reason why is because there's nothing to find.'

Norman sneered. 'Well, yeah, of course you're going to say that, aren't you?'

Hanover sat back. 'Do I look stupid? They've been watching me, and my organisation, for years. Do you really believe I would risk losing everything I have?'

Slater and Norman were both silent, but it didn't matter because Hanover was giving them no time to speak anyway.

'Think about it,' he said. 'I don't need more money, and I already have the power that comes with owning a large, successful business. I own a beautiful home not far from here, another house in France and, most importantly of all, I have a gorgeous wife I adore and two beautiful children. All this has come from building my own, legitimate, business. Why the hell would I want to jeopardise any of that?

'Now, if you'll excuse me, I think we're done here, and I have things to do. You know the way back to the car park.'

He stood up, straightened his jacket, and strode away.

'That went well,' said Slater sarcastically as he got to his feet and headed for the steps back to the car park. 'Is there any particular reason why you needed to put his back up quite so quickly?'

'I thought you said you didn't want to mess around,' said Norman, hurrying to keep up.

'I didn't say anything about going straight for his throat.'

'I thought you were being too soft on him. I mean, we know he's behind it all.'

'We don't know anything of the sort.'

'I thought Stella told you he was suspected of some bad stuff—'

'Well, I'm beginning to think maybe she's got it wrong.'

'What? You mean you believed all that crap?'

'I think what he said made a lot of sense. If you had everything he's got, would you risk losing it?'

'Yeah, but if his business was built on the back of crime . . .'

'. . . you would think the police would have found something by now,' finished Slater. 'And they haven't.'

'But these guys are good at hiding things.'

'And the police are always crap at finding them?'

'Well, no, I didn't mean that.'

'But that must be how it is if they've been looking for years and they haven't found anything yet. Unless, of course, there's nothing to find . . .'

Norman stayed silent as he plodded down the steps after Slater.

* * *

They made their way down to the car in silence, and it was ten minutes into the journey back before anyone spoke. 'If it's not Hanover behind it all, who is it?' asked Slater.

'I'm sure it *is* Hanover.'

'Look, I know you don't agree with me, but just humour me for a minute.'

'But I can't see anyone else in the frame. I'm sorry, but I don't see how it can be anyone else.'

Slater sighed.

'Okay,' said Norman. 'I'll play your game if it makes you happy. Sneaky Sam Shrivener has to be up there. He's got the car — and the driver — and he seems to be happy to dish out injunctions at the drop of a hat. He'd be my number one.'

'What about Jefferson? He creates the art. What if he directs the whole operation?'

'Honestly? I don't see him being a killer, or even an organiser. I don't think he's got it in him.'

'But he doesn't have to do the dirty work,' said Slater. 'He just says the word and someone does it for him.'

'Nah, I still can't see it. I mean, who's going to take orders from him? He's much too wet for anyone to take him seriously.'

Slater pursed his lips thoughtfully. Just as Norman was convinced Hanover was behind whatever this was, Slater was convinced he wasn't even involved. This was going to be a hard case to solve if they couldn't even agree on their main suspect.

CHAPTER TWENTY-FIVE

After a tense, moody journey home, Slater and Norman had agreed to have an early finish, take the weekend off, and reconvene on Monday morning. This had suited Slater perfectly; it meant he had plenty of time to get ready and improve his mood before he set off to Winchester to collect Stella. Now, freshly showered and shaved, he felt pretty good as he turned into the street where she lived.

He took his time getting from the car to the front door, but even so, he was seven or eight minutes early. In Slater's eyes, this was a good thing. He thought it was always better to be a few minutes early rather than keep someone waiting. He took one final deep breath and rang the doorbell.

A light suddenly blossomed beyond the door and then it swung open. A tall grey-haired man greeted him.

'You must be Dave,' he said, smiling and extending his hand. As Slater shook his hand, he continued, 'I'm Stella's father, Harry. She's not quite ready, but please, come on in.'

Slater accepted the invitation and stepped into the house.

'I was hoping to meet you,' said Harry. 'Stella has told us a lot about you.'

'All good I hope,' said Slater genially.

'All very good, actually.'

Slater felt his day had just got a whole lot better. 'Will Stella be long?' he asked.

'I'm sure she'll be down shortly. Why don't you come through and sit down.'

He showed Slater through a nearby door. Slater had expected to be shown into a living room where Harry's wife might have been waiting, but instead he found he was in a small study — and now Harry had closed the door behind them.

'I want to speak to you. I hope you don't mind.'

Slater didn't think he had much choice but to listen. He could hardly say no, could he? 'Of course, I don't mind, Harry. What can I do for you?'

'How much do you know about Stella's situation?'

Slater wondered what he had just walked into. 'Situation? I'm not exactly sure what you mean.'

'She hasn't told you, has she?'

'I'm sorry, Harry, and I don't want to appear dim, but can you give me some sort of clue?'

Harry was wringing his hands and, momentarily, he looked up to the ceiling, as if for inspiration — or courage.

'How does Stella behave if you're alone together?'

This was a question Slater hadn't expected to hear, but Harry looked genuinely upset.

'Well, now you mention it, she does get a bit tense.'

'But she's alright the rest of the time?'

Slater's curiosity had been aroused. He was only too aware of Stella's behaviour, and he suspected he knew what was behind it, but now he wondered if Harry was going to tell him. Much as he wanted to know, he found he was more concerned about what Stella would think if he did.

'Before you say any more, Harry, does Stella know you're talking to me?'

'I don't know. I haven't asked her. I'm just looking out for my daughter, that's all.'

'I think I understand where you're coming from, but maybe Stella doesn't want me to know.'

'D'you think so?'

'She's had opportunities to tell me herself, but—'

'She finds it difficult to talk about.'

'Look, Harry, I understand your concern, so let me try to put your mind at rest. I've become very fond of Stella, and I'm aware she has issues. She hasn't told me what happened, but I promised I wouldn't pry, and I would wait until she's ready to tell me about it. If you tell me now, I feel I would be breaking that promise.'

'Oh, I see. I didn't realise you had talked about it.'

'We haven't spoken in any depth, but I was a police officer for a long time. I'm pretty sure I know the sort of thing that's behind it, but I don't want to rush her.'

Harry studied Slater for a moment. 'I can see why she likes you,' he said. 'She told me you were kind — and patient.'

Slater could feel himself beginning to blush. 'I'm not going to do her any harm, if that's what you're worried about.'

'Oh, there you are,' said a familiar voice as Stella pushed the door open. 'I thought I heard the doorbell.'

'Harry was just showing me round,' said Slater guiltily.

Harry's face had been quite sad, but now, as he saw Stella, it lit up with a beaming smile. 'Don't let me hold you up,' he said. 'I don't want to make you late.'

Stella walked over to her father and kissed his cheek. 'Come on, then, Dave, let's go,' she said, heading back through the door.

'You won't tell her I said anything?' asked Harry quietly.

Slater smiled and gave Harry a conspiratorial wink. 'That's our secret,' he said, then followed after Stella.

* * *

'You seemed to be getting on well with my dad,' she said when they were in the car. 'What were you talking about?'

'We were just saying hello. I was only there for two minutes.'

'I suppose he was telling you all about my problem, was he?'

'He's worried about you.'

She tutted. 'I'm nearly forty years old, for goodness sake!'

'Yes, but you're still his little girl, and you always will be. It's nice he cares.'

'What did he tell you?'

Slater thought he shouldn't lie. 'Nothing.'

'Then why did you look guilty when I came into the room?'

'Look, he was going to tell me, but I wouldn't let him.'

'What do you mean, you wouldn't let him?'

'I told him I had promised you I would wait until you were ready to tell me. I said if he told me, I would be breaking my promise.'

'Did you? Really?'

'Yeah, of course I did.'

'That's very sweet of you. Thank you.'

'A promise is a promise.'

Slater looked across at her. It was dark outside, but as they passed under a streetlight he could see she looked pleased, and it made him feel very happy.

'The deal was that you would be doing the talking,' he said.

'Yes, I know.'

'If you don't want to, it doesn't matter. I don't mind.'

'No. I want to,' she said. 'I'm not sure what's going on here, but I don't think it's fair to keep you in the dark much longer.'

'Are you sure?'

'Yes, I'm sure, but can it wait until we walk the dog? I might get a bit upset, and it'll be embarrassing for everyone if I do that in a busy restaurant.'

Slater nodded. 'Sure. That sounds like an excellent idea.'

'So, the missing girl was the one at the mortuary?' asked Stella.

Slater had been hoping to keep the conversation about Stella, but he was obviously going to have to be a bit smarter — and quicker — if he was going to succeed. 'Yeah, that's right,' he said reluctantly.

'I'm not asking you to break the Official Secrets Act, you know.'

'Sorry?'

'You can tell me about your case. I'm not going to take it away from you.'

'It's not that,' he said. 'I'm never going to get to know you if all we ever talk about is me and my case.'

She pursed her lips thoughtfully. 'But I'm curious about it.'

'And I'm curious about you,' he said.

She glanced at him and then looked away again. 'What makes you so sure I'm worth the effort?'

'I'm not sure, but if you never tell me anything about yourself I'll never know, will I?'

In the light from a streetlamp they were passing, he could see her nod slightly, as if she thought he had a point.

'Let's make a deal,' she said after a few seconds' thought. 'Tell me about your case until we get to the restaurant, and then I won't ask again for the rest of the evening.'

'Okay,' said Slater, 'we have a deal, but this is going to be the short version.'

She clapped her hands. It could have been seen as a childish gesture, but Slater felt she had just revealed a small part of herself. He found it endearing and couldn't help but smile.

'Come on then,' she said. 'Spill the beans.'

'Alexandra Kobevko was run down by a truck driver. From what we've learned, it seems he was forced to kill her and subsequently committed suicide. However, we believe she was killed in error. The intended victim was Betty Glover, because Betty was on to what was going on and was building a story that was going to expose the whole thing.'

'Who arranged the killing?'

'Whoever is behind what we think is a pornography business. Our suspects are Jools Hanover, Sam Shrivener and Guy Jefferson. I haven't ruled out Vernon Tisdale either, although Norm thinks he's a non-starter because he's old and a bit doddery.'

They were fortunate enough to find a parking space right outside the restaurant, and now Slater parked up and switched the engine off.

'If Alexandra was murdered, I can't ignore it,' said Stella.

'You can for a few more days,' said Slater. 'If you get involved now, the chances are your lot will just say there isn't enough evidence, and it'll all be a waste of time. Give us a few more days. Let us find Betty, and then, when we have the evidence, we'll hand it over to you.'

They were out of the car now.

'What if Betty can't be found? If they meant to kill her before, what makes you think they haven't now?'

Slater held the restaurant door open for her, and she stepped inside.

'Well?' she asked. 'How do you know?'

'I don't know for sure,' he said, 'but it doesn't matter now. We're here, and we had a deal, right?'

She looked at him and pouted. 'Are you really going t—'

'Yes, I really *am* going to hold you to it.'

'But you can't do that!'

Slater grinned. 'I just did.'

CHAPTER TWENTY-SIX

As usual, the evening passed far too quickly, and all too soon it was time for them to leave. Slater escorted Stella to his car, installed her in the passenger seat, then walked round the car and climbed in next to her, just as he had each time they had been to the restaurant. Only this time, he didn't start the car and drive off. Tonight, he simply sat and waited.

She glanced nervously in his direction. 'Is there something wrong?'

He turned to face her. A nearby streetlight cast just enough feeble light into the car for him to see her worried face.

'I need to know what's going on,' he said.

'What happened to "when you're ready"?' she said stiffly, turning to face the front.

'I'm beginning to wonder if you ever *will* be ready.'

'Oh, I see.' There was a short, tense silence, then Stella spoke again. 'No one said you had to wait. I'll understand if you don't want to.'

'Come on, Stella, don't treat me like an idiot. I'm a detective. I was in the police for twenty years. You're fine until we're alone together in the car at night. Do you really think I can't work it out?'

She turned her face away from him. 'Well, if you're so clever and you've worked it all out, why do you need to humiliate me by making me tell you?' she said bitterly.

'I'm not trying to humiliate you. I just want to help.'

There was another, longer, silence, but now she had turned to the front again. Slater felt the atmosphere had changed. She had softened somehow.

'How long ago did it happen?' he asked.

She turned towards him. Her eyes were on his, but she seemed to be looking right through him. 'It was almost nine months ago.'

'In a car?'

She nodded slowly. When she spoke, her voice was a slow monotone. 'It was at night. We were on a stakeout. We were watching a house through night-vision goggles. My partner had left the car for a wee, so when the passenger door opened I assumed it was him. I didn't even look round. The next thing I knew, there were hands around my neck and I was being strangled.'

'Oh Jesus,' said Slater quietly.

'It could have been much worse,' she said. 'Once I was unconscious, he opened the door and kicked me out. Then he drove off.'

'Oh, Stella, I'm sorry,' said Slater.

'He left me for dead by the side of the road,' she said, sobbing now. 'You're not going to do that, are you?'

Instinctively, he reached for her, but she shrank back against the car door, gasping for air, her hands raised to defend herself.

Slater pulled back. 'I'm sorry, that was stupid of me,' he said, hastily. 'I wouldn't hurt you. I was just . . . I want to help, Stella, honest I do.'

She was still breathing hard, and her eyes seemed to be staring ahead, unfocused. Slowly, watching her face, he reached for her hands, gently took hold of them, and lowered them to her lap.

'Stella, look at me,' he said softly. 'I need you to slow your breathing. Come on, focus on me, and breathe with me, deep, slow breaths.'

It took a minute or two, but eventually she was calm enough to speak. 'I'm sorry,' she said. 'I know you won't hurt me. It's just . . .'

'It's okay,' he said. 'You don't need to explain. I understand.'

He was still holding her hands, and now she looked down at them as if she wasn't quite sure what was happening. He released her hands, but she quickly took hold of them, pulled them back into her lap, and held on tight. She looked back up at his face, but this time she focused on him.

'Night-time is worst,' she said. 'I can just about cope during the day, but I can't drive at night.'

Inside, Slater was feeling so sad he could cry, but he was determined to stay strong for her. 'I know, I know,' he said soothingly.

'My poor old dad,' she said with a sad little smile, tears streaking her cheeks. 'If ever I want to go anywhere after dark, he's my chauffeur. I'm just terrified of going out on my own.'

'Shh,' he said. 'You don't need to say any more. I'm sorry. I didn't mean to upset you.'

'No, it's okay,' she said. 'I'm glad I've told you. At least now you know why I'm like the Ice Queen.'

'Yeah, well, I'm not bothered about that,' he said.

She squeezed his hands. 'Thank you. Can you take me home now? Dad will be worried.'

'Of course.' He started the car and headed for her house. 'How are you managing at work?'

'Honestly? Not very well,' she said. 'I was off for three months, and when I came back I was okay, but the first time I had to work after dark I just freaked out. I've been behind a desk ever since.'

'So you didn't really get into trouble because of me and Norm?'

'Actually I did,' she said, 'but that was just a slap on the wrist, like I said. The reason I'm still behind a desk is my PTSD.'

'You'll be okay, though, right?'

In the darkness of the car he couldn't see her pull a face, but he felt it.

'It's taking a long time to recover,' she said. 'I get plenty of support and ongoing therapy, but in these days of tight budgets and continual cuts, I'm a liability they probably can't afford for much longer. I'm sure my career is going to end quite soon.'

'Oh, no. I'm sorry. I didn't realise. What will you do?'

'I have absolutely no idea,' she said. 'I'm trying not to think about it.'

'Try not to worry about it for now,' he said. 'We can worry about what to do when it happens. *If* it happens.'

'What do you mean "we" can worry about it?'

'I just meant you don't have to be alone. I'm here for you.'

She didn't say anything.

'If you want,' he added hastily. 'Or maybe you don't want me around. That's okay, of course, but what I mean is, I'm here if you want me to be. Just as a friend.'

There was another short silence before she spoke. 'I think I'd like that,' she said.

'You would?'

'If you really think you can put up with me.'

'I said I was here for you, and I meant it,' he said. 'And you can tell your dad he doesn't need to drive you around any more. I'm happy to be your new chauffeur.'

This time, when they reached her house, the atmosphere was a little less tense than it had been before.

'Thank you — for everything,' she said.

'That sounds like you're never going to see me again.'

'Don't be silly,' she said. 'Everybody needs a hero. You're going to be mine. Besides, we're walking the dog on Sunday.'

She leaned across the car and brushed her lips against his cheek. 'Ten o'clock. Don't be late.' Then she popped the door open, slid from her seat, and was gone.

As Slater watched her walk across the pavement, open the gate, and disappear inside, he raised a hand to his cheek.

CHAPTER TWENTY-SEVEN

Slater's mind had been otherwise engaged over the weekend, so when he arrived at work on Monday morning, his mind was rested, and he was optimistic he would be able to think more clearly.

'There's a letter for you,' said Norman.

Slater picked up the letter, sliced the envelope open, and unfolded the three sheets of paper inside. He felt there was something artistic about the graceful, sloping handwriting, but he didn't recognise it. It was the signature that told him.

'It's from Guy Jefferson!' he said, surprised.

'Yeah?' said Norman. 'What does he want?'

Slater began to read out loud.

Dear Mr Slater and Mr Norman, I'm writing this letter because I have learned that what you said about Alexandra being murdered is true. I intend to confront the person responsible, whatever the risk. This letter is by way of an insurance policy should anything happen to me as a result.

'When was this written?' asked Norman.

'There's no date on the letter,' said Slater. He picked up the envelope. 'The postmark on here is dated Friday just gone, posted in Winchester.'

'That would make sense,' said Norman. 'Go on, what else does he say?'

'There's a lot of it. Let me read it through first.'

Norman watched, impatiently, as Slater read the letter from start to finish. After almost five minutes of watching Slater's eyebrows raising ever higher, and hearing numerous quiet, muttered curses, he was handed the letter.

'You'd better read it,' said Slater. 'I don't think I can paraphrase all that.'

Norman took the letter and sat down. 'D'you think we can seriously believe that?' he said eventually, when he had finished reading.

'Why not?' asked Slater.

'An old guy like him and a pretty girl like her?'

'He doesn't say she reciprocated his feelings. Maybe she didn't even know he was besotted with her.'

'He was buying her gifts! I can't believe he didn't want anything in return.'

'He was getting all those innocent photos in return.'

'D'you think he was the photographer?'

'He knew where she was living, and he has all those photographs. What do you think?'

'I find it hard to understand how he can claim to have been in love with her and, at the same time, have been so happy to exploit her.'

'I find a lot of things about this case hard to understand,' said Slater, 'but if he's right, Alexandra wasn't the one who was supposed to die.'

'Yeah, but what if this is just a ploy to send us up a side street?'

'That's a possibility, but, on the other hand, if he's telling the truth, it must mean we guessed right and Betty, or Martha, as they knew her, was the real target.'

'If she was going to dish the dirt on their little operation, that would make perfect sense,' said Norman. 'What do you think happened?'

'At a guess, I think it could have been mistaken identity. Two fair-haired young women, both joggers, who wear red. What if they got someone in to do their dirty work and he chose the wrong one by mistake?'

Norman nodded slowly. 'Yeah, it could have been something like that, but you would think . . . Surely any competent hitman would make sure he got the right victim.'

'Maybe he wasn't competent,' said Slater. 'I mean, making a truck driver reverse over someone isn't my idea of the perfect way to murder someone. Or maybe he just didn't care who died, as long as someone did.'

Norman heaved a big, deeply unhappy, sigh. 'I just don't know what's going on any more. Things like this never used to happen when I first joined the police.'

'This sort of indiscriminate killing certainly seems a lot more commonplace these days, that's for sure, and we still don't know who's behind it all.'

'My money's still on Hanover,' said Norman.

'One thing's for sure, Norm — we now know it's not Guy Jefferson.'

'Yeah, well, I told you he didn't have it in him.'

'Point taken,' conceded Slater. 'But I still don't fancy Hanover for this.'

'That leaves Shrivener then,' said Norman, 'and you know what I think of that!'

'There is another poss—'

Slater was interrupted by a loud knocking on the outside door. He hurried across to open the door. A dark-haired woman was standing outside, looking pensive. 'I'm looking for the detectives,' she said.

'You've found them,' said Slater. 'Come on inside.'

'My name's Clare Hughes. I'm here on behalf of Mr Jefferson,' she said as she stepped inside. 'He said it was important.'

Slater and Norman exchanged a look. 'You know Mr Jefferson?' Slater asked.

'I only met him at the weekend, but he insisted I should come and see you if anything happened to him.'

'What do you mean, if anything happened to him?' asked Norman. 'Where is he?'

'I'm a nurse,' she said. 'I met him when he was brought into Winchester Hospital on Saturday afternoon.'

'Why? What happened?'

'Hit-and-run, apparently. The driver didn't stop.'

'Was he badly hurt?'

'His injuries were quite severe, and he was unconscious when they brought him in. He came to on Saturday evening, and for a while he was okay, but then he called me over and told me I had to give you this message. At the time, I told him he would soon be able to tell you himself, but he insisted I come and see you this morning.'

'That's no problem. We can go and speak to him,' said Norman.

'That probably won't do much good. Mr Jefferson is in a lot of pain and hardly lucid. He's going to be having a lot of surgery to repair the damage, so his condition won't improve for a few days.'

There was a brief silence as they digested this information.

'What was the message?' asked Slater. 'It must have been important if he wanted you to come all the way over here.'

'It's not really a message, just a name. Black Stock.'

Slater looked at Norman, who shrugged. 'Black Stock? Are you sure that was what he said?'

'He was really woozy from the painkillers, so I could have got the second word wrong, but the first word was definitely "black" and the second word definitely ended with a "k". Does it mean anything to you?'

Slater shook his head. 'Right now, I have no idea what it means, but it must be important.'

There was an awkward moment as they all looked at each other, wondering what was going to happen next.

'Well, Clare, thank you for delivering the message,' said Slater finally. 'It's really good of you to come all the way over here.'

'It's fine, I have a couple of days off, and my sister lives not far from here. I often see her on Mondays so it's not really out of my way, and I just felt so sorry for that poor man. Do you think they'll catch whoever ran him down?'

'Let's hope so,' said Norman. 'No one deserves that.'

* * *

'What the hell is Black Stock?' asked Norman.

'I'm just doing a search,' said Slater. He was tapping away at Norman's laptop, but then he sat back and cursed. 'Bugger! According to this it's an investment bank.'

'Does that mean we're looking for big money behind this?'

'This is a worldwide organisation,' said Slater, studying the small screen. 'If this is where it starts we'll never get to the bottom of it. Even if we *had* a name to chase, we don't have the resources.'

'Hang on a minute,' said Norman. 'All we want to do is find Betty. Isn't that what we agreed? After that, we hand it on to the police. They can handle the pornography investigation.'

'You're right. I'm getting carried away,' said Slater. 'But how does Black Stock help us?'

'Two things,' said Norman. 'One — don't forget it could be another red herring. Two — we're not even sure he said Black Stock. The nurse said it was definitely "black" and the second word ended with a "k" sound. What if it was "Black Merc"?'

Slater nodded and grinned at Norman. 'Now that's a possibility, isn't it?' he said. 'Good thinking, Norm.'

'What if Patrick is here to keep an eye on everyone, but he discovered Jefferson had found out what they had done to Alexandra? Maybe Jefferson had even confronted him about it, and threatened to spill the beans?'

'They couldn't let that happen,' continued Slater, 'so Jefferson had to be stopped. And we know they're not averse to the idea of using a vehicle as a weapon, right?'

'That's right. Maybe Patrick was the guy who organised Alexandra's death, too?'

'It all fits, doesn't it?'

'Only if "Black Merc" is really what Jefferson meant.'

'Okay, so, why don't we go and ask him?' suggested Slater. Norman made to speak, but Slater beat him to it. 'Yeah, I know what the nurse said, but maybe we'll get lucky and he'll be lucid for a couple of minutes.'

'I guess it won't hurt to try,' said Norman. 'And we've got to start somewhere.'

'We might as well go then. Here, catch.'

Norman instinctively caught the thing Slater had tossed in his direction, then grinned when he realised what it was. 'You're going to let me drive your car?' he said, jingling the keys.

Slater grinned back at him. 'My treat,' he said. 'Maybe if you're in a decent car you'll drive at a decent speed.'

* * *

Fifteen minutes later, they were heading towards the hospital at Winchester when Slater's phone began to ring.

'Hi, Stella, I didn't expect to hear from you this morning. Is everything okay?'

'When you were telling me about your case the other night, did you mention someone called Guy Jefferson?'

'Yeah, that's right.'

'Well, this might be a coincidence, but apparently someone by the very same name was rushed to A&E on Saturday.'

'Yeah, that's our man.'

'Oh. You already know? I thought I had some news for you.'

'We heard this morning. Apparently he was knocked down in a hit-and-run. We're just going over to see him.'

'You haven't heard the latest then?'

'What d'you mean "the latest"?'

'Early this morning, Guy Jefferson died because of his injuries. The "hit-and-run" has now become a murder case.'

'Oh, crap! You have to be kidding me.'

'It's not the sort of thing I joke about, Dave.'

'Sorry, of course it's not. I didn't mean it like that. I just can't believe he's dead.'

'This is connected to your case, isn't it?' she asked. 'If this is a second murder—'

'We haven't proved Alexandra was murdered, and we have no idea the person responsible for Jefferson's death has anything to do with our case.'

'But you have to admit it's a bit of a coincidence, isn't it? You really should hand it over to us, you know.'

'I told you we don't have enough evidence. We will hand it over when we find Betty Glover. She's the one who will be able to point you in the right direction and provide you with the proof you need to make a case.'

'I hope you know what you're doing.'

'So do I, Stella, so do I.'

'What's going on?' asked Norman when Slater finished his call. 'Who died?'

'Guy Jefferson.'

'What?'

'His injuries must have been even more severe than they thought. He died early this morning.'

'Crap!'

'Yeah, that's what I said.'

'This calls for a change of plan, then.'

Slater sighed. 'We can't speak to a dead man, that's for sure. It looks as if the odds are turning against us.'

'Yeah, well, maybe,' said Norman, 'but we're in Winchester now, so, while we're here, why don't we see if we can grab a few minutes with Sneaky Sam? Maybe he can tell us where his car and driver were over the weekend? We might even get to check the car for dents.'

'Now, you're talking, partner. Let's go!'

They drove in silence for a minute or two before Norman spoke. 'Can I ask a question?'

'Sure.'

'Am I right in thinking you seem to be getting pretty close to Stella Robbins? I mean you did spend half the weekend with her, right?'

'We had dinner on Friday, and we took her dog for a walk on Sunday. That's not exactly half the weekend.'

'Okay, but you are seeing her, like dating, right?'

'Well, yeah, I suppose you could say that.'

'It's not like you to be so reticent about your girlfriends.'

'I'm not sure I would call her my girlfriend.'

'You're not using her, are you? That could cost her her job. We can always use Vinnie for—'

'Relax, Norm. I'm not using her. I have actually told her to stop helping us, but she won't listen.'

'So what *is* going on?'

'We're just friends, if you see what I mean.'

'I'm not sure I do see what you mean.'

'We go out, we have fun, then, at the end of the evening, I take her home. Like friends.'

'Oh. Really? That's not like you.'

Slater turned and stared at Norman.

'Come on now, don't take offence,' said Norman. 'It's just that normally you tell me about your girlfriends, but Stella seems to be top secret.'

Slater turned to face the front again. 'Stella's different. She's not like that.'

'Okay, fair enough. I didn't mean to pry. I just want to know if you're okay, that's all.'

'I am fine, Norm, it's just a bit of a complicated situation. I promised Stella I wouldn't tell anyone, not even you.'

'That's okay. I understand.' There was a brief silence, then Norman spoke again. 'Exactly how much does she know about this case?'

'A bit.'

'How big a bit?'

'Er, well, quite a bit.'

'They're not going to muscle in and take this over, are they?'

'If you really want to know, Stella is worried that we're getting into something we won't be able to handle.'

'You mean she *does* want to take it over.'

'No, she doesn't, and anyway she can't because she's desk-bound.'

'I have a feeling there's a "but" in there somewhere,' said Norman.

'Well, Stella's worried we're going to get on the wrong side of some seriously bad people and we could get hurt. However, she has agreed to keep quiet on the proviso we get out of the way and let them take over when we find Betty, or if we find we're in too deep. Is that okay?'

Norman didn't say anything, so Slater decided to qualify what he had said. 'We did agree the other day that we would find Betty, and then hand it on to the police, right?'

'Yeah, we did.'

'So this is more or less what we were going to do. I just had to agree to keep her in the loop and yell for help if we need it.'

Norman's face broke into a broad grin. 'So she cares about you then,' he said. 'She must really like you! Do you like her as much?'

'Knock it off, Norm. You know I like her. It's just, like I said, a bit difficult.'

Norman cast a sly glance at Slater, who felt his face flush.

* * *

They had more or less expected to be turned away by Shrivener, or at least by his secretary, Angela, but that was not the case.

'Mr Shrivener is with a client right now and can't be disturbed,' purred Angela, 'but he shouldn't be much longer. If you would like to wait I'm sure he will be happy to spare you a few minutes before his next appointment.'

She pointed to a seating area. 'If you'd like to take a seat, I'll bring you some coffee while you wait.'

'D'you think he's playing for time?' Norman asked Slater as they sat down.

'I think she would have told us he wasn't here if that was the case. Besides, he knows we will only keep coming back. It's more likely he was expecting us to come and he's got a story ready in case we did.'

'Yeah, you're right. He's a brief, of course he's going to be prepared.'

Just ten minutes after Angela delivered their coffee, she was back again. 'Mr Shrivener is very busy this morning, but he can spare you ten minutes if you come now,' she told them.

They jumped to their feet and followed her to Shrivener's office. She knocked on the door and showed them in. A beaming Shrivener was waiting for them.

'This is an unexpected pleasure,' he said as they entered the room. 'Have you had second thoughts about my offer of work?'

'Work?' said Slater, who had forgotten about Shrivener's suggestion they should do some investigative work for him.

'No, actually that's not why we're here,' said Norman.

'Oh, I see. So, what do you want?'

'Can you tell us where your car was over the weekend?' asked Norman.

Shrivener frowned. 'My car? Why do you want to know about my car?'

'Guy Jefferson was injured in a hit-and-run on Saturday.'

Shrivener's eyes widened, and his mouth dropped open. 'Good God, no,' he said.

'He died from his injuries,' said Norman.

'We believe the car that hit him could have been a black Mercedes,' added Slater.

Shrivener looked blankly from Slater to Norman. It took a few seconds for him to speak. 'You mean you think I ran him down?'

'We have to consider the possibility.'

'There must be dozens of black Mercedes in this area. Are you accusing all the other owners too? Why would I do such a thing?'

'Okay, so maybe it wasn't you driving,' said Norman. 'Maybe it was that driver of yours.'

'Driver? I don't have a driver. I much prefer to drive myself.'

'Bullshit,' said Norman. 'What about the gorilla who drove you to our office?'

Shrivener let out a small snort of laughter. 'Patrick? He doesn't work for me. He's Vernon Tisdale's driver.'

'How come he was driving you that day?'

'When Vernon Tisdale asked me to take out the injunction against you, he insisted it had to be delivered that very same day. My car was being serviced, so Tisdale sent his car with his driver.'

'You mean he didn't trust you? But you're his lawyer!'

'It wasn't a case of trust. My car was being serviced, and the courtesy car they gave me was a joke. I wasn't happy driving it. Vernon Tisdale wanted a job done in a hurry, so he offered his car and driver.'

'You expect us to believe that?'

'No. I expect you to do your job and check my car was being serviced and that I had been given a poor substitute as a courtesy car. Then I will expect you to believe me.'

'Come on, Shrivener, we know you're connected to Jefferson.'

'Connected? I took out an injunction — against you — on his behalf. Tisdale told him to come to me. I had never set eyes on him before that.'

'We know he's part of this thing you have going with Jools Hanover.'

Shrivener shook his head. 'Mr Hanover told me about your accusations. Now, I know you have no proof to back up that accusation, and if you persist with it I will be bringing a defamation case against you, at the very least. You have no proof, have you?'

'It's there somewhere,' said Norman. 'We haven't found it yet, but we will. We've already linked you with Hanover, Tisdale and Jefferson.'

'It wouldn't be difficult to link me to Vernon Tisdale; I've been his lawyer for over thirty years. Even now he's retired he still uses my services from time to time, such as when he took the injunction out against you two. It was Vernon Tisdale who introduced me to Jools Hanover. At that time, Tisdale was a big player, and Hanover was an up-and-coming businessman.'

'How did they get together?' asked Slater.

'Among his many businesses, Tisdale had an advertising agency. Hanover needed marketing advice, brochures, promotional films, etc. Then, when Hanover needed a lawyer, he turned to Tisdale for a recommendation. The rest, as they say, is history.'

'Hanover provides you with a car, is that right?' asked Slater.

'I get a generous discount in return for being available at the drop of a hat.'

'Does he also supply a car to Vernon Tisdale?'

'I believe he does, but you'll have to confirm that with him.'

'Can we see your car?' asked Norman.

For a split second, it seemed Shrivener was going to refuse, but then he relented. 'Follow me, but make it quick,' he said, 'I have another appointment waiting.'

He pointed to a door and led them through to the back of the building where a gleaming black Mercedes was parked. Slater and Norman quickly walked around the car, but there was no damage to be seen anywhere.

'Are you satisfied now?' asked Shrivener.

'Er, yes, that all seems to be in order,' said Norman.

'Of course it is,' said Shrivener. 'I don't spend my weekends running people down. I am also not involved in anything illegal, nor is Jools Hanover. Now I suggest you leave, and I reiterate my warning — any more accusations against Mr Hanover will be met with a response you will wish you hadn't initiated.'

* * *

'That didn't go quite the way I was hoping,' said Norman when they got back in the car.

'D'you still think he's up to his neck in this?' asked Slater.

'He's got to be, don't you think?'

'I'm not so sure now. He seemed genuinely surprised when we told him Jefferson had been run down. And his car certainly hasn't been used to kill anyone.'

'I need a bit more convincing than that.'

'What about Patrick? We thought he was Shrivener's heavy, but it looks like we got that wrong. I'm now wondering what else we might have got wrong.'

'Has it occurred to you that Shrivener could be playing games with us?'

'Yes, it has,' said Slater, 'but I think he does that to create a shield for his clients whatever they may, or may not, have done. The cloudier he makes it, the harder it is for us to see what's really going on. I don't think it's specific to our case.'

'I thought you said they were all suspects?'

'Well, maybe I got that wrong too! Either way, I'm certainly not going to accuse him or Hanover of anything without proof. I have no desire to be crucified in court.'

Norman started the car. 'Yeah, I'm with you on that one. But where does that leave us?'

'I think we need to pay Vernon Tisdale another visit. I know you think he's a harmless little old man, but we're running out of suspects, and don't forget, Alexandra was living in his basement. In his letter, Guy Jefferson says he was paying the rent, but there was no mention of a letting agent. Maybe he was paying it directly to Tisdale.'

Norman put the car into gear and pulled away. 'I suppose we have nowhere else to go right now,' he said, 'but I can't believe that old guy is the brains behind all this.'

'Why not?' asked Slater. 'He was a very successful businessman, so he must have a good brain.'

'He might have had a good brain back then,' argued Norman, 'but he's seventy-four now, and we all know people aren't as sharp when they get older.'

'I don't subscribe to this idea people become senile the moment they retire. I think old Vernon is as sharp as he's ever been, and the fact he fools people into thinking otherwise is proof of that.'

Norman gave Slater a sharp, sideways look. 'Oh,' he said, bristling, 'so you think the old guy is making a fool of me?'

'Actually, Norm, I think he's probably making a fool of all of us.'

They continued on in gloomy silence until Slater's mobile phone began to ring. It was Stella. 'Where are you?' she asked.

'After running all around Winchester on what seems to be a wild goose chase, we're back in Tinton, hoping to speak to Vernon Tisdale.'

'Right. Well, I had nothing to do this morning, so after I heard about Guy Jefferson's death, I decided to do a bit of digging into those other names you mentioned.'

'You already knew Hanover and Shrivener were connected,' said Slater, 'and I can tell you they both insist you've got it wrong about them. Hanover admits he sails close to the line and exploits what he calls "grey areas", but he assures us he's not stupid enough to risk everything he has when he doesn't need to.'

'It's funny you should say that. The DCI who's been pursuing Hanover has just been suspended. Apparently he's been running some sort of vendetta.'

'Are you telling me Hanover's clean?'

'I'm telling you we don't have a shred of evidence to suggest he isn't, and we've been investigating him for years. I think that speaks for itself, don't you?'

'What about Shrivener?'

'He's a thorn in our sides, but that's because he's very good at what he does. Again, we've no proof of anything untoward.'

'Jesus! You mean we've been barking up the wrong tree all this time?'

Norman was only getting Slater's side of the conversation, but now he wanted to hear all of it. 'What's going on?' he asked. 'Why are we barking up the wrong tree?'

'Apparently Hanover and Shrivener are squeaky clean. Some idiot had it in for them.'

'Oh, crap! You mean you were right about them?'

'Put me on loudspeaker,' said Stella in Slater's ear. 'Norm needs to hear this too.'

Slater adjusted his phone. 'Norman needs to hear what?' he asked.

'Can you hear me, Norm?' she asked.

'Hi, Stella, yeah I hear you.'

'If you're heading over to Vernon Tisdale, you might want to hear what I've discovered about him — and Guy Jefferson — before you get there.'

'We're pretty sure they know each other,' said Slater.

'There's bit more to it than that. Did you know Tisdale was quite a big fish in marketing? He owned a very successful company and made a lot of money.'

'We knew he had been in business, but we never got around to checking him out in any depth. Shrivener told us he had a marketing company,' said Norman.

'Guy Jefferson also had his own business. He had a modelling agency.'

'Yeah, but it never amounted to anything special, did it?' said Slater. 'From what we could see, he never made a great deal of money. We thought he must have been doing something on the side, and we reckoned it had something to do with pornography.'

'You're probably not far off the mark,' said Stella. 'Back in the early eighties, Jefferson was in danger of going bust, but he was saved from bankruptcy by the intervention of another business owner, who owned a marketing company.'

'You mean Tisdale?' asked Norman.

'Exactly,' said Stella. 'Apparently Tisdale needed a photographer and an artist. He got two for the price of one when he saved Jefferson. Tisdale became the major shareholder, and with his direction, Jefferson's company turned the corner. Despite that, Jefferson's company never seemed to make much profit.'

'And yet he managed to make enough to buy that bloody great house and build an art studio that must have cost a fortune,' said Slater.

'I think that's because he was working for Tisdale on the side,' Stella said. 'His own company was just a front. And there aren't that many things he could be doing on the side that would generate that sort of money, are there?'

'D'you think Tisdale was his partner in crime?' asked Norman.

'Maybe that was why he saved Jefferson's company,' said Slater.

'I wonder whose idea it was.'

'Maybe Tisdale trapped him into it.'

'Before you two begin speculating,' said Stella, 'you might like to know that Tisdale still has a considerable income.'

'Really?' said Norman. 'That surprises me, because he lives like a pauper.'

'Don't be fooled by appearances. He owns a large amount of property and has money invested in several companies.'

'I said he wasn't as dumb as he makes out,' observed Slater.

'He even owns an old, disused airfield not far from Winchester,' added Stella.

'A disused airfield. Why did he buy that?'

'The original plan was to build a housing estate, but planning has been refused again and again because of environmental concerns.'

'What's this place called?

'Blackrock.'

Norman hit the brakes and pulled to a halt at the side of the road.

'Hang on, Stella, can you say that name again?' asked Slater.

'Tisdale owns a disused airfield called Blackrock. It was an RAF base way back when, but it's not been used for years.'

Slater and Norman were staring at each other now.

'So it wasn't Black Stock *or* Black Merc,' said Slater. 'It was Blackrock.'

'Sorry? What's that?' said Stella.

'It's a long story,' said Slater, 'but before he died, Jefferson gave a message to his nurse and told her to tell us if anything happened to him. She said she thought he had said Black Stock, but now we think it was probably Blackrock.'

'What's the significance?' asked Stella.

'Jefferson thought Betty Glover was the real target, but Alexandra was murdered in a case of mistaken identity. He also thought Betty was being held prisoner somewhere, and we believe he was trying to tell us she was being held at Blackrock Airfield.'

'There must be plenty of old buildings where you could hide someone there,' said Stella. 'It was a fully working base in the Second World War and was operational until the early eighties.'

While they were talking, Norman had put the car into gear and was on the move again. 'Where exactly is this place?' he asked. Then, addressing Stella, 'Is there anything else we should know?'

'That's all I've got so far. I just wanted to keep you up to date. I can keep on looking if you want.'

'We appreciate what you're doing, Stella,' said Norman, 'but you really want to be careful.'

'Don't worry, Norm, I seem to be invisible at the moment. I don't think anyone would notice if I walked out with half the computer system.'

'Have you ever heard of a guy called Patrick?' asked Slater.

'Who's he?'

'He drives Tisdale around and likes to play the hard man. Big guy, works out a lot. Looks as if he's done time in prison.'

'I'll see what I can find.'

'Okay, but, like Norm says, be careful.'

'You too. I'll call you later.'

* * *

Like many World War II airfields, Blackrock was surrounded on all sides by farmland, and because of the passage of time, most of it was also hidden behind trees and assorted undergrowth.

'In about two hundred yards there should be a road leading off to the left,' said Slater, studying a map on his phone.

'This car has perfectly good satnav, which is already telling me where to go,' said Norman. 'Why do you need to pull up a map on that tiny screen as well?'

'Because this map shows things the satnav doesn't. For instance, the satnav shows a road on the left. In reality it's just a track that probably hasn't been used in years, so we're not going to be cruising along there at seventy miles an hour.'

'I thought this was an off-road vehicle.'

'That doesn't mean we have to take chances and risk breaking it.'

'I thought I was supposed to be driving fast. Isn't that what you wanted?'

'Just take it steady until we see what we're up against,' said Slater.

Norman slowed as they turned on to the track. Slater had been correct in his assessment. Huge potholes attested to the fact that this was a road that no longer served the general public, and they bumped from side to side as they slowly progressed, battering through overhanging branches, towards their destination.

'Jeez, it looks like this road hasn't been used in decades,' said Norman.

'Not quite,' said Slater. 'Look, there are tracks visible every now and then, and look at those broken branches. Someone's been coming down here recently.'

'Well spotted, Hawkeye,' said Norman. 'I wonder what we're going to find down here.'

After about a hundred yards, they found a clearing containing two or three tatty old wooden buildings. Norman stopped the car and they studied the scene. 'These old huts look about the right vintage,' said Norman.

'That one,' said Slater, pointing at the largest of the buildings. 'Look at the path leading up to the door.'

'Yeah, you're right. Someone's using that place.'

He eased the car past the building where the narrow track widened, pulled off the track to the left, swung the car round facing the way they had come, and switched off the engine.

'Come on, let's take a look,' said Slater, and slipped quietly from the car.

* * *

The hut was about thirty feet wide and appeared to reach back at least three times as far. 'What do you think this is, a concert hall?' asked Norman quietly as they approached.

'Something like that, I guess,' whispered Slater.

There was a grimy window either side of the double-door entrance, and Slater peered cautiously in through the nearest. Norman raised his eyebrows questioningly. Slater shook his head in response. The window was too dirty to allow him to see much, and it was pretty dark in there.

'We're going to have to go inside,' he whispered as he moved across to the door and listened, but he couldn't hear a thing from inside. Carefully, he took a hold of the door handle, then, startled, he looked at Norman and pointed at his ears. He wasn't sure, but he thought maybe he could hear a car coming in the distance.

'There's no time to hide now,' hissed Norman. 'Come on, let's do it!'

Slater took a hold of the door handle and put his shoulder to it. He expected resistance and a fair amount of creaking and squeaking, but it opened easily and quietly. Without a second thought, they slipped silently inside, and the door swung closed behind them.

'Someone's greased the door's hinges,' observed Norman.

They were in a gloomy, long-disused hall. Dust-covered chairs and a tatty-looking stage with torn curtains at the far end bore testament to its former use as a concert hall. A dust-covered broom leaned incongruously against the wall just inside the door. It obviously hadn't been used in decades.

The acoustics were like those of an echo chamber, and every move was amplified several times over, which made it quite easy for them to become aware of a faint tapping sound. They exchanged quizzical looks. It was easy enough to hear now, but not quite so simple to figure out where it was coming from.

Slater pointed to some tables piled against a wall over to their right. Norman followed the direction and listened hard. As he nodded his agreement to Slater, they both became aware the car Norman had heard in the distance was now much closer. There was no time to lose.

As they crept cautiously towards the pile of tables, the tapping noise became louder until, finally, they could see the cause was a young woman, hiding behind the tables and shaking with fear. She huddled against the wall, her knees drawn up before her in self-defence. As they came into view she stared at them, her blackened eyes wide with fear. A wide piece of tape covered her mouth but couldn't hide even more bruises to her face. Her hands were tied behind her back.

'Jesus,' said Norman. 'What the hell's been going on here?'

Slater stepped forward and she drew back, as if she could sink into the wall and be hidden from view.

'It's okay,' he said to the terrified woman as he squatted down next to her. 'We're not going to hurt you, we're here to help.'

She flinched and let out a little squeal of pain as he gently removed the tape from her face.

'Are you Betty Glover?'

She nodded frantically. 'Who are you? Why are you here?'

'We don't have time to explain,' he said. 'We'll do that when we get you out of here.'

'How do I know I can trust you?'

'Would you prefer to wait for whoever tied you up to come back?'

She shook her head.

'Okay. Then let's try to get you out of here.'

As Slater began speaking to Betty, Norman felt sure he heard something outside. He hurried back to the entrance, took a quick peep through one of the windows, then jumped back. Hastily, he jammed the dusty broom through the door handles and dragged a table against the door. He took another peep through the window then scuttled back to Slater and Betty.

'There's a car outside,' he hissed. 'Someone's getting out. They must be heading this way.'

'Bugger,' muttered Slater, looking around for an escape route. 'Over there,' he said, pointing to a door to the left of the stage. 'Through that door at the back, quick.'

They ran down the hall and through the door, their footsteps echoing around the empty hall like thunder. Betty's hands were still tied behind her back, so Norman took her arm to steady her as they ran, Slater bringing up the rear.

As they entered the room, Slater tried to close the door, but it wouldn't budge.

'The sodding door's stuck,' he hissed. 'It's going to be obvious where we've gone.'

'That's not the only problem,' said Norman. 'Look, there's no way out.'

Slater scanned the room. Norman was right; there was no other door, just an old sash window to their left, and it looked as if it had been painted shut. That meant it probably wouldn't open easily, so it was unlikely there would be time to get it open and escape without making a lot of noise. He pointed to the floor just inside the door, pushing Norman and Betty into place.

'Get down there and keep the noise down.'

Norman put Betty furthest from the door and then lowered himself to the floor next to her.

'You'd better untie her hands,' whispered Slater as he joined them, placing himself closest to the doorway.

Norman untied her hands and they huddled together silently, but then there was a sound that made them all hold their breath. Back in the main hall someone was trying to open the door. There were two or three loud crashes, then the sound of splintering wood told its own story.

They heard the table slide across the floor as the door was forced open, and then there was no sound for a few seconds until a loud creak from a loose floorboard suggested someone was on the move. Cautiously, Slater peered around the corner, then rapidly jerked back and stared up at the ceiling.

'Oh, crap, crap, crap!' he muttered.

'What is it?' whispered Norman.

'It's Patrick, and he's got a bloody gun. You know how much I hate guns.'

'What sort of gun?'

'I don't know. It didn't have a bloody label.' Slater was wide-eyed, his breathing short and sharp.

'Is it a pistol or a rifle?'

'Some sort of handgun.'

'That's better than a sawn-off shotgun,' said Norman.

'Is it? As far as I'm concerned it can still kill. I hate guns. You know I hate guns.'

'You're not alone. We all hate guns,' said Norman patiently. 'But you need to get a grip. This is no time to panic. If we're going to get out of here we need level heads, right?'

Slater nodded his head and tried to slow his breathing. 'You're right. I'm sorry. It's just that—'

'You hate guns,' said Norman sarcastically. 'Yeah. I think we all got the message.' He immediately felt guilty. Slater's fear was genuine, and sarcasm wasn't going to help.

It would be much better to try and calm his colleague before he really lost it.

'I'm sorry,' he said soothingly. 'It's okay. I understand where you're coming from. You don't need to explain.'

'How many of them are there?' asked Slater.

'Just the one heading for the door, and the driver sitting in the car.'

'Let's hope he stayed there,' said Slater. 'We've got no chance against two guns.'

'Let's be positive about this and assume the other guy did stay in the car,' said Norman. He pointed to the window. 'That's our way out, but we're going to have to stop this guy long enough to allow us to break it and climb out.'

'How are we going to do that?'

'I'm guessing he won't want to use the gun if he doesn't have to. How about I make sure he sees me when he comes in here, and you jump him from behind?'

Slater looked around. He would have to get across to the other side of the doorway if Norman's plan was going to work.

'How do I get over there? He'll see me if I cross the open doorway.'

'There are two other rooms before he gets to this one,' said Norman, sounding far calmer than he felt. 'I reckon he will check those out on the way through. You'll have to time it so you get across when he's looking in one of those other rooms.'

Slater looked at Norman as if he were crazy.

'What?' asked Norman. 'Have you got a better idea?'

Slater swore quietly. No, of course he hadn't. 'Okay. I'll do it.'

'If you can catch him by surprise, maybe between us we can get the better of him and grab the gun.'

Slater raised his eyebrows. '*Maybe*?' he said. 'We need to do a bit better than *maybe*. We have just the one chance at this, and if we don't do it right my guess is he'll shoot us both, and I don't think *maybe* will be a consideration.'

He took another careful peek into the hall. The man with the gun was making his way stealthily across to one of the side rooms. Slater didn't say anything to Norman, but he thought the way the guy was holding the gun, he was more than ready to use it.

Holding his breath, Slater watched as the man reached for the door handle, swung the door open, and swooped inside, gun at the ready. As he did, Slater scuttled quietly across the doorway. It would have been better if he could have hidden behind the door, but there was no room with it stuck almost fully open. He just hoped Norman could get the guy's attention quick enough that he could nail him before he was spotted.

Now he was in place, Slater thought about the possible consequences if he didn't put the guy out of action. He decided the odds would improve dramatically in his favour if he had a weapon. He needed something to hit the guy that would slow him down long enough to give them time to escape. Of course, what he really needed was something heavy enough to knock the guy out. Maybe there was something behind the door.

Halfway down the hall, the gunman was now entering the second room off the main hall. There was nothing in there but some old tables and chairs, but he had a quick poke around behind the chairs to make sure.

As he emerged from the room, he scanned the hall to make sure nothing had changed and then focused his attention on the open door at the end of the hall.

* * *

Slater reached carefully behind the door and took hold of the iron bar he had spotted there. It was a couple of feet long and a couple of inches in diameter. As he lifted it, he could feel its weight. Just right, he thought. Then he had another thought; if he hit the guy on the head, he could kill him. That wouldn't be easy to explain away, whatever the circumstances. Maybe he should hit the guy across the shoulders. That should be enough to drop him to the floor, right?

On the other side of the doorway, Norman watched as Slater gave him a thumbs-up. He couldn't see what Slater had found behind the door, but from the signal he understood it was some sort of weapon. That was good. It meant they had a chance to overpower the guy and get his gun. He returned the signal, then peered carefully around the doorframe into the hall.

To his horror, Patrick had somehow managed to cover almost the entire distance from the second room and was now just a few feet away. For the briefest moment their eyes met, and the gun was raised, but then Norman, eyes wide as saucers, ducked back out of sight. He stared across at Slater, who could clearly see the terror in Norman's eyes and knew the guy must be about to come into the room.

Patrick had cursed when he saw the head duck back before he had time to fire, but now he knew exactly where his adversary was, he threw caution to the wind and rushed into the room.

Norman was standing a few feet back, the woman hidden behind him. The gunman seemed to not want to risk hitting her; she was clearly no use to them dead. He pointed the gun at Norman, indicating with the barrel that the detective should step aside.

'Over my dead body,' said Norman defiantly.

'Don't tempt me, Mister Detective. Now, step away from the woma—'

There was a dull thud as the iron bar hit him across the shoulders, followed by a clonk as it bounced up off his shoulders and met the back of his head. His legs buckled and he fell into a crumpled heap, the pistol falling uselessly to the floor.

Slater and Norman stared down at the stricken gunman. 'You hit him across the head with an iron bar?' asked Norman. 'Jeez, I hope you haven't killed him.'

'I didn't mean to hit his head,' said Slater. 'Anyway, a little gratitude wouldn't go amiss.'

Norman looked at Slater. 'Gratitude?' he said indignantly. 'It took you so long to hit him I thought you were waiting for him to pull the trigger first.' He looked down at the body again. 'I don't know how we're going to explain it if he's dead.'

Slater dropped the iron bar, knelt down, and felt for a pulse. 'He's not dead. He's got a good pulse. He'll be fine. Now, we need to get out of here before his mate comes looking for him.'

He stuffed the gun into his pocket, ran across to the window, undid the catch, and heaved upwards, but as he had expected, the window didn't budge.

'Damnit!' he grunted. 'I might have known the bloody thing would be stuck. I'll have to smash it.'

He grabbed a nearby chair and heaved it through the window. With a loud crash, the glass shattered, sending splinters everywhere. He ran back for the iron bar and used it to clean the glass from the edges of the window.

'You go first, Norm.'

'Me? Why do I get to go first?'

'Because you're not as fit as me, and I can give you a leg-up. Then I can help Betty through and you'll be there to catch her.'

He looked at Betty, who hadn't said a word since they'd untied her. Now she nodded enthusiastically.

'C'mon, Norm,' he urged. 'Let's go before he wakes up.'

'I hope you're right about him not being dead.'

'Trust me, he's fine. He'll have a headache, but he's not dead. Maybe you would be happier if I had let him shoot you.'

'If you had taken any longer he probably would have.'

'I can't believe you're so bloody ungrateful. Next time I'll be the damned decoy and you can be the hero.'

'Hero? There's nothing heroic about bashing someone over the head from behind. Now, putting yourself in the firing line, that's heroic.'

'You two can keep on bickering if you want, but I'm going to get out of here,' said Betty.

She gathered what appeared to be a pair of old curtains and threw them across the windowsill. 'To protect us from cuts,' she said, matter-of-factly, as the two detectives looked at her open-mouthed.

'Have I got it wrong?' she asked. 'I thought you said you'd come to rescue me, and we're going to escape through the window.'

'Er, yeah, that's right, we have, and we are,' said Norman, his face reddening.

'She's right,' said Slater. 'C'mon, let's get you through the window.'

Norman was more agile than Slater had realised and was through the window and dropping down the other side in a matter of seconds. Slater leaned out to check he was okay then helped Betty on her way. Once she was gone, he eased himself through and jumped down to join them.

'Where do we go now?' asked Norman.

'We need to get around the front to the car,' said Slater.

'My guess is whoever is still in the car will go looking for his friend,' said Betty. 'When he goes inside we could make a dash to the car.'

Once again, the two detectives were left open-mouthed.

'I think you should let us worry about how we're going to escape,' said Norman.

'Fine,' she said. 'So how are we going to do that?'

'Let me see now,' said Norman thoughtfully. 'How about we make our way up to the front of the building, wait for the other guy to go inside, then make a dash for it?'

* * *

It seemed to take an age to make their way through the undergrowth that had colonised the area to the side of the old hut, but eventually they reached the end of the building and could see the track before them. They could see their car, about fifty yards away to their right.

Slater peered cautiously around the corner of the building. Opposite the entrance to the hall he could see the black Mercedes blocking their exit. The doors were wide open but there was no sign of Patrick or the driver. Slater ducked back and turned to Norman and Betty.

'I think they both must be inside the building,' he whispered.

'Let's not hang around then,' said Norman. He turned to Betty. 'Are you ready?'

She nodded.

'Right,' said Slater. 'On the count of three. Norm, you lead, then Betty. I'll bring up the rear. Okay? One. Two. Three.'

They raced towards their car, and had almost reached it when they heard a shout from behind. Slater slowed down to look over his shoulder. The driver had just emerged from the building, a dazed, rather wobbly Patrick struggling to keep up with him. 'They're coming. Hurry,' urged Slater, galloping after Norman and Betty.

To Slater's dismay, he realised slowing down to look back had enabled Norman to reach the driver's door before him, and he was already inside. He also had to cover the extra ground to reach the passenger side as Norman started the car.

'We've done this wrong,' he said, as he jumped into the car. 'We've got no chance with you driving. Even a snail could overtake us. And, with them blocking the lane, we're facing the wrong way!'

Norman's face broke into a broad grin. 'Is that so?'

'You know you can't drive fast.'

'I know you're always complaining that I *don't* drive fast,' said Norman, slipping the car into reverse, 'but that's not quite the same thing, is it?'

He slammed his foot on the throttle and the car shot back. One-handed, he spun the wheel and stamped hard on the footbrake as he put the clutch in. As the car spun around, he slipped it into second gear and let the clutch out again, and they roared off down the track. It was all done in one smooth movement.

'Wow!' said Betty. 'How cool was that?'

Slack-jawed, Slater looked across at Norman, whose grin was now even wider. 'What was that?'

'That, my friend,' said Norman, 'was a J-turn, also popularised as the "Rockford Turn" thanks to the 1970s TV series.'

Slater looked hard at Norman. He couldn't quite believe what had just happened and wondered if perhaps he was dreaming.

'Crap,' said Norman, glancing in the mirror. 'They're right behind us. Okay, we have a choice coming up. D'you think we need to go left or right out of here?'

Slater looked to the front. They were accelerating hard now, rapidly approaching a junction in the track where they would have to make a sharp left or right, but Norman didn't seem to be slowing down, which was more than could be said for Slater's heartrate.

'Slow down,' said Slater.

'Come on,' said Norman. 'Do I go left or right?'

'I vote left,' said Betty, from the back seat.

'Jesus, Norm, slow down!' yelled Slater.

'Who me?' said Norman, grinning broadly. He executed a perfect handbrake turn as they reached the junction and roared off to the left. 'But I always drive slowly, remember? Isn't that what you keep telling me.'

They bounced over the grass verge at the side of the track, nearly throwing Slater out of his seat, and then they were back on an even keel and tearing off down a bumpy, tree-lined road. The sharp turn had gained them a little ground, but their pursuers weren't giving up any time soon.

'You maniac. You nearly bloody killed us!' said Slater. 'I could have been thrown out of the window.'

'Actually, I didn't nearly kill anyone,' said Norman, calmly. 'I've done a pursuit course. I know exactly what I'm doing. The only reason you nearly went out of the window was because you have the window open, and you don't have your seat belt on. I think you'll find that's your fault, not mine.'

'Pursuit course?' echoed Slater. 'When was this?'

'Years ago.'

'How many years ago?'

'More than I care to recall, but it's like riding a bike — once you get back in the saddle it all comes back.'

'But you never said.'

'You never asked.'

'But you always drive so slowly.'

'That's because I can't be arsed with all this rushing around and tailgating crap you have to put up with these days. And you never know when there's going to be a cop jumping out with a speed camera waiting to catch you out.'

'You really feel like that?'

'The truth is, if I could avoid it, I wouldn't drive at all. And, anyway, you seem to like driving, so the usual arrangement suits us both.'

They were hurtling along a bumpy, pot-holed road. The dense trees covering either side made it impossible to see anything except straight ahead.

'I hate to interrupt your conversation,' said Betty, 'but does anyone know where we're going?'

'I thought you were the one who knew your way around here,' said Norman.

'I have no idea. I've been trapped in that damned hut all the time.'

'But you suggested we turn left!'

'You asked someone to choose a direction, so I did.'

'Going by the state of this road,' said Slater, 'it's not exactly a well-trodden path, which probably means we're heading into the middle of nowhere.'

The trees seemed to be thinning out as they approached a bend ahead. The sixty miles an hour they were doing seemed more like a hundred and sixty as they bumped along, but Norman was quite relaxed as he eased the car into the bend and followed the road.

'Holy crap, hold on,' he yelled, suddenly.

Up ahead an ancient wooden pole, painted with red and white stripes, stretched across the road with a large *No Entry* sign off to the side. It looked like the sort of barrier you would expect to find at an old military site. There was no way they were going to be able to stop in time, so Norman put his foot down and aimed for what he thought would be the weakest point — right in the centre.

The pole was at windscreen height, and Slater ducked as they approached, half expecting a heavy collision, but after decades of woodworm invasion the pole was nothing but a painted shell. As the car passed through, it disintegrated into a dusty powder that briefly hid their pursuers from view.

'Well, would you look at that?' said Norman. 'We're on the military part of the base. Look, you can still see the footings where the old buildings used to stand.'

Slater was looking for a clue that might suggest which direction they should follow. The old roads seemed to form a grid pattern. Norman took the straightest one that took them through the middle.

'It's a bit overgrown now, but I guess this must have been where the offices and kitchens were,' said Slater. 'There's nothing to tell us where to go.'

'We'll just have to go with it and see where it takes us,' said Norman.

Suddenly they were through the grid and its scrubby old building footings and emerging into a large clearing. Straight ahead, a wide strip of tarmac stretched off into the distance.

'It's an airfield, isn't it?' said Norman, pointing ahead. 'We must be on the old runway.'

He aimed the car down the centre of the runway and put his foot flat to the floor. They were soon nearing a hundred miles an hour.

'How fast does this thing go?' he asked Slater.

'I don't know. I've never tried to find out.' Slater looked over his shoulder. 'Whatever, you need to go faster,' he said. 'They're gaining on us.'

'I wouldn't want to blow your engine apart,' said Norman.

'And I wouldn't want Patrick to blow my head apart,' said Slater, 'so just put your foot down. We'll worry about the engine another time.'

Something whizzed by, catching the front wing on Norman's side a glancing blow as it passed.

'Was that what I think it was?' asked Norman.

Slater looked over his shoulder again. 'We're in the shit now,' he said. 'They're shooting at us.'

'I'm gonna be upset if they damage your car after I've tried so hard to look after it,' said Norman. 'That just better not happen.' He began weaving from side to side.

'What are you doing?' yelled Slater, leaning forward to brace himself against the dashboard.

'Trying to make us more difficult to hit, of course.'

'You'll turn it over.'

'I will not. These things are designed to swerve much more than this.'

The Mercedes had been gradually gaining on them and was creeping up next to them on the driver's side. In the mirror, Norman could see Patrick was lining up a shot at him from the passenger seat. He just needed to get a little closer . . .

'Hold tight,' yelled Norman. 'I'm sorry about your tyres.'

'My tyres?'

'Yeah, we're going left.'

Norman swung the wheel left, and the car began to skid, but with a skill Slater had never seen before, Norman drifted the car broadside, its tyres squealing loudly as they left a trail of black rubber on the tarmac. And then, suddenly, they were heading across the open ground, away from the runway. Caught unawares, the Mercedes driver was still heading straight on down the runway while Norman was executing his skid manoeuvre, and now a huge gap had opened up between them.

Norman steered them in a huge circle, finally re-joining the runway, but now heading in the opposite direction. In the distance they could see the Mercedes had turned and was heading after them, but now they were a good four hundred yards behind.

Slater's mobile phone had started ringing and he fished it from his pocket.

'You're going to answer your phone, now? Seriously?' asked Norman, incredulously.

'Why not,' said Slater. 'I can't do anything else right now, can I?'

'You could call for help.'

'This is help. It's Stella.' He put the phone to his ear. 'Am I glad to hear from you,' he said. 'You'll never guess what's happening—'

'I know where you are,' she said. 'You're at Blackrock Airfield.'

'How do you know that?'

'You told me you were going there, and I've been tracking your phone.'

'You've been what? Are you even allowed to do that without my permission?'

'Listen to me. Patrick isn't Patrick. His real name is Hal Bravona. He's wanted for a whole host of crimes, including murder.'

'But he's just a driver.'

'Trust me, he's so much more than just a driver. We had him on our radar for murder, and then he vanished.'

'That will be multiple murder if he catches up with us,' said Slater.

'What do you mean?'

'We're currently being chased up and down the runway at this old airfield. He's got someone driving him, and he's taking potshots from the passenger seat.'

'Keep on running,' she said. 'I've got cars and a helicopter on the way.'

'You've what?'

'I haven't got time to explain now. Help is on the way. Just try to stay safe until they get there.'

'Yeah, b—' But Stella had ended the call. 'Help is on the way,' said Slater. 'Stella has sent cars and a helicopter, but we need to keep away from Patrick until they get here.'

'No problem,' said Norman, bumping them off the runway and back onto the open ground. 'We can keep on the rough stuff far enough out that he can't hit us. I don't think they'll risk bringing that Merc out there. It'll get stuck.'

As they headed away from the runway again, Slater looked back at the chasing car. It seemed to be slowing down, and soon came to a stop where they had left the runway. The passenger door opened and Patrick emerged. Slater watched as the now tiny figure shook a fist in their direction.

'He looks a bit pissed off,' said Slater.

Norman slowed the car down and brought it to a gradual halt, so they were facing the Mercedes in the distance. Now the engine was no longer racing, and the car was no longer bumping across the rough ground, it was almost deathly quiet, apart from the quiet burbling of the powerful engine. Norman pushed a button and his window glided down.

'Let's get some fresh air in here,' he said. Then, a few seconds later, he added, 'Listen. Hear that?'

Slater wound his own window down. Now he could hear a faint thrumming in the distance. 'Helicopter,' he said.

In the distance, Patrick had heard the noise, too, and they watched him rush back to the Mercedes and climb inside. The Merc began to pick up speed as it headed back down the runway.

'Uh oh,' said Norman. 'They've left it too late. Here comes the cavalry.'

He pointed to where a host of blue lights could be seen speeding up the runway. They watched in silence as the Mercedes slowed, turned and headed back down the runway, pursued by three police cars.

'There ain't no escape that way, unless that car's gonna grow wings,' said Norman quietly.

A helicopter came into view at the far end of the runway, hovering low. 'And now even wings won't help,' Norman added.

'I think we can head back now,' said Slater.

An unmarked car had stopped on the runway.

'It looks like someone's waiting for us,' said Norman, as he put the car into gear.

CHAPTER TWENTY-EIGHT

It was just coming up to 8 p.m. It had been a week since Norman had astonished Slater with his driving prowess, Patrick had been arrested and the police had taken over the case. In that time, Slater had agreed not to contact Stella, and although he had desperately wanted to see her, he had kept his side of the bargain. As he sat at the bar sipping an ice-cold orange juice, he hoped she was going to keep her side of the deal and meet him here, as they had agreed.

A large mirror filled the wall behind the bar, and Slater had chosen a seat that allowed him to see the door even though he had his back to it, so he saw her the moment she entered. It was icy cold outside, but she was snug in a huge coat, her head covered in a knitted woollen hat that he thought probably had its design origins in Peru, or somewhere similar.

She looked around the restaurant anxiously, but then relaxed into a smile when she caught his reflection in the mirror. She slipped off her hat and coat, and he turned and stood up as she approached. To his great surprise, she slipped her arms around him and briefly hugged him close. This was the first time there had been any real physical contact between them, but then she suddenly stepped back hurriedly, looking embarrassed. In an effort to save her blushes and disguise his delight at the hug, he turned to the barman and ordered her a drink and pulled another stool across.

'Thank you for keeping your promise,' she said when she was settled with her drink.

'It wasn't easy,' he admitted.

Now she blushed a deep red.

'I can't help it, Stella. I like you, and I like being with you. I'm not going to pretend otherwise.'

'But you did it anyway,' she said.

'I did it because you asked me to.'

'It would have complicated things at work. It hasn't been easy, and . . .'

'I understand,' he said. 'You don't need to explain.'

'Not everyone would understand.'

'But I'm not everyone, am I? I used to do the same job, remember?' There was a brief, awkward silence but Slater soon filled it. 'It's good to see you. I missed you.'

She looked up at him and smiled. 'It's only been a week.'

'Yeah,' he said, with a wry smile, 'but it's been a very long one.'

* * *

'Your statements have been really helpful,' she said when they were sitting at their table, a few minutes later.

'What made you think of tracking my phone?'

'When you asked me to check out Patrick, I soon realised he wasn't Patrick at all but was Hal Bravona. Bravona has been on our wanted list for a long time.'

'It must have been embarrassing to find he's been hiding right under your noses.'

'Yes. I'm sure there's going to be a shit storm over that when the dust settles.'

'Who was driving the car?' asked Slater.

'I think you know him as Adrian Davies, or perhaps Adrian Reynolds.'

'Bloody hell! He was trying to get us to find Betty so he could bump her off? We guessed he wasn't kosher, but he had that photo of her as a teenager! How?'

'Well, Betty says it isn't actually a photo of her, although there is a striking resemblance.'

Slater shook his head in wonder. 'That explains why we had so many problems identifying her. As for Adrian Reynolds, we thought he might be a rival journalist after her story.'

'Oh, he is a journalist, or at least he *was*, until he had the misfortune to cross swords with Patrick. He was easily persuaded not to write the story, and he was also happy to tell Patrick about Betty. The thing is, Betty had never really trusted him, so he had no idea where to find her.'

'You mean, he actually came to us so we could find her for Patrick?'

'That's about the size of it.'

'And if we had succeeded, Patrick would have killed her too?'

'Exactly. She was a lucky girl who escaped death twice. She was the one who was supposed to die when Alexandra was killed.'

'What?'

'It was a case of mistaken identity.'

'The girl in the red tracksuit,' muttered Slater.

'Sorry?'

'Someone was told to kill the girl in the red tracksuit, but they didn't realise there were two of them.'

'You knew that?' asked Stella.

'Not for sure, but I thought it was a possibility. I still don't understand why Patrick didn't kill Betty when he caught her at the airfield.'

'Because he needed to know where her laptop was.'

'That's why he beat her up?'

Stella nodded. 'He wanted to stop the story getting out. Ironically, she can't write it now because of the court case.'

'So, where was Betty before Patrick took her to the airfield?'

'He didn't take her there. He found her there.'

Slater frowned. 'I don't get it.'

'Let me explain,' said Stella. 'When we identified Bravona, we sent a car to Vernon Tisdale's house to see if he was there. He wasn't, of course, but we did find Tisdale. Bravona had beaten him up and left him for dead, but Vernon's a tough old boy. He was barely conscious when we found him, but he was able to tell us Betty was hiding at Blackrock. What he *didn't* know was that Bravona had already found that out from Guy Jefferson before he murdered him.'

Slater was puzzled. 'But I thought Tisdale was behind it all.'

'He was, at first. He had a nice little thing going. He took the sneaky, innocent photos of whoever was living in his basement, and Jefferson painted them. It was all going nicely until they let the basement to Alexandra. She had been smuggled in by Bravona, who somehow figured out what was going on. He then blackmailed Tisdale and Jefferson, and they found they were working for him.'

'He posed as the driver so he could keep them in line?' asked Slater.

'Exactly, and being two old men, they weren't able to argue with a much younger and stronger man, who had no qualms about killing people who crossed him. The thing was, these two old guys weren't into murder. They knew Betty was an occasional visitor to the flat, although they didn't know why, but when Alexandra was killed, they realised Betty was probably in danger too. Then she turned up looking for Alex, threatening to tell her story. Tisdale persuaded her she was in grave danger from Patrick and offered to hide her away at his airfield.

'Unfortunately, Tisdale didn't realise Jefferson had fallen in love with Alexandra and had been buying her gifts. Bravona knew about this, and after a while he put two and two together and guessed Jefferson might know about Betty and where she was hiding.'

'Betty had been safe there?'

'She would have been quite safe, but then two private detectives started nosing around.'

'But why did Tisdale and Jefferson keep her there? Why not get her away?' Slater asked.

'That was their dilemma. They didn't want her to die, but they didn't want her to tell her story either.'

'So Davies brought us in to find her, and all the time Tisdale had her safely hidden away!'

'Yes, that's right, but when you started getting close enough to the truth, he thought he could work it out from there. He told you to back off, but you didn't, did you?'

'We had enough reasons to be worried about Betty by then. We couldn't let it drop, knowing her life was probably in danger.'

Stella nodded. 'When you kept on coming, Bravona started to get worried you were going to get there first. But then you went to Guy Jefferson and not long after Jefferson was dead, but not before Bravona had forced him to reveal where to find Betty.'

Slater frowned. 'You make it sound like it was our fault Jefferson died.'

'It was unfortunate, but you had no way of knowing what was going to happen. Don't forget, if you hadn't kept on chasing this, Betty would be dead by now too.'

'Yeah, I suppose there is that,' said Slater gloomily. 'So Samuel Shrivener and Jools Hanover really *were* both innocent — at least in this case. I still don't trust Shrivener as far as I could throw him. But how did Betty meet Alex in the first place?'

'She was investigating how illegals were arriving in the country. She had been given a tip-off that Alex was an illegal, so she introduced herself.'

'Who told her that?'

'She's a journalist, remember? She's claiming all her contacts are confidential.'

'Was she living with Alex at any point?'

'No. She thought that would have been too risky for both of them. She just visited now and then.'

'What about the envelope with her name on it?'

'According to Betty, she brought it with her. There was originally a letter inside with her journalism credentials and real ID, etc. She used it to convince Alex to trust her.'

Slater took a moment to process all this. 'I never understood why she used the Martha Dennis ID,' he said eventually. 'I get that she was undercover, but why choose a dead kid's ID?'

'She claims she didn't want *anyone* to know which ID she was using, so she went to a forger and bought one!'

'You said "she claims". Does that mean you don't believe her?'

'It means she can't prove it because she won't give us a name. It's not up to me to make a decision about whether I believe her: I'm not in charge of the investigation.'

'D'you know what's going to happen to Pam Bristow, the truck driver's wife?'

'She did herself a big favour by bringing the money in and making a statement. She's not really done anything wrong, and we have enough of a case to be able to keep her husband's name out of the papers at least.'

'That's good to hear. I think she's suffered enough.'

'D'you want to hear something funny?' Stella asked, grinning.

'Go on,' said Slater.

'Bravona wants to have you charged with assault because you attacked him with an iron bar!'

'What?' he said indignantly. 'You're joking. He was about to shoot Norm. What was I supposed to do, stand and watch?'

Stella was laughing now. 'It's alright,' she said. 'We told him he was wasting his time and it wasn't going to happen.'

He smiled at her laughter. It was good to see her looking so happy. 'So, what happens now?' he asked.

She looked quizzical.

'I take it you've redeemed yourself at work, after all this?'

'Ha! Now I have to explain how I knew about this case when I was supposed to be on desk duties, and why I didn't bring it to anyone's attention sooner.'

'But that's crazy. You've just caught a guy who's been wanted for ages, and you've stopped a pornography business in its tracks.'

'Yes, well, that's not quite how everyone sees it. Bravona is just a small part of a big people-smuggling operation. By taking him out, we've sent everyone else running for the hills, so I'm not exactly flavour of the month with everyone. It seems I can't do anything right at the moment.'

'I wouldn't say that,' said Slater. He reached across the table and took her hand. She stared at his hand, and instinctively she began to draw away, but something made her stop.

'You make me happy,' he said. 'So, that's one thing you're doing right.'

She looked up and studied his face for a second or two, then relaxed into a smile and allowed him to hold onto her hand.

'That's good. It works for me too, you know.'

He smiled at that and gave her hand a little squeeze.

'Right,' she said. 'I've filled in all your blanks, now there's something you have to tell me.'

Slater looked at her, puzzled. 'There is?'

'If your mother's funeral has passed, and you didn't tell me . . .'

'Oh, that.'

'Yes, that,' Stella said. 'Have I missed it?'

'No, you haven't. Apparently it's a winter thing. More people die, so there are more funerals, which means you have to wait a bit longer.'

'How much longer?'

'It's next Wednesday, but you don't need to worry about coming. I'll be fine.'

'Nonsense. I didn't offer my support so you can refuse it.'

'Yeah, but—'

'No "buts". I'm owed some leave, so I'm coming.'

Her stern look, and one raised eyebrow, dared him to challenge her decision, but he wasn't going to argue. He would never have asked her to come and ride shotgun, but this was different; she had volunteered.

'So that's next Wednesday agreed then,' she said, with a smile. 'Now, back to tonight. Shall we order?'

THE END

THE JOFFE BOOKS STORY

We began in 2014 when Jasper agreed to publish his mum's much-rejected romance novel and it became a bestseller.

Since then we've grown into the largest independent publisher in the UK. We're extremely proud to publish some of the very best writers in the world, including Joy Ellis, Faith Martin, Caro Ramsay, Helen Forrester, Simon Brett and Robert Goddard. Everyone at Joffe Books loves reading and we never forget that it all begins with the magic of an author telling a story.

We are proud to publish talented first-time authors, as well as established writers whose books we love introducing to a new generation of readers.

We won Trade Publisher of the Year at the Independent Publishing Awards in 2023. We have been shortlisted for Independent Publisher of the Year at the British Book Awards for the last four years, and were shortlisted for the Diversity and Inclusivity Award at the 2022 Independent Publishing Awards. In 2023 we were shortlisted for Publisher of the Year at the RNA Industry Awards.

We built this company with your help, and we love to hear from you, so please email us about absolutely anything bookish at feedback@joffebooks.com

If you want to receive free books every Friday and hear about all our new releases, join our mailing list: www.joffebooks.com/contact

And when you tell your friends about us, just remember: it's pronounced Joffe as in coffee or toffee!

Printed in Dunstable, United Kingdom

71203357R00145